www.alohalagoonmysteries.com

ALOHA LAGOON MYSTERIES

Ukulele Murder
Murder on the Aloha Express
Deadly Wipeout
Deadly Bubbles in the Wine
Mele Kalikimaka Murder
Death of the Big Kahuna
Photo Finished

BOOKS BY BETH PRENTICE

Invitation to Murder
Killer Unleashed
Deadly Wipeout

DEADLY WIPEOUT

an Aloha Lagoon mystery

Beth Prentice

For Gemma—thank you for giving me the chance to be a part of this amazing world!

CHAPTER ONE

I looked in the mirror behind the bar of The Lava Pot at Aloha Lagoon Resort and cringed. My hair that I had spent ages blow-drying this morning was now a frizzy mess. Sweat had broken out on my forehead and upper lip, and I had wet stains under the armpits of the blue shirt I'd chosen to wear. Great. Not the best first impression I would choose to give a prospective employer. I signaled the bartender.

"Could I get a glass of water please?" I asked in my friendliest tone.

"It's just on the bar, love. Help yourself," he said in a thick English accent, nodding toward a large glass water pitcher sitting amongst a dozen glasses, all nicely presented on a silver-looking tray.

To be honest, if I hadn't been so nervous about the job interview I was about to undertake, I might have noticed how sexy he was. Well, actually, of *course* I noticed how sexy he was. I was preoccupied, not blind.

"Oh, thank you," I replied, slightly embarrassed I hadn't noticed it myself.

"You're welcome."

I wasn't an expert on English accents, but based on all my knowledge of Ricky Gervais, I guessed he was from somewhere in the south. His electric blue eyes twinkled at me as his lips broke out in a smile. My heart missed a beat, but I figured that was just nerves taking over.

I got off the stool and moved to the pitcher. Downing several small glasses of water, I took the time to look around me. The bar was just like any other tiki bar I had ever been in. Alright, it was the *only* tiki bar I'd ever been in.

The front opened out to the beach, displaying lots of wood and sea grass—and alcohol. I guess they had the most important things covered. Other than the bartender and a lady vacuuming the wooden floors beneath the tables, I was the only other person in the bar. Mornings were obviously their quiet time.

My palms sweated profusely, so I discreetly wiped my free hand on my new white jeans. Ooh, actually I shouldn't have done that. I twisted to look at my backside, and sure enough I now had a great big dirty mark. I guess my hand wasn't as clean as I thought it was. Great.

I had no idea why I was so nervous. It wasn't like this was the first job interview I'd ever had. True, it was the first job interview to be a surfing instructor I'd ever had, but I still shouldn't be this nervous.

I'd only moved to the island a week ago, but my mum and my brother had lived here for years now, and they loved it. Previously I'd been living in a small one-bedroom apartment overlooking the high-rises in Sydney, Australia.

Don't get me wrong—I love Sydney, but when my God-awful boss had fired me for something that hadn't even been my fault, I'd decided it was time for a sea change. I missed my family like crazy, so when Mum begged me—okay, maybe beg is not the *actual* word I should use—to move to Aloha Lagoon, I handed my notice to my landlord, had my belongings shipped out, and used all my savings to buy a plane ticket.

So far I was not regretting my decision. Well, I wasn't until the large man with islander heritage came walking toward me with a serious-looking folder under his arm.

Mr. David Mahelona, I presumed, the head of the resort's Human Resources department and the man who was here to interview me.

"Samantha Reynolds?" he asked, looking sternly at me.

I gulped. "Y-yes," I replied, plastering a big smile on my face.

I moved to put my empty glass on the timber bar, ready to shake his hand, when I tripped on the leg of the nearest barstool and fell forward. I put out my hand, praying to any god that would listen that I wouldn't break the glass I held.

I needn't have worried though. The tray holding the other eleven clean glasses broke my fall, sliding off the bar and hitting the floor with an almighty crash. On the upside, the glass I held still remained intact.

I felt the heat race up my neck and stop at my ears as the sweat on my top lip switched up to maximum saturation.

I closed my eyes and hoped that when I opened them, I would be at home in bed and this would be nothing but a bad dream.

Opening them, I realized I could never be that lucky.

David Mahelona frowned, releasing a very big sigh as he did so.

"I'm so sorry," I mumbled, carefully placing the unbroken glass on the bar and attempting to move behind it. "I'll clean up the mess. And I'll...I'll pay for the damages," I stuttered.

The bartender, who'd witnessed my complete humiliation, moved closer to me as I tried to open the wooden gate separating us.

"Umm...could I have a broom please?" I asked, avoiding eye contact with him altogether.

"Samantha! Leave it. Casey will clean it up," yelled Mr. Mahelona, moving over to a nearby table.

I looked up, shocked by his tone. Okay then, I wouldn't be arguing with him.

I hated making a mistake. I *hated* it. And I hated someone else cleaning up my mess even more. I looked at Casey and gave him a small smile. I also made a note to come back later, if I could pluck up the courage, and buy him a drink for his inconvenience.

"Sorry," I mumbled, moving away toward Mr. Mahelona.

He placed the folder on the table, signaling for me to sit. I immediately sat in the chair he held out for me.

"Thank you," I mumbled again.

He sat down opposite me and opened the folder. He took up a lot of air space. His skin was dark, his shoulders broad, and his expression downright intimidating.

"Now tell me, why do you want to be a surf instructor?"

"Oh, umm..." *Be more confident.* "I have always had a love of the surf. I grew up in Sydney, but I was actually born near the beach in LA, so I guess you could say surfing is in my blood."

That was a statement I'd prepared earlier, and I praised myself for remembering it. He stared back at me, his thoughts unreadable.

"I know I have no experience as an instructor," I continued, "but surfing is something that comes naturally to me. If I can surf, I can teach someone to surf." At least I hoped I could.

"So why should I give you the job? Your résumé says you've been working for an accounting firm for the last three years."

"Yes, that's correct. I was a personal assistant, but I promise you that every afternoon you'd find me at the beach surfing the waves."

Actually that wasn't quite true. I have surfed. In fact, at one point it was something I did a lot, and I was very good at it. It had just been a very long time since I'd surfed. But I was sure it was just a practice thing. Two minutes in and I'd be a pro at it again. However, now didn't feel like the right time to mention that.

Why was I applying to be an instructor then? Because I was desperate, that was why. Moving my entire life across the world was expensive—far more expensive than I'd anticipated. And now I was broke. No, I didn't mean just short on cash this week. I meant my bank balance was a big fat zero. And as much as I loved my mother, living with her for any longer than necessary was going to kill me—or her, not sure which.

So as anyone could see, I needed cash. Fast. And it seemed that I'd moved here in the off-season, so work was limited. Hence I'd applied for this job. The job advertisement had said the position was teaching kids. How hard could that be?

"I have a current first aid certificate," I said, giving him my biggest smile, "and a Certificate II in Public Safety (Aquatic Rescue)." Should I have added that I'd gotten that when I'd been fifteen? "I'm very good at organizing people. I'm a team player with an *extremely* high regard for public safety, I can follow safety policies and procedures, I'm excellent with paperwork, and I can plan your ass…er, backside off. My communication skills are prolific."

I did a quick assessment of whether or not I was getting my point across. "And, sir, I possess a quality you can't learn—I'm completely at one with the water. It's really like an extension of me." God, even I'd hire me.

David Mahelona looked at me, almost as if he thought staring at me hard enough would tell him if I was lying or not.

I gave him a big smile and straightened my shoulders, hoping I conveyed a woman filled with confidence. I caught a glimpse of myself in the mirror again and grimaced. I actually looked more like a woman possessed. The humidity seemed to be having a very big influence on my current hairstyle. I made a mental note to stop by the Aloha Lagoon Resort hair salon and see if they had any product that could combat humidity. Either that or some very strong hair ties.

David Mahelona sighed. "Our senior surf instructor is away with appendicitis and will be off work for the next few weeks. We've managed to reschedule the adults who were booked in, but the parents are a little upset that the children are missing out. I need someone who can start immediately."

I didn't think the parents were really worried about the kids missing out. I think it probably had more to do with the fact that they'd planned time without their little cherubs and were now stressing out.

"I can start immediately."

"Okay. I'll give you a trial. You can start tomorrow morning at eight, but be assured that I'll be monitoring you closely."

I let out a very big breath. "Thank you. You won't regret it."

He probably would, but all I could do was my best, right?

He stood and held out his hand for me to shake. "Human Resources will contact you shortly in regards to the paperwork and uniform. Welcome to the Aloha Lagoon Resort." With that he picked up his folder, stood, turned his back to me, and walked away.

Casey, who'd been listening in on the entire interview, walked toward me, drying a glass and smiling from ear to ear.

"He made that decision fast. I must have impressed him," I said, relaxing for the first time since I'd arrived.

"It helps that you were the only applicant for the job."

I should have been insulted by that comment. "In that case, well done, me."

* * *

Okay, don't panic. It'll be okay.

I was sure I had enough time to reconnect with my surfing skills and learn how to teach them before eight o'clock the next morning. And YouTube had all sorts of interesting videos. Surely one of them was a "learn to surf" tutorial.

I swiped at the iPad in front of me, waiting for the search to finish. I gave a sigh of relief as 91,400 results came swooping in. And first up was "Learn to Surf—lesson one." I noted it had 446,097 views, so it must be good.

My brother, who was sitting at the table opposite me, had tears streaming down his cheeks from laughing so hard. *Humph.*

I'd left the resort in a bit of a haze and made my way back to my mum's house, where I presently lived until I found myself somewhere permanent. It was a bit cramped, as my brother was also living there until he found somewhere permanent. He'd been there a year. Geez, I needed to be out before then.

Mum walked up behind him and clipped him around the ear. "Luke! Stop laughing at your sister."

He sat up straight and wiped at his face with the back of his hand, reminding me of all those years ago when we were kids.

Luke and I were twins. We were both almost carbon copies of Mum, with dark brown eyes and long sandy blond hair—yes, even Luke—and we were both twenty-eight years old and back living at home. At least we were both working.

"It's not funny," I said, staring at him.

"Yes, it is."

"Really, Samantha," said Mum, "why did you take a job as a surf instructor?"

"Because I have no money."

"Yes, but why didn't you apply at the Loco Moco Café in the resort? I believe they're looking for servers at the moment."

I had a memory of how I smashed all the glasses at the tiki bar this morning, and shuddered.

"I'm not server material," I replied.

"And you're surfing material?" asked Luke, laughing still. "When was the last time you were even *in* the water?"

"Last night. I had a bath."

Luke laughed harder still. "Okay, I'm off to sign up for lessons," he said, standing and kissing Mum on the cheek.

"You can't. I'm only teaching kids." Plus, he'd better not. I'd kill him.

I probably shouldn't have been joking about things like that. Tomorrow morning I would be standing in front of a group of kids who were about to enter the water, and I would be responsible for them and their safety.

I groaned. When I'd seen the notice for the job, I'd thought it would be easy. Now I wasn't so sure this was a good idea.

"Mum, they have lifeguards on the beaches here, don't they?"

Mum shook her head as her way of saying she disapproved of what I was doing. "I'm going to work. Remember I have a double shift today, so I'll be doing the late shift too."

Mum worked at the local nursing home. She'd been working there ever since she'd returned to Hawaii. It was a reasonably smallish home, and the nursing staff wasn't huge, which is why Mum occasionally did double shifts. Plus she always appreciated the extra money. For as long as I could remember, Mum had been a single parent, our dad having disappeared when we were just four. Sure, she now had a boyfriend, but he seemed not to help her very much. In fact, if you asked me, I'd say he seemed a bit of a leech. But Mum seemed to like him, so who was I to judge?

I had a moment of guilt, thinking about Mum's tight budget and the extra burden Luke and I were putting on it. I sighed and remembered that was why I'd taken a job that I felt a little underqualified for. Lucky I was a fast learner.

I watched as Mum pulled her blonde hair into a ponytail. The only sign of her aging was the grey hair just above her ears. Mum had turned fifty on her last birthday, but she didn't look a year over forty. Her figure was better than mine—I had no idea who I inherited the chunky thighs from—her hair was longer than mine, and her skin was smoother than mine. On more than one occasion I'd been asked if we were sisters.

I smiled for the first time today, feeling safe again now that I was home. Eight years ago, before Grandma had passed away, Mum had packed up and moved back to Hawaii to look after her. At the time I didn't realize I'd miss my mum so much. Sitting in her kitchen once again, I knew I'd made the right choice coming here. My life in Sydney had just been a chapter in the book of my life.

I looked at the YouTube clip and felt my stomach flip. I wasn't sure if it was a good flip from excitement or a bad flip from fear of what might happen tomorrow.

I closed my eyes and prayed it was a good flip. This new chapter was going to be exciting.

* * *

Job number one was to buy myself a new bikini and wet suit. After watching three hours of *Learning to Surf*, the only thing I'd really learned was that a lot of surfers wore wet suits. And they made them look really professional.

I needed all the help I could get, so I grabbed Mum's bike and swung my leg over the seat. Riding a bike was something else I hadn't done in a very long time, but seeing as how I didn't have a car, it would have to do. I hoped the saying about never forgetting how to ride a bike was true.

The handlebars of Mum's red cruiser were wide, and the seat leaned back, making it difficult to ride. By the time I reached the main road heading into town, I'd happily mastered the steering and my balance. Before that, I'd just plain scared myself.

The tropical paradise of Aloha Lagoon was nestled along the coast of Kauai. The town mostly relied on the resort for work and income. There were a few local, family-run businesses, but they too relied on the tourists to keep food on their tables. At least that was what Mum had told me.

I had to admit it was actually a really lovely place. I understood why my family loved it here so much. The weather was great (even if the humidity was a bit high for my liking), and the locals were a multicultural bunch. Some were native Hawaiian's, some were imports from the mainland, and some were from countries around the globe who'd visited and never left. What they had in common was that they were all really friendly. Not that I'd met too many of them so far, but the ones I had met were lovely. Actually, that wasn't quite true. Mr. Mahelona scared the bejeezus out of me, so maybe I should rephrase with *mostly* everyone was really friendly.

Mum lived on the outskirts of town in a small three-bedroom, timber-clad house. Driving, it would only have taken me five minutes to reach my destination. Riding the bike it took me closer to twenty, but I couldn't complain. The landscape was magnificent. I took some deep breaths and enjoyed the fresh air as I smiled. I listened to the birds calling each other and looked at the backdrop of lush green mountains as I pedaled along the road lined with palms and pines. We had palms in Australia, but I'd never seen any as tall as the ones in Hawaii.

My mind drifted to Mum and how all those years ago she'd left the States to follow Dad across the world to Australia and how hard that must have been to leave her family behind. I remembered how hard it had been for *me* when she'd left Australia and moved to Hawaii, but I understood her reasons. Now I was just glad that I'd eventually followed her.

I pulled my bike to a stop outside Lahela's Surf, got off, and leaned it against the wall, the sweat tickling my face as it ran its way down my cheek. Lahela's wasn't a big chain surf shop. It was a small shop founded by Lahela herself. I'd called Mum earlier asking her where the best place to buy a bikini and wet suit was, and this shop was what she'd recommended.

Apparently Lahela was now a resident of the nursing home where Mum worked, but the business was still family-owned and operated by her granddaughter, Alani.

I heard the little jingle of a bell as I opened the door and entered. Thank goodness she had air conditioning.

I looked around the racks of T-shirts, spotting a couple I liked. I was definitely a T-shirt kind of girl. I picked up a hanger and found some shorts to match, wondering if my budget could stretch to paying for them. I was just browsing the bikinis when a woman about my age popped her head up from between a pile of boxes at the back of the shop.

She screamed. "You scared me!" She stood, dropping the bag she held. "Darn it," she cursed, bending to retrieve it.

I took the few seconds to assess her. She was short— well, a lot shorter than I was anyway. She had sleek black hair, islander dark skin, and was completely gorgeous. I blinked in the wattage of her smile.

"Sorry," she said. "Can I help you with anything?"

"Oh. Yes, please. I'm looking for a wet suit."

"Sure. What type were you after?"

"Umm, what types do you have?" I had no idea there was more than one type.

"We have the wet suit jacket, the Short John wet suit, Long John wet suit, the Springsuit with short *and* long arms, the Short Arm Steamer, and the Full suit."

She stood looking at me, smiling, obviously waiting for my answer. To be honest, I had no idea what she'd just said. After a minute of awkward silence, she stepped out from her pile of boxes and moved toward me.

"How about I show you. They're all on the wall at the back of the shop."

"Thank you," I mumbled, following her through the store. We stopped at a rack overflowing with wet suits of all different sizes and styles. Even though the beach was a very popular place I'd visited as a teenager, in the last few years, I hadn't spent too much time there, and I'd *never* worn a wet suit. I coughed, clearing my throat.

"What would you recommend?" I asked, my tone sounding much more professional.

"I'm assuming you want it to use immediately?"

I nodded.

"And for surfing?"

I nodded again.

"Are you here on vacation?" she asked, flipping through the suits as she spoke.

"No. I just moved here a week ago." I quickly brought her up to date with my current living situation.

"That's so exciting! Oh, you're going to love it here. Mostly everyone is just so friendly."

That was definitely the impression I'd gotten so far.

"Okay then," she said, turning back to the wet suits, "I'd suggest the Short John, which has no arms, or the Springsuit, which is short in the leg with the full arm coverage. Or did you want full sun protection? If so, definitely the Full suit. Only not too many people want the full suit, as the water is always warm."

"I'll try the short one with the long arms, thank you."

She looked me up and down and chose the appropriate size for me. Walking me to the changing room, she ushered me in.

"We ask that you leave underwear on, but if you need any assistance, just call me. I'm Alani," she said as she pulled the curtain closed.

Okay. I could do this. I did think she had chosen a size too small, but I'd take that as a compliment. I peeled off my shorts and tank top, leaving my push-up bra and G-string on. I didn't normally wear G-strings, but this morning I hadn't wanted any underwear lines in my jeans for my interview, and even though I'd changed my clothes, I'd left the underwear on. Now I wished I hadn't. I checked that the curtain was pulled *all* the way over.

Taking the suit off the hanger, I stood on one foot and pushed the other into the suit. It was a bit of a squeeze, but I guessed they were meant to be tight.

Two feet in—it was time to pull it up. I pushed my arms into the sleeves and attempted to pull the suit up past my thighs. *Okay, don't panic. It'll come up.*

Finally. Now all I had to do was pull the zipper up. I reached behind me and grabbed at the extra-long end on the zipper. I wiggled and jiggled, and as the zipper got higher, the suit got tighter. Was it meant to be *this* tight? Halfway up, I gave up the fight and called for Alani.

She came immediately and stuck her head inside the curtain. "Oh wow!" She sounded happy, but I could see the shock in her eyes. "That's great. Let's see if we can get the zipper *all* the way up." Alani stepped into the changing room, and after a few minutes of me wiggling and her huffing as she pulled on the zipper, she gave up. "Maybe we need the next size," she said, wiping her brow.

You think?

She pulled the curtain back, and I attempted to pull my arms out of the suit, but after ten minutes of sweating in my attempt to get it on, it seemed that it was now not coming off. Oh geez. Did I mention I was claustrophobic?

Sweat dripped down my temple toward my neck. My reflection in the full-length mirror was not a pretty one. My face was red and blotchy, and my eyes were wide and showed a hint of hysteria. I hoped the job would be a lot easier than buying the outfit.

Thankfully, Alani returned quickly with another suit, and after a few more minutes of pulling and tugging in the opposite direction, I was free.

"Now would you like to try the next size up?" she asked.

"No!" I yelled a little too vehemently. "Sorry, I mean no," I finished in a much more civilized tone. "I don't think I'll worry about a wet suit after all. Surely a surfing instructor can just wear a bikini. In fact, look at this one right here. It's super cute and no-nonsense." I grabbed at a bikini on the nearby rack. It was navy blue and white and had a very nautical theme to it.

"Are you a surfing instructor?"

"Yes. I'm the new children's instructor at the resort."

"Oh wow. That's awesome," she replied excitedly. "You'll love it there."

"Thanks. I hope so." Somehow, I doubted it.

CHAPTER TWO

———

I opened my eyes and looked at the clock next to my bed. It showed 4:30 a.m. I didn't normally wake up that early, but my body hadn't adapted to the time change between Sydney and Hawaii yet. I groaned and rolled over, closing my eyes tight and willing sleep to come back to me. What would today hold, I wondered as I lay there in the dark. It was then that it hit me. Today was the start of my brand new job.

I sat up in bed and rubbed my eyes as my stomach did a gymnastic routine. I groaned. What the heck was I doing?

No, that was not the attitude to have. I needed to be positive! Today was going to be amazing. It was the start of my new life.

I found my new bikini and the uniform I'd been given by Human Resources and got dressed. The uniform consisted of khaki-colored shorts and a polo shirt with the resort logo embroidered over my left breast. I then pulled on some sandals and made my way out to the kitchen.

Mum's house wasn't flash. In fact, in my opinion at least, it really needed to be renovated. Not because the fixtures and fittings were old and decrepit but because they were old and ugly. Nevertheless, Mum loved it, and as she was still only a few years into paying off the mortgage, I figured it would stay like this for a while longer yet.

Luke stood in the kitchen, pouring a cup of coffee. He looked over his shoulder as I approached.

"Morning," he mumbled. He wasn't a morning person.

"Morning," I sang.

"Do you have to be so cheery?" he asked. I smiled. Even though I was now an adult, I still loved annoying him.

"I start my new job today. Why shouldn't I be cheery?"

"Should I remind you that you can't surf?"

"I can surf! In fact, I used to be better than you. I just haven't done it in a while," I added quietly. The coffee smelled delicious, so I pushed past him and poured myself a cup. My stomach was still tied in a very elaborate knot, but coffee might help that.

"Whatever you need to tell yourself to get through the day, I guess."

Humph. I wouldn't let Luke's mood influence my day. Instead, I ignored him, poured my coffee into a travel mug advertising the resort, and quietly opened the back door.

"Have a good day!" I sang to Luke, waving. He grumbled something incoherent back as I shut the door behind me.

It was still quite dark, but the sky was a lighter shade of dark than it had been an hour ago. It wouldn't be long until the sun broke the horizon. I really loved being up to see the sunrise—I just normally hated *getting* up to see the sunrise, which seemed to be a bit of a problem.

I grabbed Mum's bike and swung my leg over it, balancing the travel cup in between my fingers and the handlebars. Not my best move. Within minutes I had tipped it over, and it scalded my legs as it trickled to my ankle.

Argh!

The Aloha Lagoon Resort was probably the most beautiful place I had ever visited. Its size and luxury should have made it feel unfriendly, but instead it felt almost village-like with its shops and restaurants. The walls were rendered cream cement, the roofs were terra-cotta tiled, and the pools were crystal clear and blue. And that was just the man-made stuff. Nature outshone it in spades. Every time I caught a glimpse of the ocean, I found myself stopping what I was doing just to stare at it.

I felt the nerves settle in place as I locked the bike up in the staff parking area. It would have been good to have a practice surf before I started, but I figured I would keep the kids out of the water today and get Luke to tell me where to find a good beach that wasn't visible from the resort. I'd borrow his board and head there straight after work for a much-needed practice.

Yesterday HR had handed me the keys to the surfboard shed, so I pulled them from my pocket, found the resort map they'd also given me, and headed there.

The shed was located not too far from The Lava Pot tiki bar, which was probably so that parents could enjoy a drink whilst watching their kids in the water. Or maybe it was for the stressed beach staff at the end of a long day. Who knew? I unlocked the door and flipped the light on. And then sucked in my breath at the number of boards I saw there. Geez, did a resort really need this many boards? My mind ran at a thousand miles an hour, trying to remember which board was which.

I grabbed the trolley used to transport the boards and loaded it up with what I remembered to be a suitable range for kids. I then grabbed one for myself. I moved it all out of the shed and down the cement path leading to the sand. Daylight had broken even though the sun had not shown itself yet, and I smiled at a few early morning joggers. It actually felt good to be holding a board again.

By the time I had everything set up and all the boards waxed, I checked the time on my watch. Ten past seven. At least the sun was up now, but I still had fifty minutes before I had to start work, and an hour and fifty minutes before any kids were to arrive.

I adjusted my uniform and looked around me, pulling my sunglasses on against the glare of the morning sun. The Lava Pot came into view, and I remembered the disaster of the broken glasses from the day before.

The bar didn't officially look open, but I did see the tall timber-and-glass paneled doors had been partially pulled back, opening it to the beach. I could also see staff moving around, so I headed across the grass to it, ignoring the landscape gardener walking my way. He looked pretty friendly with his dark hair and beard. At first glance I guessed him to be around my age, yet he had a self-assurance and presence that was unusual for twentysomething.

"Hi," he said, smiling and stopping on the path in front of me.

"Hi," I said, giving him a small wave.

"I haven't seen you around here before." He was still smiling, so why did I feel like I was about to be told off?

"No. It's my first day," I answered, stopping next to him. On closer inspection he was actually quite good-looking in an intense kind of way. I gulped.

"Ah. Well, I'm Nick, head of landscaping and gardens." He offered his hand for me to shake.

"Pleased to meet you, Nick. I'm Samantha, the new children's surf instructor," I replied, accepting his gesture. I hoped to portray confidence, but even I could hear the nerves in my voice.

"I'm not sure if you've had a chance to read the staff rules yet," he continued, letting go of my hand, "but the resort likes the staff to walk on the paths. They think it looks more professional." He shrugged when he said it, and I got the impression he was happy for me to enjoy the grass.

"Oh, I'm so sorry," I said, quickly jumping off the grass and onto the cement path he was on. "I haven't had a chance to read them yet. I only got hired yesterday."

"That's okay. I only mentioned it because Human Resources has been clamping down on staff rules lately. If it's your first day, you'll be wanting to make a good impression."

Geez, I hadn't even officially started work yet, and already I could have annoyed HR.

"Thanks for the warning," I said appreciatively. "I'll make sure I read the rules tonight. I definitely don't want to upset anyone." Especially Human Resources. They were, after all, the ones responsible for my pay.

"Enjoy your day, Samantha. I'll look forward to seeing you around." Nick smiled and continued down the path. I sighed and moved in the direction of The Lava Pot.

The bar didn't look quite as intimidating as it had yesterday, but I figured that was because yesterday I was waiting to meet Mr. Mahelona, my fingers crossed that he would employ me. If I kept walking on the grass, maybe he'd change his mind. Then again, he hadn't seen me teach yet, so walking on the grass could be the least of my worries.

Reaching the bar, I saw the same lady vacuuming the wooden floors who had been there the day before. Casey worked behind the bar, restocking the shelves, lining up bottles as he moved. I actually didn't really think I'd find him here this early. I wondered if I could pluck up enough courage and actually buy him the drink I'd promised myself I'd buy him.

He noticed me and smiled. I smiled back, slightly breathless.

He waved to me. I waved back. I should move my feet either *away* from the bar or *into* it, but somehow they didn't want to move. Casey's smile had stopped me in my tracks.

He was, without a doubt, the best-looking guy I had ever seen. He stood over six foot tall, had light brown-blond hair, and even from this distance I could see his amazing blue eyes. He wore the Aloha Lagoon uniform, and I was mesmerized as it pulled tight over his biceps as he moved.

"Would you like a drink?" he called to me.

"What?" I replied. Focus, Samantha, *focus*.

"A drink. Would you like one?" he asked, his thick English accent rolling off his tongue.

"Isn't it too early to be drinking?" My watch hands were pointing at the seven and the three. "It's not even seven thirty yet."

"Nah," he said, waving his hand in front of his face. "It's five o'clock somewhere in the world. And it's not every day you start a new job."

He remembered today was my first day. My stomach flipped, but I was sure that was from nerves. For the job. Not for anything else.

My brain finally got a message through to my feet, and they moved closer to him. "You're here early."

"Yeah, got a delivery coming in, and the geezer couldn't come any later in the day."

I nodded, smiling at his colloquialism. "Are you allowed to serve alcohol before opening hours?"

"No, but it can be our secret." He winked, and I actually stumbled over my own feet.

"Sorry. Wet floor," I mumbled, my cheeks flaming. The cleaning lady looked at me and scowled.

"That floor is not wet," she snapped.

Casey laughed. "What would you like?"

I managed to reach a barstool and get myself onto it without falling on my ass, but hearing his laugh, deep and masculine, I felt myself slip. *Good God, girl. Get a grip!*

"I probably shouldn't have anything alcoholic anyway," I managed to say. "I'm going to be responsible for a group of kids soon." And even though I hadn't read the employment contract, I'm sure there would be a clause in there stating I must be sober.

"Okay. How about I make you a Coffee Cola Cooler?"

"A what?"

Casey laughed again. It seemed to be something he did a lot. "It's just coffee and cola with a splash of maple syrup. It'll give you a boost for the start of the day." I thought about the disastrous cup of coffee I'd had on the ride in to work.

I nodded, thinking Casey's offer sounded good. Caffeine and sugar—what more could a girl want first thing in the morning? I looked at Casey's back as he turned away to make the drink. *Well, I could think of something...*

I groaned, disgusted with myself.

"Sorry, what's that?" said Casey, looking at me over his shoulder.

"Nothing! Just coughed." I added a little cough to cover my lie.

I watched, mesmerized, as he made my drink and handed it to me, smiling as he went. He then made one for himself.

Shaking myself, I reached into my pocket for some money, ready to pay for the drink.

"It's on the house," he said. "We never officially met yesterday. I'm Casey." He held out his hand for me to shake. I noticed his long fingers and short nails, his personal grooming immaculate.

"Oh, umm. Samantha. Samantha Reynolds," I replied, feeling his palm slide into mine.

"It's a pleasure to meet you properly, Samantha."

His skin felt cool against mine, and I wished I wasn't feeling so clammy. I could only imagine what he was thinking. I groaned inwardly as he let go.

"Same," I said, grateful to have my hand back. I really wanted to wipe it on my shorts now, just to remove the excess moisture, but I thought that would be rude. Plus, it now felt kind of tingly, and that was nice.

"I haven't seen you around here before," he continued, placing his elbows on the bar and leaning his body forward.

I blinked as I felt him enter my personal space. "I only moved here a week ago," I explained, grabbing at my glass. Moisture broke out around my hairline, and my hand shook as thoughts became jumbled. I watched as he lifted his glass to his lips and emptied it in one go.

I took a sip of my drink and felt calmer the second the sweetness touched my tongue. *That's what his tongue would taste like*, I thought, my mind jumping to places it didn't usually go.

"Samantha?"

"Huh?" I asked, pulling myself back to reality.

"I asked you where you're from. You have an accent," he said, laughing.

"Sorry. I'm from Sydney, Australia, but I was born in the States. I only just moved back to be closer to my family."

"Cool. I spent two years in Sydney training at the European Bartender School in Chippendale. Then I worked at the White Rabbit for a year."

"Oh my goodness! Really? I've been there—to the White Rabbit, that is. Not the bartender school." I probably didn't need to clarify that, but there you go.

"Wow. I don't remember seeing you there."

"I only went once. It was a work party thing. Personally, the White Rabbit was a bit too nice for my liking. I'm more of a casual sort of girl," I rambled.

Casey smiled. He was just teasing me. Bugger. I felt my cheeks flame.

I cleared my throat. "Where were you from before that?"

"Portsmouth, England. Not quite as sunny as Sydney."

I nodded. I'd never been to Portsmouth, but I realized I was right in my earlier assessment of him being from the south of England. At least that was where I thought Portsmouth was.

"But we can't complain about the weather here," he finished.

Just at that moment I heard someone coughing behind me. I pulled my eyes away from Casey and turned to see Mr. Mahelona frowning at me from his spot on the boardwalk outside the bar. The distance wasn't that far. I could see him clearly. I quickly checked my watch to make sure I was still on my time and not his. Yes. Still had half an hour to go.

"It's okay, Dave," called Casey. "It's nonalcoholic." He lifted his glass in the air to demonstrate what he was referring to.

Mr. Mahelona kept frowning, but he did continue on his way. I made a mental note to remember his promise to be watching me today.

"Does he always frown like that, or is it just me that brings out the best in him?" I asked.

"He's always like that, but you do seem to bring out the best in him."

I groaned. Great, I hadn't even started yet, and I'd already made HR frown. Could today get any worse?

"I should go," I said as I put down my empty glass. I could already feel the caffeine kick in. "Thanks for the drink. It helped a lot."

"No problem. Glad you enjoyed it. I have a double shift today, so pop back when you've clocked off, and I'll make you something stronger."

He gave me a huge smile. So big I felt the ground move. Or maybe that was the electric floor polisher the cleaning lady was now using. Either way, the ground definitely shook.

My stomach lurched at the thought that shortly I would be standing in front of my very first class, and I had never felt so underqualified for a job in my life. I certainly hoped that Casey couldn't see me from his spot behind the bar.

* * *

Alright, this wasn't so bad. I don't know why I was worried.

I had my back to the water, my board in front of me. I had ten boards lined up on the sand, all with the decks facing up, and ten preadolescent children standing beside them, all beaming at me expectantly. I also had twenty parents all walking away, waving as they went.

My lesson was planned out. I was going to teach them the correct names of the parts of the board, some beach safety, and the proper names for the waves. All I needed to do was drag all that out to last an hour. I was sure I could do it.

These kids weren't getting anywhere near the water today, but I'd already checked the location of the lifeguard Malie, and I'd introduced myself to her just to be on the safe side. I did have my first aid certificate; I'd just never had to use it. I wasn't about to start needing it today.

"Okay, guys. Who's ready for their first-ever surfing lesson?" I asked the group excitedly.

"It's not our first lesson," said a boy who was so big, I didn't even think I could call him a boy.

"Pardon?" I asked.

"It's not our first lesson," he replied, attitude dripping from his every word.

"What do you mean? Of course it's your first lesson." I laughed to cover my shock.

"No. We've already had three lessons with Brad."

They had? No one had told me that! In fact, I distinctly remembered being told that they were newbies, but I guessed that didn't mean they'd had no lessons at all. Crap! Now what was I going to do?

"Oh," I said, taking some deep, calming breaths. "Okay. Of course you have. Silly me for forgetting."

"You're really pretty," said a sweet little girl with dark curls.

"No, she's not," said another boy, who stood taller than me. "She's hot!"

God help me.

The class consisted of four girls around the age of ten, and six boys who I was assured were all under the age of fourteen. The boys all started to snicker. I hoped my next classes were all *pre*pubescent.

"Okay," I said, panic starting to bubble. "Maybe today we can recap what you've already learned!" Was that quick thinking or what?

"But Brad's already taught us," complained the boy with fluff growing on his lip. "It'll be boring."

"Shut up, Nathaniel," said his mate, slapping him on the back. "If she has to help us in the water, that means she'll have to take her shirt off." He said this as a whisper, but everyone in the group heard him. The other boys all snickered again.

My head started to pound. I moved my neck from side to side, hoping to alleviate the tension building there, and noticed Casey standing on the terraced deck, overlooking the sand. He was opening the beach umbrellas over the tables, and I could see his smile from here. *Shoot me now.*

"Alright," I said, attempting to get the lesson back on track. Even though, if it kept going along like this, I had no worries about them getting into the water. "Why don't we start by introducing ourselves."

"We already know each other," said Nathaniel, obviously the smart mouth of the group.

"Well…yes, but I don't know you, do I?"

"Where's Brad?" asked one of the girls.

"He's got appendicitis," I explained. "Now, my name is Samantha, but you can all call me Sam." I waited for the "Hi, Sam" to come back to me, but when they all stood staring at me, I figured it wouldn't be that easy. "So, what's your name, sweetie?" I asked the girl who'd been speaking.

"Emily."

"It's lovely to meet you, Emily."

I turned to the girl next to her. Her name was Bree. By the time I'd gotten around the group, I found I also had identical twins, Kayla and Shayla (I'd never be able to tell them apart), Nathaniel (the loud mouth), Mitchell (the one who thought I was hot—wasn't sure if I should be insulted or flattered), James, Elliott, Lee, and Nyall. I just needed to remember them all.

I looked at my watch. The lesson had been going for five minutes. *What?* It felt like the hour should be up already!

"Okay, now we all know each other…" I said.

"Of course we know each other. She's my damned sister," said Nathaniel, pointing to Emily.

I wanted to pull him up for his language, but I also wanted him to think I was cool. Casey was frowning.

"Nathaniel, please don't swear. Your mother might hear you," I added quietly so Casey wouldn't hear me. Mr. Mahelona had moved to stand behind Casey.

Nathaniel quickly turned around to see if indeed his mother was standing within earshot. Relief swept his face when he realized she was nowhere to be seen. Relief swept *my* face when Mr. Mahelona moved away. He may not be my boss, but I remembered his promise to be monitoring me.

"Alright! Time to start!" I chimed. "Now first thing's first. Are we all wearing sunscreen?"

"I'm not," said Mitchell. "Could you rub some all over me please, Sam?"

Nathaniel laughed. I sighed. "James, could you please rub sunscreen on Mitchell?" Mitchell and James simultaneously scowled. "Anyone else not wearing sunscreen? Hmm?" The remaining boys kept quiet.

"Good. Now, let's have a rundown on the terminology of the board. It's very important to use correct terminology so that nobody gets confused as to what we are talking about."

One minute later, we all knew the correct terminology.

"Beach safety is very important," I continued, undeterred. "Now before you ever get into the water, you should do a check of the conditions. First of all, survey the water. Are there any rips you need to avoid? Which way is the tide going? Look for other surfers in the water. What they are doing can give you a lot of clues as to what is happening out there." Thank goodness I remembered *Learn to Surf* lesson three. I mean, I knew to do this stuff. I just had to think to tell the kids to do it.

Kayla put up her hand (at least, I think it was Kayla).

"Yes, Kayla?" I asked hesitantly.

"I'm Shayla."

Crap. "Sorry, Shayla. What's your question?"

"What's a rip?"

Ha. Brad hadn't taught them everything! "A rip," I said, racking my brain as to how the heck I could describe it, "is where the water coming into the beach is being pulled back out to sea."

"That's an ocean," said Nathaniel.

God, I'd be ready to kill him by the time the lesson was over. "Yes, thank you, Nathaniel. I'm well aware that it's an ocean."

"But you said it was the sea."

"Forgive me. I used the wrong word."

"You said that it was very important to use the correct terminology," he added.

"Yes. Thank you for reminding me," I replied through gritted teeth. Somehow this lesson was going downhill fast.

"Can we get in the water yet? I'm hot," complained Bree.

"Oh, I thought we would stay on the sand today, to make sure we go over everything important."

"But we know it all!" added Lee.

I distinctly got that impression.

"Look," he said, bending to his board and standing it up. "This is the deck." He pointed to the deck. "This is the rail." He pointed to the rail. "The nose and the tail."

Bree started to laugh. "Ha-ha-ha, that's funny. You made a rhyme!"

Ten kids joined her laughing. I didn't.

"Well, yes," I said, attempting to take control of the now giggling class. "But can you identify the rip out there?" I asked. "Huh?"

I had my hands on my hips, losing patience by the second. I was also starting to panic, because it appeared that these kids *did* know everything I had planned to teach them. I still had forty-five minutes left in the lesson, and it seemed I was not going to be able to avoid them getting into the water.

"Yes," Lee replied. "It's over there. The lifeguard has signs out for it."

I turned to where he was pointing and saw the sign on the beach about a hundred meters up the sand. "Great, I'm glad you noticed that. Very good."

To be honest, I hadn't seen the bloody sign. I was sure it wasn't there when I'd set up the class. I felt my stomach flip with the knowledge that I was going to have to get into the water. And it had been a good couple of years since I'd last been on a board. Why, oh why had I applied for this job? The Loco Moco Café would have been easier than this.

"Alright, do we all know how to get up on our boards once we are out there? And what to do once you have caught the wave?"

I'd had a brain wave of an idea that might keep them out of the water for a bit longer. I could teach them the one-foot-forward-squat-on-your-board thing.

Ten faces smiled back at me as they all nodded. I sighed. So much for that idea.

It appeared I had no other options. "I don't know how Brad did this, but this is how *I'm* doing it! We will get into the water one by one." There was no way I wanted them all in the water at the same time. "I'll get in first, and then Emily, you can join me. Together we will paddle out, and I'll help you catch a wave back to shore." Sounded easy, right?

I pulled off my shirt and shorts, throwing them on the sand behind me. Tomorrow I would go back to Lahela's Surf and buy a one-piece swimsuit after I realized a bikini was a really bad idea when Mitchell's mouth hung open, and the other five boys all stood staring at me in silence.

I turned my back to them, tied on my leg rope, and picked up my board.

Signaling to Emily to wait until I was in the water before following me, I tucked my board under my arm and made my way into the water. The size of the waves had grown slightly since I'd been standing on the beach, and they were now about a foot and a half high. Not huge but big enough for my heart to palpitate thinking Emily would soon be joining me.

I waded out into the surf. A larger wave rolled in, making me lose my balance and knocking me off my feet. I suddenly remembered the part of surfing I hated. Spluttering, I stood back up and saw eleven faces laughing at me. Ten were kids. One was Casey.

The water rushed back out to sea, the sand moving as it went, giving me the sensation I was being moved with it.

I regained my composure and signaled to Emily when a second, bigger wave came in. Once again I was knocked off my feet. Argh!

Emily waded out to meet me. When we were both out past the breakers, I helped Emily onto her board. Not that she needed it. She got on a heck of a lot more elegantly than I did.

We waited for the perfect wave to come along, and I pushed her board with all my might. I beamed as she held on tight to her board and rode the wave in. I made a mental note to remind her that this was not body boarding and that she needed to stand up, but she was lost in the water as it crashed to the shore. Only when I saw her huge smile beaming back at me did I let out the breath I'd been holding.

Sitting on my board, I checked my watch, thinking this lesson must nearly be over. I still had half an hour to go. I tapped the face of it, hoping that it had stopped working. The second hand ticked away. I sighed and rode my own board to shore.

"Okay, who wants to go next?" I asked, moving my attention back to the kids. "No volunteers? Okay, then I choose Mitchell."

He looked happy as he stepped up to his board, his smart mouth now gone. Maybe I was going to be okay at the teaching thing after all. I had a small moment of victory that I'd at least achieved that.

"Okay, Mitchell, stay here until I signal for you, okay?" He nodded his agreement, and I waded back into the water, my board firmly under my arm.

Reaching the depth I wanted, I did a quick head count of the kids on the sand. That was when I noticed the female lifeguard, Malie, running down the beach toward us. Panic took over for a moment as I saw the faces of ten children looking back at me, horrified.

What was wrong? Was a shark coming for me? I squealed and looked over my shoulder out to the ocean, but as I did, a wave came in causing someone to slam into me.

The person knocked me into the shallows, and I took in a lungful of salt water as I went. My board hit me in the leg, and I knew a bruise would appear later. I cursed the person who wasn't watching where they were going.

As the water rushed back out, I stumbled to my feet, spluttering out what I'd inhaled. I hated the taste of salt water. *Hated it.* I could feel my bikini bottoms filled with sand and made sure they hadn't moved down my legs. That would be embarrassing. My board was still caught in the water being pulled back out, dragging my leg with it as it went. I was unprepared for it, and the water pulled it from under me. I fell, landing on the person who'd knocked me over.

Rolling onto my back, I managed to pull at my leg rope and control my surfboard before the next wave brought it back to shore, hitting either me or the person facedown in the sand. I was about to stand and help him to his feet, when Malie reached us and pulled the man onto his back. I watched in horror as she put her arms under his shoulders and dragged him to shore.

It was only as the water rushed back in that I realized why the man hadn't been watching where he was going.

This man was dead.

CHAPTER THREE

———

Thank goodness for Malie. She acted fast and professionally. Not like me. I wanted to crumble to the ground, crying and freaked out, but Bree, Kayla, and Shayla beat me to it. I'd never seen a dead body, and honestly, I didn't want to see one now.

The resort's head of security, Jimmy Toki, and Mr. Mahelona had run down to the beach as soon as word reached them. I watched them from a distance as Malie recounted what had happened, her hands doing a lot of the talking for her. She was tiny, but judging by the way she had dragged that body from the surf, she was strong.

I'd managed to keep my Coffee Cola Cooler in my stomach and had rounded the kids up away from the body. I'd moved them up to the grassed area above the sand and used my cell phone to call for their parents to come back for them.

I struggled to remember my first aid training. I'd finished my course top of the class, but under pressure was a whole different story. The day was hot enough, but I knew that shock could set in, so I found the kids' towels and had them all wrapped up nice and warm.

I was grateful they were all okay and unharmed. Unlike the poor guy on the beach.

The flashing lights of the police vehicle and ambulance moved down the wide path and came to a stop next to the surfboard shed. The paramedics couldn't help the dead guy now, but I gratefully stepped back and allowed them to check the kids.

Two uniformed police officers walked past me dressed in black, their badges displayed on their left breasts, their gun belts heavy around their hips. As they moved to Malie, another car pulled onto the path behind theirs. This one wasn't marked as a police car, but it did have a flashing light, so I guessed it was allowed to be there.

An islander stepped out of the vehicle and moved toward us. He wore a very loud Hawaiian shirt and slacks. I guessed this, along with his air of authority, was his uniform. His gaze raked me over as he passed. If this were a movie, that would have been the scene that would have been played in slow motion. I swallowed the lump forming in my throat as he stepped up to Malie.

I was distracted from what he was doing as parents started to arrive to collect their kids, and I busied myself giving them any information I knew. Which wasn't much, but it was a lot less embellished than the story the boys were peddling. I did tell the parents not to go very far, as I wasn't sure if the police needed to speak to the kids, so they made themselves comfortable on the reclining chairs overlooking the beach and the ocean, their backs turned firmly to the deceased.

By the time I looked back to the sand, the coroner and her team had arrived, and the police had used a tarp to section the body off from onlookers. I gave a small sigh of relief and sat my backside on the grass, a chill working its way to my bones despite the warm morning air. The girl from the surf shop sat down next to me, dropping a surfboard onto the sand as she moved.

"It's Alani, isn't it?" I asked her, completely impressed with how I remembered her name. I wasn't usually that good with names. She nodded.

"Not working today?" I asked.

"Day off," she responded, looking toward the tarp. Her warm personality radiated from her and made me feel warmer inside. "What happened?"

I quickly brought her up to date.

"Geez, that's not good karma," she said.

Great. Just what I needed.

"Are you okay?"

"Yeah, I guess so. I'm hoping I still have a job though. Mr. Mahelona didn't look too impressed with me today."

"Oh, I wouldn't worry about him. He just looks scary."

She was telling *me*.

"I'd be more worried about Detective Ray Kahoalani, or Detective Ray, as we call him." She nodded to the man in the loud Hawaiian shirt.

I gulped. "Really?"

"Yeah. He has a reputation around here. Likes people to know that even though this is paradise, the law still applies."

I looked at the man in question. As he spoke to the coroner, he scribbled in his notebook. He did look intimidating.

"Is there anything I should be worried about?" I asked. "I'm sure he'll be questioning me soon."

"Nah. Just tell him the truth. He isn't known for jumping to crazy conclusions, but he's thorough."

"Okay. Thanks."

We sat in companionable silence until the detective moved toward me. Sitting on the grass with him standing over me, I felt the fear rush from my stomach to my throat.

Alani stood. "I'll leave you to it," she said before smiling at the detective.

I was grateful for her support and wished she had stayed.

"Samantha Reynolds?" the detective asked, wiping sweat from his brow with the back of his hand.

"Yes. That's me," I replied, also standing. Detective Ray Kahoalani was a lot taller than I, but I felt a lot better at this height.

"Do you mind if I ask you a few questions?"

He asked this as a question, but I got the distinct impression that it wasn't negotiable. I nodded.

"Can you tell me what happened?"

I quickly recounted my version of events. He nodded a few times and scribbled in his notebook, but mostly he frowned. I had no idea what he was thinking, but it scared me anyway.

Why? It wasn't like I'd done anything wrong. I shook off the thought and pulled myself up to my full height of five foot five. If he could look intimidating, then so could I. Oh, who was I kidding? I was about as intimidating as a church mouse.

When I had recounted my story no less than four times, he seemed satisfied with my answers. "Okay. That's enough for now, but I may need to ask you more questions later, so make yourself available."

"Can you tell me who that man was?" I asked quietly. The man in question had just been zippered into a body bag.

"Not at this stage."

"Was he old?"

Ray Kahoalani frowned. "Why do you want to know?"

I shrugged. "It just feels better if he was old. Like, he'd already had a long, fulfilled life."

The detective sighed. "Yes. He was old. I'm just not sure how old at this stage."

"Oh, okay. Thank you. That's good to know."

He gave me what I took to be a smile and turned, moving away toward the children.

I let out the breath I'd been holding. Probably a bit prematurely, as at that moment David Mahelona walked over to me.

"Samantha!" he barked.

I jumped.

"Yes, sir?"

"Not a good start," he continued accusingly, his dark brows reminding me of a very hairy caterpillar sitting on his forehead. I shuddered.

"No. Not really." What did he want me to say? I mean, it wasn't exactly my fault a dead guy washed up on the beach

"I'm going to have to suspend you."

What?

"Why? I had nothing to do with what's happened," I pleaded.

"Regardless, the beach is going to be closed for a few days. Until the detective has finished with his investigations, no one is allowed on here. The police will be taping it off."

"But that's not fair. I need this job. Is there anything else I can do?"

"Well, as it appears you're not responsible, you will be stood down for now with full pay."

My eyebrows shot up to somewhere around my hairline.

"Don't get too excited," he continued. "You will be expected to be available any time you're called in. And as soon as the police tape is removed, lessons will be rescheduled. The resort will not be losing money over this. Those lessons will have to be made up, so you will be working overtime without the overtime pay. Understood?"

"Yes, sir." I understood alright. I was going to be doing a double shift without the double shift pay rate. But the upside was I would have a few days to hone my surfing skills.

"And don't forget you're still on probation. I'll be watching you, Samantha."

He turned his back and moved to the group of parents, his expression filled with concern and compassion. Completely the opposite to when he was looking at me.

* * *

I slowly moved toward The Lava Pot, pulling my shirt on over my head. My body ached, my head ached, and I was tired. And it was only lunchtime. A bruise the size of a saucer had started to appear on my upper thigh from where my surfboard had hit me, sunburn made my shoulders sting, and I had sand in my bikini. I was a wreck. There was no other word for it.

I'd locked the shed filled with surfboards and noted the police tape sectioning off the beach in front of the tiki bar. I wondered how this would affect the bar business. From the crowd that gathered on the terrace, I figured it was helping it.

I pushed through the crowd and found a barstool. Lifting myself onto it, disappointment sat in my stomach as a female bartender wandered over to me to take my order and Casey was nowhere to be seen.

"Hi, what can I get you?" She smiled a super-white smile, her shimmering blonde hair shining under the lights.

"Ummm…lunch. I think I need lunch."

"Sure. Here's our menu. I can recommend the fish tacos or the nachos. Both are delicious. Actually everything on our menu is delicious. Our cook is amazing." She beamed.

I skimmed the menu, and she was right. Everything sounded delicious, but after the events of the morning, my stomach felt like it could only handle something light.

"I'll have the caesar salad with chicken please."

"Good choice. Anything else?"

Casey flicked to mind, but then I caught a glimpse of myself in the mirror behind the bar. My wet hair was still tied in a ponytail, and I was grateful for small mercies.

"A drink maybe?" she continued.

"Oh, a cola please."

"Okay. It won't be long."

"Thanks."

Fiddling with a napkin, I noticed Alani wander in. She spotted me on my stool and waved.

"You survived," she said, smiling as she took the seat next to me.

I smiled back. "Yes. My interrogation wasn't so bad."

"That's because you're innocent. Detective Ray isn't so nice when you're guilty."

"Lucky I have nothing to worry about then."

The bartender placed my drink in front of me.

"What are you drinking?"

"Just cola. Even though I feel like something much stronger."

Alani laughed and signaled the bartender that she would have what I was having.

"How come you're not working today?" I asked.

"My cousin Hani fills in for me so I can take some time to myself. She's a bit ditzy and can be quite annoying. It usually takes me a full shift after her just to get the cash register to balance again." Alani gave a dazzling smile. If this was her annoyed mood, I wasn't sure if I could handle her happy. "But I do get some time off, so I can't complain, right?"

I nodded.

"So," she continued, "you've got some spare time on your hands."

"How do you know that?"

"I have another cousin, Anela, who works in reception here at the resort. She told me." Word got around fast. "Don't worry though—I also heard Dave was really impressed with how well you handled the kids after that body washed up. And he doesn't impress easily."

"Dave?"

"Mr. Mahelona."

"Really? I impressed him?" I thought back to the frown he gave me. Alani nodded enthusiastically. "Wow. He didn't seem impressed."

Alani waved her hand dismissively. "Don't worry about him. He's always like that."

"Do you know him well?"

"Not really. Only through Anela. She's always complaining about him and telling me everything he does around here."

"But you called him by his first name."

"Yeah. It's easier than calling him Mr. David Mahelona."

I laughed. "But you're local. You shouldn't have any problems pronouncing names."

"I don't. It's just quicker this way."

"Maybe I should try that. Some of the names are really tripping me up."

"Like the surf," said Casey, his voice filled with humor, as he placed an empty glass on the bar next to me.

My heart missed a beat, and I nearly fell off my barstool as I glanced his way and saw his deep-blue eyes twinkling back at me. He reached out and placed his arm around my back to prevent me from slipping.

"Goodness, where did you come from?" I asked, slightly breathless, my hand jumping to smooth my hair into place as I spoke.

"Just cleaning some tables." He moved his arm away and stepped closer to the timber gate that prevented clientele from entering the bar area.

"Sorry. I didn't see you."

"No need to be sorry."

I was sorry because I hadn't seen him, and I'd been looking.

He moved aside as my caesar salad arrived. "Are you ready for a cocktail yet?" he asked. "From what I hear, you're officially off duty for a few days."

Geez, did everybody know about that?

"Cocktail?" I asked, fatigue sinking into my shoulders.

"I recommend the Lava Flow! It's awesome," said Alani. "It's got rum and pineapple juice and more rum. I think it has some strawberries and banana in it too, so it's kind of a health drink really."

"It would go great with your salad," added Casey.

I thought about it as I looked at my watch. It was one fifteen. Was that too early to drink? I quickly calculated the time difference between Kauai and Sydney. If I was correct, it was 4:15 p.m. in Sydney, and as my body clock hadn't completely adjusted yet, I figured it was perfectly acceptable to start drinking. Plus, I'd had a really bad day, and alcohol would hopefully take the edge off.

"Sure. Why not?" I said.

Casey's grin grew as he stepped away from me and poured several different ingredients into a blender and strawberries into another. I watched as he moved effortlessly around the bar, taking a few other orders whilst the blender did its thing, smiling at the ladies and remembering their names. I could see why he was in the job he was in. He seemed to love it. And the clientele loved him. I was so wrapped up in watching him that I completely missed what Alani said to me.

"Huh?" I said, my brain not coming up with anything better. To be fair, it'd had a lot of stress today, so I could understand why it couldn't summon a thesaurus when it needed to. And yes, it was stress related and nothing to do with Casey. Well, that was my story anyway.

"I asked what you're going to do with your time off."

"Oh. Probably surfing. And sleeping. I don't mind which order they come in."

Alani laughed hard, slapping me on the shoulder as she did so. I felt the sting from my sunburn and winced.

"Oh, my, you are so funny!" she said.

I was? I didn't mean to be funny. I was actually being serious. Best to smile along with her, I guessed.

I'd admit that smiling did make me feel better. Until I looked over at Casey and noticed him staring at me. Then my stomach flipped and cartwheeled, the butterfly circus performing a matinee.

My salad suddenly became the most interesting thing in the world as I picked at it and listened as Alani filled me in on the comings and goings of the resort and who was dating whom. When Casey handed me my drink, I thanked him and pretty much downed it in one go. Big mistake.

Coughing and spluttering as the rum burned my throat, I felt my eyes water. Unfortunately, the watery eyes turned into crying, which then turned into sobbing pretty much. I guess the stress of the day had caught up with me. But that wasn't the embarrassing part. That came when everyone around me realized I was not a quiet crier. Nope, with this girl, you got lots of liquid, lots of hiccupping, and lots of noise.

I tried desperately to stop it, but the harder I tried, the more I hiccupped, and the more I hiccupped, the more I cried. Casey looked around wildly, probably looking for any exit he could find, and took off for the other end of the bar. Thankfully, Alani reached over and put her arm around my shoulders, pulling me in close and holding me tight.

"You poor thing," she cooed. "It's been a really bad day, hasn't it?"

I nodded against her shirt. "I…I'm…s…sorry," I said.

"Now don't be. It's okay to let it out. In fact, my tutu always told me it's better out than in."

I wiped at my nose with the back of my hand and sat up to look at her. "*Tutu*?" I asked. It was a term I had never heard of.

"Yes. My *tutu*, my grandmother."

"Oh, that's cool." I sniffed. "I just called my grandmother 'Gran.' *Tutu* is so much nicer."

Alani smiled.

Casey returned, handing me some napkins and a bar of chocolate. I accepted both gratefully but raised my eyebrows at the chocolate.

"I have a lot of sisters. Whenever they cried, they wanted chocolate. It seemed to make them feel better." He shrugged, his eyes soft and compassionate.

I felt the pull in my stomach, thinking just how sweet that was. I smiled.

It might have been a bad day, but I had the distinct impression that if nothing else, I'd made two new friends.

CHAPTER FOUR

———

Apparently time flies when you were having fun, as I lost quite a few hours in The Lava Pot. The sun was starting to drop in the sky by the time I got home. I'm not sure if drunk cycling was illegal in Aloha Lagoon or not, but happily I didn't see Detective Ray or any other police officers along the way. And I didn't fall off once, so all in all, not a bad effort.

I pushed the bike up the path and leaned it against the house, quietly making my way inside. I was grateful Mum was pulling a double shift today and I wouldn't have to sneak inside doing my best to pretend I was sober. Which I wasn't. Turned out I quite liked the Lava Flow cocktail.

The last time I had done the sober act I'd been sixteen, and my friend Kelsey and I had snuck out without our parents knowing. Mum hadn't been fooled one little bit, and even though she'd grounded me for a month, she had looked after me when the hangover had hit me big-time the following morning. At least this time she couldn't ground me.

I straightened my back and walked into the kitchen, thinking a nice cool shower was just what I needed, when I saw Luke sitting at the kitchen counter, staring into a bowl of cereal. He looked lost.

"Hey, Luke. What are you doing home? Shouldn't you be at work?" I said.

Luke worked at the same place Mum did, only he was a cook. It obviously didn't pay well, or you would think he would have moved out by now.

He looked up at me, his expression grim. "I've finished for the day. Where have you been?" he asked.

Oh boy. I wasn't getting the lecture from him, was I? "I've been at The Lava Pot."

"I've been trying to call you."

He had?

"Why didn't you answer your phone?"

Pulling my phone from my pocket, I switched it off of silent mode, noticing the missed calls and voice messages. I dialed the number for my messages and listened to the six voice calls from Luke asking me, "Where the hell are you?" and "*Call me, it's urgent.*"

Uh-oh. "What's wrong?" I asked, ending my call, the cocktails swirling in my stomach, mixing with anxiety.

"It's Mum."

"Is she okay? She's not sick or hurt, is she?" My stomach lurched, and I had to calm my breathing.

"No, but she's at the police station. They took her in for questioning."

Okay, that made no sense. My stomach settled with the knowledge that a misunderstanding had taken place. Mum never did anything wrong. Never. She lived her life by the book. She'd told me it was one of the reasons she and Dad had separated.

"What? Why?"

"Did you hear about the old guy who washed up on the beach today?"

Did *I* hear about it? "Yes. I was the one who found him." Technically.

Luke looked shocked. "Really? I heard he was pushed in with the tide."

"He was. He knocked me over on his way in."

I saw the grin flick at Luke's mouth. It was only momentary and was quickly replaced with a frown.

"Well, he was a resident at Aloha Ohana, the nursing home where Mum and I work. They've taken her in for questioning about him."

The anxiety switch flipped in my stomach again. I sat heavily on the cane stool next to Luke, dropping my phone on the counter as I moved. "Why? What would Mum know about him?"

"Apparently he went missing last night, and she was the last nurse to sign off, saying he was safely in his bed. She was the last one to see him alive."

"But couldn't he just have wandered off? Old people do that all the time in Sydney!"

"He was in a wheelchair."

"So?"

"So he couldn't wander off without someone either hearing him or noticing him."

"That still doesn't mean Mum knows anything about it."

"Yeah. I know that, you know that, but at the moment the police don't seem to know that. Anyway, I didn't want to panic you, as I'm sure it's just routine. But we should go to her and make sure she's okay."

"What are we doing sitting here then?" I asked, my voice reaching the stratosphere.

"I was waiting for you!"

"Well, I'm here now, so let's go."

Luke sighed heavily and stood, glaring at me as he went.

*   *   *

Argh! Why are they so slow? Did they not know how boring it was waiting in a police station? You'd think it would be interesting, with all sorts of people coming and going—but it wasn't. It was frustrating.

I looked at the police officer behind the counter. He tapped away at his keyboard, completely unfazed by the fact Luke and I patiently (I use that word loosely) waited for the good detective to finish questioning Mum.

Sure I'd seen the detective leave the interrogation room and walk down the hallway to a separate office, but that had been an hour ago. What the heck could he be doing in there that was taking so long? And why wouldn't they let us see Mum?

I stood and paced, backward and forward, the only sounds the tapping of the keyboard, the hum of the air conditioner, and my sandals slapping on the vinyl floor.

"Far out, you have noisy shoes," complained Luke. "It's worse than Chinese torture! Sam, please sit down. I can't take it anymore."

I looked at the clock on the wall. It read 8:45 p.m. We'd been here for nearly two and a half hours.

"No, I can't sit down! I don't understand why we can't see her."

"Neither do I, but you pacing like that won't make them move any faster."

"I know that," I snapped. "But at least I'm doing something!"

"Yeah, you're annoying the crap out of me!"

That wasn't hard. I'd had a whole childhood of practice at it. I pulled the band from my hair, releasing the ponytail I had tied it in this morning. Ah, that felt good. I massaged my scalp where the band had been, relieving some of the tension that had built up. After being in the surf this morning, I still hadn't showered, and my hair felt awful and my skin sticky, but then the humidity wasn't helping either. Thank goodness for air conditioning.

Luke looked at me and let out a bark of laughter. "People reckon we look alike. Man, I hope not."

I caught a glimpse of my reflection in the window and bit my tongue on my retort. Luke had a point. I did look pretty horrible. I used my fingers to comb my hair back, retied the ponytail, and wandered over to the police officer at the counter.

"Excuse me. Is there a restroom I can use anywhere around here?"

He looked up from his computer and nodded toward a door about halfway down the hall. "Sure. It's the first door on the right."

I thanked him and headed in the direction he'd suggested. Walking down the hall, I did a sticky-beak glance into any offices with open doors. Unfortunately, the restroom was located pretty close to the front of the station, so there weren't too many I could look into.

I pushed the door open and made my way to the vanity. Turning the water on, I splashed my face and used it to tidy my hair as best I could. I could hear a woman on the phone in one of the stalls. I guessed she was close to the person on the other end of the line, or maybe it was a Hawaiian thing. I'd never had a conversation while answering the call of nature.

"This isn't the first time we've had to watch that nursing home," she said.

My ears pricked up, and I quietly turned off the tap. I heard the rustle of clothing, and then the toilet flushed.

"Something funny is going on, but don't worry—Ray will get to the bottom of it."

I wondered if she was talking about Mum. The cubicle door opened, and out stepped a uniformed officer. She was short, dark, and looked like she'd eaten too much McDonald's. Or was that only Aussie police who ate too much Macca's? Who knows? Whatever it was, she needed to slow down on it.

She saw me, and shock registered in her eyes. She'd obviously thought she was alone. "I've got to go," she said into the phone, instantly shutting off the call. She pushed past me and exited the room, without even washing her hands. Eww.

That was interesting. I quickly finished what I was doing and ran back out to fill Luke in on what I'd just heard.

I found him with Mum, Detective Ray glaring down at her.

"Ah, Samantha," he said turning to me. "Just the person I want to talk to."

My heart palpitated at his words. "Really? Why do you want to talk to me?"

"Follow me," he said, turning and walking down the hallway where I had just been.

Dutifully, I followed him. This time I got a much better look inside the offices. In fact, he opened the door to one of them and ushered me inside. I guessed it to be the room that Mum had just spent the last few hours in. I sat in the chair closest to me as he shut the door and sat down opposite.

"For the record, can you please tell me your name?" he commanded.

I felt the moisture break out on my lip.
"Ummm…Samantha Jane Reynolds. I was named after my grandmother on my dad's side of the family. Not that I know my dad. He left when I was four."

Detective Ray glared at me, his brows drawn almost in a single line. He probably didn't need to know all that. "Just answer the question please."

I gulped and nodded. "Sorry."

"Can you tell me where you were last night at approximately eleven p.m.?" Oh geez, that sounded official.

I thought back to last night. "Yes. I was at home."

"Were you alone?"

"No. Mum and Luke were both there."

"You were with your mother?"

"Yes. Sort of." I had to be careful what I said. I didn't want to incriminate Mum in any way. "She went to bed as soon as she got home from work with a headache."

Should I have said that? This was difficult, and I was almost panting with the strain. How did criminals do this? I was only being questioned in regard to Mum. I hadn't even done anything wrong!

"How do you know she was in bed? Could she have left at any point without you knowing?"

"No." *Maybe.* "I know I went into her room at ten o'clock. She was in bed then."

"How do you know it was ten o'clock?"

"Because I'd just finished watching a rerun of *Friends*. It finishes at ten. You can check that." Ha, at least I knew that for a fact.

"I intend to."

Crap.

"Go on."

"Oh, well, Mum got annoyed at me because I turned the light on and woke her up. She'd only just got to sleep, but I wanted to borrow these really cute shorts she has, and I couldn't find them in the dark." Was that enough of an alibi? Did I need to explain what the shorts looked like so he would know I wasn't lying?

"So that was at ten o'clock?"

"Yes."

"Did anyone go in to see her after you woke her up?"

"I don't know. Maybe Luke. You could ask him."

"I intend to."

I shifted uncomfortably in my seat. "Detective, why are you questioning Mum?"

The seconds ticked away as he debated whether to share anything with me. "I'm sure you know that your mother's patients have a higher death rate than most?"

"They do?" I asked, surprised.

"They do."

Oh no!

"But you don't have any evidence, right?"

"The coroner will have her report to me ASAP. I'm sure it will tell me everything I need to know." Detective Ray threw his pen on the table and looked at me, his gaze piercing. "Tell me, Samantha, how is it that you found the body of the same man your mother was the last person to see alive?"

I had no idea how to answer that.

"What are the chances?" he asked.

Exactly. What were the bloody chances?

"Umm, Detective? There is no way I could have known that body would wash up when and where it did."

He shifted in his seat. "Yes, well, I think I have enough for now. But make yourself available if I need any more questions answered. I believe you'll have a lot of free time on your hands over the next few days."

Had David Mahelona broadcast it? Detective Ray stood and showed me to the door. I waited quietly in the waiting room with Mum whilst he did the same routine with Luke. Once he'd finished with us all, he showed us to the front door.

"I'm sure we'll have more questions for you, Ms. Reynolds. Don't leave town."

Mum nodded, biting her lip as she did so, a habit she had whenever she tried to stop herself from saying something she shouldn't. I had a good idea of what she wanted to say. I was just glad she chose not to say it…at least until we'd exited the building.

Once outside, she let loose. "I can't believe that stupid man!" she yelled.

"Mum, turn it down a bit. You don't want them to haul you back inside for being rude about a policeman, do you?" I asked, thinking I'd had enough of sitting around waiting for one night. I really wanted a shower and then bed.

"No, I won't turn it down. I've been in there for hours, biting my tongue. Look at it!" She stuck her tongue out for us to see, and both Luke and I got a good view of it. Even with the only light coming from the streetlamp we did indeed get to see that it looked like it had been bitten more than once.

"And I've hardly got any skin left on the inside of my lips. I've been chewing it off all afternoon!" she finished, thankfully refraining from showing us that.

"It's over now," said Luke, attempting to pacify her.

He should've known better. Whenever she got a head full of steam, it was far better to let her get it out of her system.

"It is not over, Luke. Let God be my witness when I say that man is looking for blood. My blood!"

"Why do you think that?" I asked.

"He thinks I'm responsible for that man's death, and from what he told me, he's not going to rest until he proves it."

"How can he prove something that isn't true?" asked Luke.

"I don't think something like fact will get in his way!"

I thought back to what Alani had told me about the detective. "I'm sure that's not right, Mum."

"Well, they have no evidence against me. Other than a resident leaving unnoticed, they don't even *know* if foul play is involved."

"They're waiting on the coroner's report," I explained, reaching the car and waiting as Luke beeped the doors open. I moved to the back and got inside.

"When will they have that?" Luke asked.

I shrugged. "ASAP, apparently."

"Good. The sooner the better," said Mum. "And I bet when it shows that Albert died of natural causes, I won't even get an apology."

I closed my eyes and said a silent prayer to any god who was listening to please let that be the case. There was a nagging feeling in the pit of my stomach though as I wondered how a ninety-two-year-old man with limited mobility could get himself all the way from Aloha Ohana to the ocean and die at sea from natural causes, without anyone helping him along the way.

* * *

The day started sunny and warm. It appeared that was the weather in general here. Not too many cool days or wet days, which suited me fine.

It had been two days since the body of Albert William Johnstone had washed up on the beach, and the police had yet to remove the tape. I wasn't sure what evidence there would be left, as the beach was excellent at renewing itself daily. You know…tide came in—tide went out. It generally washed everything with it. But there you had it. The tape was still up.

Mr. Mahelona had been asking the good detective daily when it would be removed, and apparently if it wasn't removed by tomorrow, he wanted me to start the surfing lessons somewhere else on the beach. To be honest, I'd wondered why he hadn't done that from the start, but I guessed there was method in his madness. I was just enjoying the time off with pay.

I decided to use it preparing myself for the job. Today I was going back to Lahela's Surf to buy a more appropriate swimsuit, and then I was going to hone my surfing skills by spending the afternoon in the water practicing. Good plan, right? I thought so.

I got out of bed and padded to the bathroom to do the morning routine. After that, I headed to the kitchen in search of food. Thank goodness Luke was a cook and he'd put amazing leftovers in the fridge.

I retrieved the leftover pizza he'd made and padded my way out to the back deck. I sighed contentedly, looking at Mum's garden as the scent of frangipani wafted my way. Frangipanis were my all-time favorite flower, and just smelling them made me feel happy and calm.

I wondered where Mum was this morning. I'd already checked the house for her, with no luck. Luke had gone to work, but I didn't think she was due to start her shift until the afternoon. Oh well, she'd turn up when she was ready.

I'd popped the last of the food into my mouth when Mum's boyfriend, Mark, walked through the back gate and up the path. Inwardly, I scowled.

I didn't particularly like Mark. To be fair, I hardly knew him. I simply felt Mum could do better. He wasn't bad looking for a man in his fifties. He still had a full head of hair at least. His stomach could be a bit smaller, his overbite could be less pronounced, and his shorts could be a little longer in the leg, but other than that, I couldn't really put my finger on what it was about him I didn't like. He smiled as he approached me, and his super-white teeth shone in the morning sunlight.

"Good morning, Samantha," he sang. "How are you today?"

"Well, thanks. You?" I'd made a promise to myself and Mum to be nice to him.

"It's another gorgeous day in paradise, and I'm looking at the second most beautiful woman in the world. How can I not be anything but exceptional?"

I nodded. I wanted to groan out loud but remembered my promise. "What are you doing here?" Oops, that actually sounded ruder than I'd hoped it to.

"I'm looking for Rita. Is she around?"

"I don't actually know where she is. She'd gone by the time I got up this morning."

"Ah. She's probably just gone to the farmers' market, I'd say. She loves her fresh food. Personally, I can't tell the difference between the fresh stuff and the packaged stuff, but that's just me, I guess."

"Probably. You should have called before coming over. It would have saved you the trip."

"I was already out on my morning walk when I thought to come over, and I don't have a cell phone. Don't like the radiation and all that."

"Well, I don't know when she'll be back," I said, looking at Mark and wishing he would bugger off.

The front doorbell rang. I put my plate on the side table and made my way through the house to see who was there. The timber door was open, but the fly screen door was securely closed.

I could see a man standing on the opposite side of the door, his cream-colored suit two sizes too big on his frame, his beady eyes framed by his tortoiseshell glasses. He pushed them up the bridge of his hawklike nose as he shuffled his feet. He looked hot, and I don't mean in a sexy way. I'd be hot in that awful suit too.

"Hello," I said, greeting him with a smile.

"Hello," he replied as I pushed the screen open.

Mark, who'd followed me through the house, moved to stand behind me. I sighed.

"Can I help you?"

"I'm looking for Rita Reynolds."

She was popular this morning. "She's not here at the moment, sorry. I'm her daughter, Samantha. Can I help at all?"

He reached into his pocket and pulled out a business card. Handing it to me, I turned it over in my hand and read the words *Edward Fathersham, Estate Lawyer.*

"I've been trying to contact your mother all morning, but it appears I can't find her phone number."

"Oh, that's because it's not listed."

"Well, can you ask her to contact me please? It's rather urgent."

"Yeah, sure. As soon as she comes home I'll pass the message along."

Mr. Fathersham pulled a handkerchief from his trouser pocket and mopped his top lip. I didn't even know they still made handkerchiefs.

"Would you like to come in for a drink?" I asked, feeling sorry for the man.

"No, no. That's very kind, but I must be going."

"Alright. I'll tell Mum that you dropped by."

He seemed satisfied with that and turned to make his way back down the front path to the gate, allowing the hot breeze to close it behind him.

Once he was out of sight, I walked back into the house and closed the screen behind me. I stuck the business card to the fridge, using one of the pineapple magnets to hold it in place, and made a mental note to ask Mum what an estate lawyer would want with her.

Mark was obviously thinking the same thing as he stared at the business card, not even blinking. I could almost hear the cogs turning in his mind. My skin prickled.

"So, Mark, I need to go out," I said, hoping he would take the hint and leave.

"That's okay. You do whatever you need to do. I'll just wait for Rita. I'll make sure I pass the message along for you."

It appeared I had no option other than leave him in the house. I didn't feel very comfortable with the idea, but it was Mum's house, after all, and if she trusted him, what right did I have to question it?

"Alright, I'll see you later, I guess," I said, actually grateful to be getting away from him.

He waved happily as I made my way out the back door. I grabbed the bike and swung my leg over it, ready to head back into town to Lahela's Surf. I looked back over my shoulder as I pushed off on the pedal, and I could have sworn I saw the curtains in Mum's bedroom move. I wondered what he was doing in there.

CHAPTER FIVE

    My ride along the coast into town was a slow one, only because I stopped four times along the way.

    My first stop was because I'd noticed some kayakers offshore and watched them for a while, wondering where they were going. As they made their way into an inlet of water, I lost them in the foliage and made a mental note to ask Alani where they would have been going. I hadn't had a chance to do any of the touristy things yet, and now that I was working at the resort, which was primarily a tourist destination, I figured I needed to get up to speed with what was what around here. Plus, that looked like fun.

    My second stop along the way was when I was flagged down by a couple who appeared to be lost. They stopped me to ask me directions. It didn't take long for them to regret it. Once I'd sufficiently confused everyone, including myself, they thanked me and took off quickly, most likely to look for someone who could give them the correct instructions.

    I tried riding and looking at the ocean, but it seemed I wasn't that coordinated, so my next two stops were simply to stare. Would I become immune to that view? I hoped not.

    Finally reaching Lahela's Surf, I propped my bike against the wall and made my way inside. I was really there to buy a new swimsuit, but I kind of hoped Alani would be working. I wanted a friend to talk to, and even though we didn't really know each other, I hoped she might become one. Plus, she could hopefully help me with my surfing skills. Turned out I needed more than practice.

The little bell above the door jingled as I entered. A girl in a bright yellow Hawaiian-print shirt and the shortest shorts I had ever seen smiled at me from behind the counter.

"Hi," she sang.

I guessed her to be in her late teens. "Hello."

"How can I help you today?" She walked around the counter and moved toward me.

I wondered if this was Alani's cousin, Hani. "I was looking for a new swimsuit, but I was hoping to see Alani."

"She's on her break. She'll be back soon though, and I can help you with the swimsuit in the meanwhile. I'm Hani."

She beamed, and I could see the family resemblance. "I'm Samantha," I said, smiling back at her. She looked young, but she seemed really sweet.

"Oh my goodness! You're *the* Samantha! The one who got knocked over by the dead guy at the resort."

"How did you guess?" Was I wearing a sign or something? Oh wait, that was right—Alani's cousin, island grapevines. Apparently news traveled fast.

"Not too many Samantha's around here."

I felt the blush start at my ears. "Ummm…well, yes, I guess I am *the* Samantha."

"Wow!" she squealed, almost jumping on the spot. "Oh, I wish I'd been there. My friend, Jess, said she was sitting on the beach further down, and she saw the whole thing. She said she saw you, and you had no idea the dead guy was coming in on a wave, and whoosh—you were backside in the air."

That was probably one way of describing it.

"She only saw it because she was actually watching Casey, the gorgeous bartender at The Lava Pot, and he was looking at something in the ocean. So she turned to see what he was looking at and got to see the entire thing!"

I picked a one-piece swimsuit off the rack, distracted by the knowledge that Casey had seen me with my backside in the air. The swimsuit was enormous. I looked at the tag. Oops, wrong size.

"Wait till I tell her I've met you. Oh, you're not thinking of that suit, are you?" Hani asked, continuing to serve me at the same time as pulling her phone from the pocket of her shorts.

She took a quick selfie, me in the background holding the enormous swimsuit, tapped at the keys, and pressed send.

At that moment Alani appeared from behind the racks. "Hani! What are you doing?" she yelled.

Hani jumped and pushed her phone back into her pocket. "Nothing…other than helping a customer."

"So why was your phone in your hand?"

"I was just sending a quick Snapchat to Caitlyn."

"While you were helping a customer?"

"Yeah, well, she was in it."

Alani paled.

"Don't worry," continued Hani, "She looked really good in the photo."

I did? I wouldn't mind seeing that photo. "It's okay, Alani," I said as my way of pacifying the situation. "I don't mind."

Alani looked from me to Hani and sighed. "Why don't you take your break now, and I'll finish helping Sam."

Hani shrugged. "Yeah, whatever."

She beamed at me again and left, pulling her phone from her pocket once more. I inwardly groaned and hoped that whoever her friend was, she didn't have any video footage of me with my rear in the air.

Once she was gone, Alani turned to me. "I'm really sorry about that."

"It's all good. Don't worry."

"You're not thinking of buying that swimsuit, are you?" Alani asked, her expression one of horror.

I hurriedly put the suit back on the rack. "No, but I am looking for a one-piece."

"Didn't you like the cute bikini you bought the other day?"

"Yeah, I did. So did the adolescent boys."

Alani smiled her megawatt smile.

"I need something with a bit more coverage for work."

"Ah, okay. I have a few options for you. We just got some new stock in, and I haven't put it out on the racks yet. There's one I think will be perfect."

Alani led me to the back of the shop, where she rummaged through a few boxes and came up with what she was looking for.

"Hey, Alani," I said, plucking up the courage I needed to start a new friendship. "Would you like to go surfing with me sometime?"

"Sure, that would be awesome. I finish at two today. Is that too early?"

"No, that would be great!"

"Do you have a board, or would you like to use one of the spares I keep here?"

"Thank you. I'd love that. I need to buy one soon, but I need to get paid first." I handed Alani what was close to being the last of my cash to pay for the swimsuit.

"Sure thing. Don't worry though. You can use one of our boards for as long as you like."

I felt that happy glow only a new friendship could give you and smiled. I may not have had the best start in Aloha Lagoon, but things seemed to be looking up.

* * *

I killed some time while I waited for Alani to finish work by wandering around town and getting some lunch, walking whilst I ate. I hadn't had much chance to see the town properly, so I used my time well.

As I walked I admired an old church with its whitewashed walls and brown tiled roof, making my way to the window of a local gift shop. Sure I had no spare money, but I could window shop. I was grateful for the overhanging trees shading the road and dropping the temperature by a few degrees, giving me a momentary break from the heat.

The town was reasonably quiet, as this was the off-season, but I smiled at a smattering of tourists as they meandered past me, stopping to take photos of the many flowering trees and shrubs, looking like they were completely in awe of how green Aloha Lagoon was.

I tried my hardest to not be a tourist, but it was difficult, and before long, I made my way into the gift shop, threw my budget out of the window, and bought myself a yellow T-shirt with *I heart AL* written in white across the chest.

At two o'clock I walked back to Lahela's Surf and met Alani, where we picked up our boards, and she led the way to a secluded spot on the beach where the waves were perfect.

It took me most of the hour and a half that we were in the water, and much tuition from Alani, to get the hang of it again. Fortunately, no one else was around to see my many fails at catching the wave.

By the time we finished, I was exhausted but happy.

"You looked a bit rusty out there," commented Alani, walking out of the water with me and dropping her board to the sand.

I gave her a sheepish grin. "Yeah, I felt better at the end though," I said, copying her with the board and grabbing my towel to dry my face.

"You looked it. I thought you were the surf instructor at the resort?"

"I am." I quickly filled her in on my interview and why I'd taken the job. By the time I finished, Alani had her head back, laughing a deep belly laugh unlike anything I'd ever heard.

"High five to you," she said, holding her hand up for me to palm slap. "That's initiative. I'm always talking to Hani about stuff like that. Don't let fear get in your way—just do it."

"Fear did get in the way for a while. I was terrified one of the kids would drown or something equally horrific. I guess I was right."

"Well, I'm impressed."

"Really? I feel like a fraud."

"Don't. You may never have taught surfing before, but keep going at it like you did today, and you'll be as good as the regular instructor, Brad, in no time."

I beamed at her encouragement.

Alani wrapped her towel around her waist and picked up her board. "Come on," she said. "I'm going to introduce you to Kahoni. He makes the world's best juice."

I liked the sound of that. Wrapping my towel around me, I carried my board up the beach.

Walking across the sand dunes, we came to a stop in a parking lot where an old lime green van stood opposite us with the words *The Juice Guy* written in large letters across the rear. I figured that must be Kahoni.

"Another cousin?" I asked as he smiled a megawatt smile at us.

"Yep. How did you know?"

"Good guess."

"Hello, ladies!" Kahoni beamed. "How are the waves this afternoon?"

"You haven't been down there to check them out?" asked Alani.

"Too busy!"

"Well, we're going to make you busier. I'll have my usual, and what would you like, Sam? My shout," she said, turning to me.

"Umm…just an apple juice please." I felt uncomfortable accepting her gesture, but her body language suggested I shouldn't argue about it.

Kahoni looked offended at my choice of drink. "Just apple juice? I can't tempt you with something better?"

I wondered what was wrong with apple juice. "Maybe." I didn't want to upset him.

"Do you like mango?" he asked.

I nodded.

"Then how does a Mango Sunset sound?"

"What's in that one?"

"Mango and honey mixed with my very best yogurt."

"Okay. Sounds nice."

Kahoni shook his head, looking at me as if I was crazy for suggesting I'd just have apple juice, then busied himself making our drinks. I stood back and allowed the people who'd moved in behind me to step up and place their order. It didn't take long for their conversations to waft my way.

"I visited Grandpa at Aloha Ohana this morning," I heard one lady say.

My ears pricked up immediately. That was the facility that Mum worked at. This woman looked to be a bit older than

Mum, her dress style consisting of a kaftan and leather sandals. Obviously her friend shopped at the same place.

"I requested Nurse Rita be kept away from him. Thankfully, she's been suspended," she continued. "Her patients die very quickly because she helps them along the way."

"How did you know that?" asked her friend, surprised. "I always thought they took great care of loved ones up there."

"Do you remember Joan Sullivan? She was Aloha Ohana's oldest resident. She didn't die of old age, you know. Grandpa told me that Nurse Rita helped her along the way. He said she has a great belief in euthanasia."

"Why didn't you tell the police about it?" asked her friend, horrified.

"At the time I thought Grandpa was making it up. But now…if Rita hadn't been asked to leave, I would have moved Grandpa home. I mean, we would have loved to have kept him with us from the start, but…" she explained.

I didn't want to hear about her grandpa. I was stuck on her words about Rita. Anger rumbled in my belly. She had no right to say things like that about Mum. No right.

"You're wrong!" I blurted out before my brain could stop me. My mouth did that at times—opened up and said whatever the heck it wanted. "That man on the beach died of natural causes."

The woman looked at me, shocked. "No," she said, her tone stern. "*You're* wrong. He did not die from natural causes. He was murdered."

I wanted to continue to argue my point, but her words slapped me backward. *Murdered?* The nagging gnawing in my stomach kicked up a notch. Alani put her arm around my shoulder and squeezed. I think she saw the look of shock on my face.

"Come on, Sam. Let's get out of here."

She called to Kahoni to cancel our order and turned me around back toward the beach. Once we were on the sand, she looked at me.

"Do you believe what that woman said?"

I shook my head, but doubt must have been written all over my face. "No, I don't believe her. About Mum anyway.

Mum wouldn't hurt a fly. The bit about the old guy being murdered? Maybe. I mean, I haven't heard anything official, but then I don't suppose I would. It was only a coincidence he washed up on the beach at the exact moment I was there. Detective Ray has no reason to tell me anything."

Alani nodded, leading me back down the beach.

"I'd heard that rumor about the murder too," she said quietly. "I visited my *tutu* yesterday, and she whispered to me that she thought the man had been murdered."

"Did she say anything about Mum?"

"No! She loves your mom. She's always telling me how Rita is the best nurse that they have."

That was good to hear. "Don't worry about them, Sam. It's just gossip. In a couple of days, they'll have something else to talk about."

I hoped so, for Mum's sake.

* * *

My soul relaxed the minute I walked in the door at home. Mum was busy cooking at the stove—something that smelled delicious—and Luke was sitting on the sofa, laughing at a rerun of *Friends*. He loved Chandler's sarcastic humor. Personally, Ross was my favorite—his mannerisms cracked me up.

"Hi," I said to Mum, walking over and giving her a kiss. She hummed as she worked. "You must have had a good day."

"Hello, Samantha. Did you wipe the sand off your feet before coming inside?"

"I lost most of it on the twenty-minute bike ride from town. That smells good. What are you cooking?"

"Chicken long rice. I thought what we don't eat now can be put in the fridge for leftovers."

Sniffing the air, I didn't think there would be much going into the fridge. I dropped my phone and house key onto the counter next to the door.

"Can you set the table please, Samantha?" asked Mum.

"Sure." I grabbed three plates, forks, and knives and put them on the table.

"Don't set a place for me," said Luke. "I have to get going back into work. Paul, the other cook, has just messaged me. He's going home sick." Luke sighed.

"Well, grab yourself a bowl now and eat it while you're getting ready," directed Mum.

You didn't have to tell Luke twice. He jumped over the back of the sofa and joined Mum at the stove.

"I actually wanted to talk to you two over dinner, but I guess we'll have to do it now."

Oh no. That didn't sound good, even though Mum looked more happy and relaxed than I'd seen her in days. I felt the blood drain from my face. "What's wrong?" I asked.

"Nothing's wrong. I just saw a solicitor today."

"Oh, yeah, one stopped by. I left his card for you."

"Yes, thank you. Mark gave it to me. He came with me on my visit. It turns out that Albert—the man who died in the surf a few days ago—named me in his will."

"Go, Mum!" said Luke, smiling and giving her a high five. "That's awesome!"

I wanted to share his enthusiasm, but the gnawing in my stomach started again as I remembered what the woman at the beach had said.

"Why did he do that?" I asked. "Did you know him well?"

"Who cares why he did it," said Luke. He grabbed Mum and pulled her in for a big hug. I heard her bones crack from two feet away. "How much did he leave you?"

"Quite a bit actually. Enough to pay off my mortgage. Apparently he appreciated how I treated him, and as he had no family, he decided to leave whatever he had to me. Honestly, Hawaii has been so lucky for me this last year. Remember that radio contest I won a few months ago? And I didn't even remember entering…" Mum trailed off.

"But this is a lot more than a few dollars from a radio competition," I said.

Mum nodded. "I agree. This just blows me away."

I was happy for her, I really was. If I could just get the gnawing to stop.

"Mum, did you know he'd put you in his will?"

"Of course not! I try not to discuss monetary affairs with people. What you don't know won't hurt you," she added.

I wasn't quite sure that was right. "But what happens when Detective Ray finds out?"

Mum looked thoughtful. "I hadn't considered that. I was just so excited that Albert remembered me." She stopped stirring the contents of the pot and wiped her hands on the nearest tea towel. "But I didn't ask Albert to. He did it of his own free will."

"I hope the detective sees it that way."

"Well, it's the truth. I don't even know how long ago Albert wrote it. I mean, he's been at Aloha Ohana for about six years now. He could have changed it at any time."

I didn't know when Albert had changed it either, but I would bet my new paycheck that the good detective would find out.

* * *

In exchange for surfing lessons, I'd promised Alani I would help her rearrange her stock that night, so after dinner I borrowed Mum's bike again and headed into town. It was the first time I had ridden the bike in the dark, and I was embarrassed to say that I wasn't very good at negotiating the road with the only light coming from a small headlamp on the handlebars. But I got there and only fell off once, so I couldn't complain.

"If we finish in time, we should go and grab a drink at The Lava Pot," said Alani.

That sounded like fun, and maybe Casey would be working, so I'd get to see him too. I'd never bought him that drink to repay him for cleaning up my mess at the interview. I mentioned this to Alani. She smiled and made a plan for us to work at super fast speeds so we could get the job accomplished and still make it in time for that drink.

I looked at my watch. It said seven thirty. I looked around the shop at what needed to be done and figured it wasn't possible to get to The Lava Pot that night. That was before I knew Alani possessed superstrength and could lift boxes that weighed as much as I did. By the time nine thirty came around, everything was done, and I was exhausted.

"Okay, time for a drink," said Alani, smiling as she looked around. "Oh," she said, her gaze stopping on me. "Maybe we need to fix you up a little bit first."

I moved to the full-length mirror in the changing room. My heart sank. My shirt was filthy, my hair was frizzy, my elbow was covered with dried blood from my fall off the bike, and my makeup had run. Plus the bruise on my leg was now turning a deep shade of purple. I couldn't let Casey see me looking like this.

"Don't worry," said Alani, sensing my distress. "It's okay."

That was easy for her to say. Her hair was still neatly tied up in the French braid she had taken all of two seconds to do earlier, her makeup was still where she'd put it, and her clothes were clean. How the heck had she managed that when she'd lifted twice as many boxes as I had?

"How do you do it?" I asked.

"Do what?'

"Look that gorgeous all the time. Actually, don't answer that. I know how. Good genes. You have gorgeous skin, lovely thick hair, and the smile of a goddess. I shouldn't even bother trying, really. Standing next to you, nobody will even see me."

Alani laughed. "You have no idea what I have to do to keep this look going. It takes me hours."

"So does this," I said, smiling and sweeping my hands down my body as I spoke.

Alani laughed again, a deep throaty sound that came from her belly, grabbed a dress off the rack, and handed it to me. "Here, put this on. It'll look amazing on you."

I knew the dress. I'd had my eye on it all night. It was a white cotton dress with spaghetti straps. I took the dress and held it against my body as I moved into the changing room. No harm in trying it on, right?

It was perfect as it fell low on my bust and skimmed my leg midthigh. But it was also out of my budget. I never should have tried it on. "Alani I can't afford this," I said, admiring the way it showed off my tanned legs, despite the bruise.

"Consider it payment for working here tonight."

I turned to her, stunned. Before I could argue, she grabbed my elbow and started to clean it with a piece of gauze soaked in antiseptic lotion. I winced at the stinging.

"Ouch!"

"Now for your hair. Come and sit down over here," she commanded.

I did as asked, mainly because she was a bit pushy when she wanted to be. Within minutes my hair was woven into a gorgeous braid, and she'd fixed my makeup with some of hers. I stood to look in the mirror. Wow. She was good.

"Thank you," I said, emotion clogging my throat.

I looked at Alani's reflection standing behind me and knew I'd found a new best friend. She smiled at me, hopefully thinking the same thing.

"Okay," she said. "Let's go before Casey goes home. Although, I know where he lives, so we could always go and watch him through his windows. He never closes his curtains."

I raised my eyebrows at her.

"Well, that's what I've heard. It's not like I've ever sat in the long grass opposite his house and watched him or anything. I'm sure it's just a myth that he walks around his kitchen with his shirt off and that he has amazing abs. And pecs. Oh, and biceps." Alani sighed.

"Is there something I should know about you and Casey?"

"No," she said, smiling. "I just think he's hot. I haven't told anyone this yet, but I have my eye on someone else." Alani turned and moved to pick up her bag.

I smiled, relieved that it wasn't Casey she was interested in. Not that I thought I stood a chance with him, but when your best friend likes a guy, he's off limits, even for a crush.

"So who is it that you like?" I asked, suddenly curious.

"Just someone."

I raised my eyebrows, questioning.

"I don't want to say just yet. You know, in case I jinx it."

Fair enough. I could understand that. "Okay. But I want to be the second to know. Right after him, of course."

CHAPTER SIX

The Lava Pot was pumping by the time we got there. Five nights a week Benny Hoku and his Ukulele Wahines appeared playing traditional music. Tonight was one of those nights, which meant the bar was crowded and the cocktails were flowing. It looked like a fun scene.

Alani and I pushed our way past the girls in grass skirts taking food orders, made our way through the crowd, and found a table nearest to the bar. I ordered a Lava Flow cocktail, and Alani ordered a mocktail. She was driving after all.

I couldn't see Casey, but it didn't take long for a group of Scottish backpackers to make their way to us, pulling up barstools from every direction. Their accents were broad.

I enjoyed the male attention as they casually flirted with me, buying me whatever drinks I wanted. Even though, I think I only got the attention because one guy, Harley, who I assumed to be the leader of the group, was the first to put dibs on Alani. I knew she wasn't really interested in him, but I guessed she enjoyed the banter.

Eventually though, I gave up trying to figure out what they were saying, and they got distracted by the band, so I left Alani happily chatting to Harley and made my way to the beach.

The Aloha Lagoon Resort was a beautiful place, even at night. The fairy lights blew gently in the trees, and the scent of the frangipanis wafted toward me, making the air smell tropical. The torches had been lit earlier, and the flames danced in the breeze, and the salt air stuck to my skin. I was grateful that Alani had tied my hair back quite tightly, so any stray frizzies caused by the humidity stayed securely held by the band.

I slipped my sandals off, made my way to the sand, and sat down, my arms behind me propping me up. I took a deep breath and felt my soul relax. The full moon reflected on the water, and I squished the sand between my toes. I noted how it was much coarser than the sand in Sydney.

My mind flicked back to the life I'd had there. Did I miss it? Not really. I missed some of my friends and the familiarity of knowing my way around, but that was outweighed by the excitement of living in Aloha Lagoon. There was no place on earth more beautiful. And I had my family now. While living in Sydney, I'd missed them more than anything.

I closed my eyes and sighed with contentment. The sound of the waves lapping the beach had almost lulled me into a sleep, when I heard the rustle of clothing behind me and snapped my eyes open, sitting up straight as I did so. My heart stuttered when I saw Casey.

"Sorry. I didn't mean to startle you," he said, his voice deep and extremely sexy. "You looked so happy I wasn't sure whether I should disturb you or not."

"Oh, you're not disturbing me." I didn't add that he was the reason I was even at the resort tonight.

"Do you mind if I sit down?"

"Please do."

Casey sat shoulder to shoulder with me. If I moved even a couple of inches, I'd be touching him. The beach wasn't lit up—the only light we had came from the full moon and the torches on the boardwalk outside The Lava Pot. It was enough for me to see his expression soften. He dazzled me with his smile, and I felt my stomach flip. I probably needed to admit to myself that I had a serious crush on the man. But who wouldn't? He was gorgeous.

"You have a good spot here."

I nodded. "It'd be nicer if the police tape was removed," I commented, looking the twenty meters or so down the beach to where it swayed gently in the wind.

"True. Have you heard any more about what actually happened to the old guy?"

I shook my head. "Not really, but it seems the old guy— aka Albert—left Mum some money in his will."

"That was nice of him."

"Yeah, it was nice. Mum was touched by the thought."

"How is she?"

"She's okay." I turned my head back to Casey, confused by the questioning tone in his voice. "Why? Do you know something I don't?"

Casey looked out at the water. It suddenly seemed to become very interesting.

"Casey?"

"I just heard some rumors—that's all," he said, shrugging like it was nothing. "Just some stupid gossip."

"What did you hear?"

"I wouldn't worry about it, Sam. It was just that Rosemary—the lady who cleans the bar—she said she'd heard that Rita killed him. Rita apparently has strong opinions on euthanasia. I don't believe it. It's just what I heard."

Actually, he was right when he said Mum had strong opinions about euthanasia. I'd been stuck more than once listening to her rant about it.

"You're kidding, right?"

"It's just gossip. I shouldn't have mentioned it."

"Yes, you should have. If people are talking about Mum, I want to know about it."

"Is she okay though?"

"Yeah, she's okay. She won't be happy when I tell her this."

"Rosemary's just a gossip. I wouldn't put any stock into what she's saying."

"From my experience, if one person is saying it, others are too."

Casey sighed.

"If they knew Mum, they wouldn't be saying it," I continued. "She's the most caring, beautiful person the world is lucky enough to have. The residents of Aloha Ohana are fortunate to have her there."

"I know. She has to be. She's Luke's mother, and he's one of the nicest people I've ever met."

Was he talking about the same Luke I knew? "You are talking about my brother, right?"

Casey smiled that dazzling smile again. "Yes."

"I didn't realize you knew Luke."

"Yeah, he arrived here about the same time I did. I met him at the bar one night when we were both admiring the same woman. We kind of hit it off after that, usually comparing…well, that doesn't matter. We just hit it off."

Why hadn't Luke mentioned Casey to me? Actually, hang on a minute, I think he had. I just hadn't been listening, as I figured the Casey he was talking about to be a girl at the time.

"He'd be the closest friend I have here."

Wow. Lucky Luke.

"Anyway, enough of the man-love," said Casey, laughing. "I have work to do." He stood, and I looked up at him from my spot on the sand.

I watched him walk. His legs were long and covered the ground effortlessly, his gait relaxed. As he reached the boardwalk running along the front of The Lava Pot, he looked back at me and waved. Oh boy!

* * *

Normally I was a really positive, proactive person. I was a problem solver. I always remembered Mum telling everyone I had to be the problem solver, as Luke was the one who created the problems to start with. The universe had seen to it that he had someone who could solve those problems for him. Not sure that I loved that role, but there it was. It was obviously my destiny.

But this time I was worried about Mum. If what Casey had just told me was correct, then the rumors needed to be stopped. And I knew they weren't true. Mum loved the world and everything in it. Her destiny was to help people. There was no way she had anything to do with Albert dying. Yes, the rumors were correct in saying she believed in euthanasia, but it was more than that. Mum believed we had the right to die with dignity. What happened to Albert was not dignified.

I thought about what Casey had told me. His words about Luke surprised me. I knew I teased Luke and said he was a bugger, but Casey was right about him. He was the kindest, most considerate man I knew. He just didn't show that side of himself to too many people. Casey had to be pretty special himself to know that about Luke.

Of course, I would never tell Luke what I thought of him. No, I'd never hear the end of it. He got his caring nature from Mum. To be honest, I didn't know what traits either of us got from our dad. Mum never talked about him.

When I was ten I'd asked her to tell me some stories about our dad—you know, how they met, how he proposed—that kind of thing. She got all prickly and said that being a dad meant more than turning up for conception (at the time I'd had no idea what that actually meant. I asked my friend Jade, and when she told me, I'd nearly fainted). Being a dad meant being there for your family, through the good times and the bad. He'd never been there, so in her opinion he didn't deserve the title. I'd felt like I was being told off, so I never asked her about him again. I'd asked Gran instead.

She hadn't told me much other than that she could understand what Mum had seen in him. He'd been tall, athletic, and extremely good-looking. He'd also been popular with the ladies and left Mum for another woman more than once. I guessed that had hurt her a lot. So much so that Mum had destroyed every photo she'd ever had of him. To this day I couldn't tell you what he really looked like.

Anyway, me thinking about Dad wouldn't help her right now. First, I needed to figure out a way to stop the gossip mill talking about her, stop her hearing what they were saying, and make sure that Detective Ray didn't agree with them.

I was still trying to decide how to do that when I heard voices on the boardwalk, pulling me from my thoughts. I checked my watch, thinking I really should be going home and getting some sleep. 11:30 p.m. I needed to find Alani. I'd left the bike at her shop and had gotten a lift here with her. So unless I found her, I was in for a long walk home.

I stood and brushed the sand from my backside and made my way toward the boardwalk. Movement in the shrubbery caught my eye. I had to squint to see, as it was out of range of the torches, but the moon was bright. A figure ducked back into the shrubs, and I wondered what they were doing that they didn't want seen.

I had just stepped up onto the boardwalk when a very tall man with red hair rushed past me, nearly knocking me over. He ran down the beach toward the person who had just stepped out of the shrubs again, their silhouettes highlighted by the moon.

I had visions of a secret romantic affair he was running late for, but those were shattered when they walked down the beach away from me, their body language anything but friendly. Within seconds they looked like they were yelling at each other, the tall man then pushing the other until they fell.

My heart palpitated. Should I call security? Probably. Instead, I ran back down to the sand and screamed out to them to cut it out. I was unsure if they would hear me, as they were a good forty meters or so down the beach, but the tall one doing the pushing obviously had good hearing, as he looked my way and then turned and ran in the opposite direction. I took a few steps toward them, hoping to help the one on the ground. He saw me, got up quickly, and ran after the first man. I guess he didn't want any help.

I sighed as the breeze picked up, and turned back in the direction of The Lava Pot. I found Alani still chatting to the backpacker, her cheeks glowing. She saw me and waved me over.

"Hi," she sang. "Did Casey find you?" she asked.

"Yes, thanks. He did." I couldn't stop the smile that spread across my face. "Are you ready to head home?" I asked, looking between her and the backpacker.

"Harley was going to a private party up the beach. I wasn't going to go, but I thought it would be fun," she explained with a shrug.

"Aye, you can come," said Harley, his Scottish accent thick.

I didn't really want to go. The day had taken its toll on me, and I was tired. I wanted to go home to bed. By myself. I saw the look Harley's friend gave me, and shivered. "Alani, can I have a quick word? In private."

She stood, and we moved closer to the bar, out of their earshot. "Are you really going to that party?" I asked her, thinking how a girl should never do something like that alone.

"Yeah. It's okay. Kahoni will be there. Nobody messes with him."

I sighed, relieved. "Good."

"You're coming, aren't you?"

I shook my head. "Sorry. I'm going home. I'm buggered."

She gave me a quick squeeze. "Here, take the car then. I'll get a lift home with Kahoni."

"Thanks."

She turned and left, Harley's arm slung over her shoulder.

Hang on a minute. How was I going to drive? I'd had at least four cocktails in about an hour and a half. Sure, I felt okay to drive, but I'd bet I was over the legal limit. I sighed and sat heavily on the nearest barstool. Casey walked up behind me.

"That's a big sigh," he said, leaning across the bar, placing some dirty glasses on it.

I looked at the clock. It was now eleven forty-five. I could call Luke, but he had to be up for work at four in the morning, so he wouldn't appreciate a call at this time of night to disturb his beauty sleep. Even though he disturbed mine all the time with his snoring.

"Is there a taxi service around here?" I asked.

"Do you need a lift?"

"I have keys, but I think I'm over the limit to drive."

"I can give you a lift. If you don't mind waiting till I finish my shift?"

Now let me think this through. "Sure. That would be awesome." Yeah, didn't take me long to think about it, did it?

* * *

The drive home only took a little over five minutes, which was disappointing.

The moon was high in the sky, shining down on the ocean, creating a path of light for the waves to dance in. It was such a pretty sight I could have sat on the hill watching it until the sun rose, preferably sitting in the car with Casey.

However, that fantasy was crushed the second we pulled into Mum's drive and saw Luke sitting on the front steps, his head in his hands, the porch light illuminating him from behind.

Casey turned the engine off and jumped from the car even before I could get my seat belt undone. That wasn't hard. It appeared that my seat belt was stuck. I pushed the little button that was supposed to release it, but nothing happened. I pulled on the belt, hoping that it would just pop out. Still nothing. Damn.

I looked out the windscreen at Casey's back. Luke had stood, and from what I could see, he appeared distressed. I also noted the look he gave Casey. I'd seen that look before. It was the one he reserved for any boy who brought me home whom he disapproved of. I sighed, thinking I really was too old for that rubbish and that I could look after myself perfectly well without his help.

I desperately pulled on the belt, willing it to release. Luke's raised voice drifted my way. He was pretty agitated about something, and I didn't think that something was my ride home. Anxiety swirled in my stomach, wondering what he was even doing awake at this time of night.

Casey turned back to the car to see what had happened to me. Understanding flashed across his expression, and he sprinted over to help me.

"Sorry," he said, opening the car door for me. "I forgot the seat belt sticks sometimes."

He leaned into the car, right into my personal space. *Whoa.* The butterflies that usually lived quiet lives in my stomach awoke and started doing laps, completely eradicating the anxiety. Casey's scent filled my senses as he reached across me and worked his magic on the belt buckle. That wasn't the only thing he worked his magic on, but I'd keep my hormones out of this for now. Luke ranting over his shoulder was kind of killing any mood they might be working up to.

I heard the click as the belt released, and Casey smiled at me, his lips only inches from mine. Even in the dim light I could make out the color of his eyes, and if it wasn't for Luke's' voice, I think my heart would probably have beat right out of my chest. I really wished the butterflies would just settle the heck down. The whole effect made me breathless.

"Why don't you carry your phone like a normal person?" Luke screamed at me over Casey's shoulder. "I've been trying to call you. I thought you were with Alani."

"I do carry my phone," I protested, getting out of the car to face him. He waved my phone in the air, showing me I obviously didn't.

"Really?"

Argh! I hated it when he was right. There'd be no living with him now. "I must have forgotten it," I added weakly, thinking I must have left it behind this evening. "And I *was* with Alani."

"Well, she didn't answer the shop phone."

"That's because we went to The Lava Pot."

"Luke, why don't you calm down and tell us what's going on?" said Casey, grabbing Luke by the shoulder and steering him away from me.

Which was probably a good thing, as Luke looked like he was about to throttle me in a way only a brother can.

"It's Mum," said Luke, glaring at me.

The butterflies in my stomach freaked out for a completely different reason, allowing the anxiety to rush back in.

"The police turned up quite a few hours ago and took Mum back to the station for more questioning. Apparently the autopsy on the dead guy showed he died from an insulin overdose."

"So?"

"He wasn't a diabetic."

* * *

Thank goodness for Casey. I'm not sure who he helped the most—me or Luke. He sprang into action, getting Luke and me back into his car and driving us to the police station. Unfortunately, we were outside of visiting hours, and they wouldn't let us see Mum. We did find out that she hadn't been arrested—yet. Which was a good start, but the good detective hadn't finished questioning her.

Nothing could be done until she either called us for a lift or the morning arrived—whichever came first, so Casey drove us home again. By that time, it was two thirty a.m., and I was drained.

"Thanks for your help, Casey," I said, yawning, as Luke made his way inside, mumbling about getting some sleep because he had to be up for work in a few hours' time. Poor Luke. "Sorry. I'm not yawning because of the company. It's just been a long day."

"That's okay. I'm glad I was here to help. Not that I did much," he said, matching my yawn. It was contagious. "Go and get some sleep. I'll call you in the morning and see how everything went."

He leaned in and kissed my cheek. It was light and friendly, yet it was enough to wake up my hormones. I felt the pull in my belly as his breath whispered over my skin. What I wanted to do was grab hold of him and kiss him right back. Properly kiss him. None of this cheek stuff. But I didn't. Casey was Luke's friend, and I'd seen the warning look he'd received earlier when I'd turned up in his car. I made a mental note to ask Luke about that.

"Good night," I said.

Casey smiled and made his way to the car. As I watched his taillights retreat into the night, I reprimanded myself all the way to my room. *Good night?* Was that the best I could come up with after that amazing moment? I was opening my bedroom door when Luke stepped out of the bathroom.

"What's going on with you and Casey?" he demanded.

See? Bloody brothers. "Nothing."

"Bull. What were you doing in his car earlier?"

"He gave me a lift home. That's all."

"He doesn't give women a lift home. Unless he's interested in something other than her company, that is."

The butterflies stirred at Luke's words. "Yes, and I'm your sister, aren't I? And isn't he your friend?"

"Humph." Luke obviously hadn't thought of that.

I knew that all I was going to be thinking of all night was Luke's words about Casey only giving lifts to women he wanted to…you know. I wanted to ask Luke how many women that was exactly, but I knew he would see straight through me, so

I chose to close my bedroom door on him and stew on it all night.

By the time morning came around, I wished I'd just bloody well asked him. The bags under my eyes showed exactly how little sleep I'd had. It really wasn't much. Sure, I'd lain in bed until seven, which should have given me at least five hours sleep, but my mind decided sleep wasn't necessary and it was much better to lay awake and imagine Casey with all those women. Mum had played on my mind too. I was really worried that the evidence Detective Ray had was going to bury her. Trouble was, I didn't know what that evidence was. But I was going to find out.

I stood under the shower using more than my share of the hot water, but bugger Luke. It was partly his fault I was so tired. And grumpy apparently. Argh!

I wanted to be at the police station early, but I needed to eat first. My mood wasn't the best when I was hungry, and I figured that I needed to be in a good mood to face Detective Ray.

Walking to the fridge, hoping to find something I could eat and run with, I noticed Mark's home phone number written on the notice board next to the fridge. He'd written it there in case Luke or I ever needed him. Well, I guessed if ever I was going to need him, now would be the time. I mean, I could ride my bike into town, but I was tired, and the thought didn't really appeal to me. Plus, I was hoping that Mum would be coming home with me, and she wouldn't appreciate being doubled on the handlebars. I pulled my cell phone from my pocket and dialed him, hoping he hadn't left for an early morning run.

"Hello," he answered, his voice sounding tired.

"Hi, Mark. It's Sam. Could I get a lift with you to the police station please?"

"The police station? Why on earth do you need to go there?"

Oops. I'd forgotten that we hadn't called him last night to tell him what was happening. "Oh, Mum's been taken in for more questioning. It sounds really serious, and I want to be there so that I can find out exactly what's going on."

"Hmmm. Has she?"

"Yes. She has." Annoyance prickled. I'd expected Mark to be as outraged as us, but he certainly didn't seem upset. "So—can I get a lift?"

"Yes, yes, of course. Ummm...I'll be there as soon as I can." With that he hung up the phone. No pleasant good-byes then.

It took him longer than I thought necessary, but we eventually reached the station just as Mum was being released, her new lawyer by her side. I had no idea where he'd come from, but I was happy to see him anyway. He was middle-aged and balding and looked very efficient.

Apparently Detective Ray had already left the building. Damn. I wouldn't be able to ask him any questions. Oh well, I'd see what Mum had to say first.

She looked tired as she walked toward us. I rushed to her and pulled her close for a hug. I knew Luke wanted to be here, but he'd had to go to work. I had my phone in my pocket, and as soon as we were outside, I would phone him and put Mum on.

"Hey, sweetie," said Mum quietly.

I felt the tears swell as she rubbed my back, as if I were the one in trouble. "Everything's going to be okay."

"I certainly hope so," bellowed Mark, his voice reverberating around the foyer of the police station. "I'll be suing for this, you know!"

Mum's lawyer glared at him and ushered us out the door. Once outside, we all spoke at once. Well Mum, Mark, and I did. It appeared the lawyer kept his cool, even under pressure from us.

"Thank goodness I'm out of there," said Mum.

"They haven't stopped the inheritance, have they?" asked Mark.

"It's okay, Mum. We'll figure this out. We'll find out who the real killer is!"

I was all talk, and Mum saw right through my bravado, pulling me in for another much-needed hug. No matter what the situation, she would always be a mother.

"Look," said the lawyer, his voice controlled. "Rita has had a difficult night. Why don't you take her home and make her some breakfast? She can fill you in on any details you need to know. Anything else, here is my card. You're welcome to call me anytime."

I took the card and read his name. Michael Chatsworth.

Before I had a chance to question him, he turned his back to us and made his way down the path toward his car. We decided to follow his advice and take Mum home. She did look beat.

"Mum, where did the lawyer come from?"

"I called him last night."

"Why? Weren't they only questioning you?"

"Yes. But I didn't like the way that the questions were going, so I thought I should have some professional advice when answering them."

"But doesn't that make you look guilty?" I wrung my hands as I spoke, nerves making me feel very jittery.

"Samantha, I have some extra money that I keep in my safe place at home. I plan to add to it by taking some savings out of my bank account. That way, if this doesn't turn out the way we hope, at least you'll have access to some money."

"But, Mum, that's not a good idea," I said, thinking how Mark snooped around her bedroom.

"Maybe having it at home isn't the best place to keep it," she said to me, "but under the current circumstances, it's the wisest."

"No, Mum, it's all okay. Leave your savings in the bank, deposit the other money, and we'll work it out later."

Mum didn't respond as Mark pulled her under his arm, and they walked ahead of me. I could almost see the cogs in his mind working overtime. He kissed Mum above the ear and asked, "Was it awful?"

"Only because I know just how set Detective Kahoalani is on proving my guilt. Other than that it was kind of interesting," said Mum. "I didn't get any sleep, as there seemed to be a lot of hours between questions, but I certainly learned a lot. For starters, I thought Aloha Lagoon was a quiet place. Apparently I was wrong. All sorts of people were being pulled in all night. There were a few really interesting Scottish backpackers who seemed to have gotten up to some hijinks that they shouldn't have gotten up to. I didn't get to talk to them, but I could hear them shouting about discrimination. Apparently the local man—Kahoni, I think they called him—didn't get arrested, and he was the one throwing the punches."

My mind flipped to Alani. "What?" I asked, running to catch up with Mum and Mark, who were striding ahead of me.

"Yeah, they'd gotten into a fight over a woman. The police were called, and they were placed in lockup. Anyway, that's over now."

"But what did Detective Ray say to you? Why did he take you in? Did you tell him it was a misunderstanding?"

Mum turned to me and smiled. "Samantha, calm down. I'll fill you in on all of that once I get in the car."

Argh! I hated waiting, but I knew better than to argue with her. Instead, I ran ahead to the car and tapped my foot impatiently as they walked up.

Mark unlocked the doors and helped Mum into her seat, and I climbed into the back, ready to hear all about what happened. Once we were all in the car, Mum started to fill us in.

"Albert's autopsy showed that he died from an overdose of insulin, and he wasn't a diabetic," explained Mum, clicking her seat belt in as Mark started the engine. "I asked how they thought he ended up in the ocean, and apparently they're still investigating that, as the video security feed from the nursing home had been switched off that night due to some maintenance."

"That was convenient," added Mark.

I had to agree with him.

"They think I killed him for the inheritance," Mum continued, "and that I knew an autopsy would show how he died, which is why I had to dispose of his body." Mum's ears went red as her anger kicked up.

"Supposedly, once he was dead, I got him into his wheelchair, pushed him out to a car, and then drove him to the beach, where I threw him into the ocean, hoping nature would take it from there."

"How did they think you were strong enough to do that?" I asked, shocked.

"I lift patients on my own all the time. I did tell him that, yes, I could lift a patient on and off the toilet, but into a car? And when they were a dead weight?"

"How did they explain that?" asked Mark, concentrating on the road ahead.

"They didn't. Apparently they're still looking into the evidence."

"The evidence doesn't exist because you're innocent," I almost yelled, my own anger stirring.

"It doesn't matter," said Mum. "They aren't looking for evidence to support that someone else did it. They are only looking for evidence to support that I did."

Maybe they were, but it wouldn't stop me from looking for anything that would clear Mum's name.

CHAPTER SEVEN

As soon as we got home and got Mum settled, I phoned
Alani to make sure she was okay. She was, thanks to her cousin,
Kahoni. It turned out that more than one of the Scottish
backpackers had liked her, and Kahoni overheard them talking
dirty about her. That was when he'd stepped in to teach them to
have more respect for women, and things got out of hand from
there. I wondered if I should point out to her that even though it
had been Kahoni who'd saved her, it had also been Kahoni who
had started the fight? Probably not. I brought her up to date with
what had happened in my night.

"So I guess what I'm asking is, would you help me? I
just want to ask around the nursing home and see if anyone there
saw something that might prove Mum's innocence."

"Well…" She hesitated. "Why don't you let the police do
that?"

"Because I think they're looking at the wrong person. I
can't just sit here and do nothing!"

I heard Alani sigh over the phone line. "Okay. What do
you want to do?"

"I want to chat to the residents of Aloha Ohana. Your
grandmother is there, so I wondered if we could get in on the
pretense that you're visiting her." I bit my nail as I anxiously
waited for Alani's response.

"Yeah, that's okay. I have another bottle of *okolehao* I
want to take to her anyway."

"A bottle of what?"

"It's basically homemade brandy. My brothers make it
for her. She loves it, but it's illegal to make, so we have to hide it

in a Paul Masson brandy bottle. I only took her one last week, but she shares it around, so she goes through it pretty quickly."

My heart jumped. "Oh, sure. Great!"

Hey, I didn't have anything against Lahela having a quiet drop. I was just nervous about this investigating thing, and now I was aiding and abetting the illegal distribution of alcohol to the elderly residents of Aloha Lagoon.

Alani picked me up within the hour. Aloha Ohana wasn't that far from home, the drive only taking ten minutes. Apparently the waiting list to become a resident was pretty long. Getting out of the car and looking back out to the view across the ocean, I couldn't blame people for putting their names down early.

"Tutu is in the Hibiscus wing." That sounded nice. "Do you know which wing Albert lived in?"

No, I didn't, but one quick text message to Luke told me he was in the Oleander wing. Apparently all the wings were named after flowers. My sandals slapped on the asphalt driveway as I ran after Alani toward the entrance. The big automatic doors opened, and we were greeted by a friendly staff member who knew Alani by name.

"Hi, Alani, how are you today?" Her smile was as big as Alani's.

"I'm well, thank you, Ania. You?"

"I can't complain. I'm surprised to see you. This isn't your usual day."

"No, I'm doing an extra visit. This is my friend, Samantha. She's Rita's daughter."

The security guard sitting behind Ania looked up from his newspaper. He was obviously very busy. *Did he not know a killer was running around here?* Okay, I was a bit anxious.

"Oh! Hello, Samantha," said Ania.

Her big smile froze as she looked at me, and I felt the air around us change and become less friendly. She'd obviously heard about the police questioning Mum. Geez, news traveled fast. The security guard, however, didn't seem upset at all. His smile got bigger, and he walked around the desk to greet us.

"Hi, Tony," said Alani, sensing the change.

"Alani," he said, but it was me he focused on. "Hello, Samantha." He held out his hand for me to shake. "I'm very pleased to meet you. You look just like Rita. Has anyone ever told you that?"

"Ummm, yes. I get that a lot." I smiled as I shook his hand.

He was a strange man to look at—really tall and quite overweight. In fact, I'd say he was almost bordering on obese. His dark hair framed his bloated face, making his eyes small and difficult to see. He seemed friendly enough though. And his face lit up at the mention of Rita. I figured maybe he had a bit of a crush.

"Why don't you both sign in the visitors' book, and I'll walk with you to visit Lahela?"

Did we need an escort? Maybe he was more suspicious of Mum than he was letting on.

Alani moved to the visitors' book and signed us both in, and we followed Tony as he walked ahead of us, occasionally looking over his shoulder to check that we were still there.

"How is Rita?" he asked me as we walked. "I heard the awful news of how the police are questioning her."

"She's okay. She's at home, sleeping. She didn't get much sleep last night."

Tony nodded. "Ah, it's such a shame though. I, for one, don't believe it for one minute. Rita is far too nice a person to ever hurt one of the residents. They all love her. Not that I've ever met her myself. We always seem to have different shifts. But I hear things." I guess I could cross off the crush idea.

"Yeah, I think Detective Ray has it wrong too, and I'm going to prove it."

"He was here yesterday asking all sorts of questions and taking away evidence. Apparently he had a tip-off telling him how she supports euthanasia. I've got a feeling I know where that came from."

"Really? Where?" I asked, my own detective skills kicking in.

Tony shuffled uncomfortably and adjusted his belt. "Well…I shouldn't really say anything. Police investigation and all."

Yes, but how was I going to get the answers I needed with that attitude? I decided to let it rest for now and ask Lahela if she'd heard anything like that. Maybe I would have a better chance with her. After all, she didn't have a job she needed to worry about keeping.

I thought of the alcohol Alani was smuggling in for her and made a note to ask Alani what time she drank it. Maybe I should come back after that and ask my questions. Tongues might be a lot looser after consuming it.

We walked down many corridors until I was completely lost, but eventually we stopped in a large common room filled with tables and people playing board games. Alani smiled at Tony. He reminded me of someone. I just needed to figure out who.

"Thanks, Tony. We can take it from here."

"My pleasure, ladies. Enjoy your visit."

Alani led me through the maze of tables to the best seat in the house. A table on the far side of the room overlooking the view.

Alani smiled down at a lady who appeared to be in her seventies. She was large boned and had a mop of frizzy hair pinned at the ear with a bright pink hibiscus flower. Her skin was dark, showing the signs of years of being in the sun, and she had Alani's smile.

"Tutu!" said Alani, her own smile growing bigger than I'd ever seen it.

"Alani! It's about time you turned up for a visit. I don't see you nearly enough!"

She said it with love, and I instantly got a gauge on the type of person she was. She was loud, happy, and still full of life.

"Tutu, I only saw you a few days ago."

"Yeah, and it's not enough. Now sit down, and I'll deal you into the game. Move over, Mallory," she said to the lady sitting opposite her.

Mallory looked not a day over a hundred. She was whiter than a ghost and had shriveled-up skin and large teeth. Actually, I think her teeth were probably the right size once upon a time, but age had shrunken her face, giving them the illusion they were now too big for her.

Mallory looked at us and sighed. She struggled to get up out of her chair, and I wondered if I should help her or if that would be insulting. I didn't have much experience with the elderly.

"What are you playing today?" asked Alani.

"Cards. Five hundred, to be exact."

"Uh, oh. Really? And Mallory is still talking to you?"

"Of course she is. Aren't you, Mallory?"

Mallory was still shuffling to move over one seat to her right. She glared back at Lahela. "I would be if you didn't cheat."

Lahela sighed and looked at me, mouthing the word *dementia* and nodding toward Mallory. I stifled a giggle.

"Who are you, you gorgeous little thing?" she asked me.

"I'm Samantha. Alani's friend."

"Come over here so I can get a better look at you."

I did as Lahela asked and stepped closer. "Hmmm, you look familiar."

"Sam is Rita's daughter. You know, Rita the nurse," explained Alani.

Lahela clapped her hands together loudly, pleased with that. "That's it! You look just like her." She beamed at me.

She obviously liked Mum, which would help me a lot with my investigation.

"Is what I heard about her true?" she asked, her expression turning somber.

I nodded. "Yes, if what you heard is that she's being questioned for the murder of Albert Johnstone."

"Tsk, tsk," she murmured. "Come and sit. Mallory, move over one more so Samantha can sit down."

Mallory had only just sat down after struggling to move the first time. She sighed and shuffled her feet again.

"Oh, no, that's okay. I'll sit over there," I quickly said, indicating a chair on Lahela's left.

"No, you won't," said Lahela. "I can see better out of my right eye, so I want you sitting on my right, next to Alani."

"Tutu, why don't you put your glasses on, and then you'll be able to see out of both eyes?"

"Because I'm not old. Only old people wear glasses."

"I sometimes wear glasses when I'm reading, and I'm only twenty-eight. That's not old." I hoped.

"Yes, and if I had some fancy ones, then maybe I would wear them."

"I'll organize to take you to get some," said Alani. "We can have a shopping day if you like?"

Lahela beamed. "That would be great! So long as it's not on a Monday. I play bingo on Monday. Or Wednesday. That's Tai Chi. And Friday I go swimming."

"Okay. How about I organize it for next Tuesday?"

Lahela looked thoughtful. "Nope, sorry. Tuesday is my television shows."

"Thursday?" asked Alani, not giving up.

"I'll have to see what's on the menu. Don't want to miss a good lunch like last week. I had to go to the hairdresser, and I missed pizza. Luke makes the best pizza."

I nodded in agreement. I wouldn't want to miss Luke's pizza either.

Alani sighed. "Just let me know which day I can take you."

"Okay. Great. Now, are you sitting down so I can deal the next hand?" she asked, referring to the card game we had interrupted.

"Sure," said Alani, smiling at Mallory, who had just sat back down.

I sat next to Alani. It had been a long time since I had played five hundred, and I really hoped I could remember the rules. Turns out it didn't really matter. Lahela pretty much made up the rules as we went along, but we did have fun and definitely laughed a lot.

Only when Mallory nodded off to sleep in her chair did I bring up the subject of Mum. "Lahela, do you mind if I ask you a couple of questions about the man who died?"

"Sure, what do you want to know?"

"Well…" I wasn't really sure what questions I should ask, as I'd never led an investigation before, so I decided to start with the basics. "Did he have any enemies?"

"Albert was an idiot, but he was caring. He'd give you his dinner and starve if he thought you needed it."

"Do you have any idea how he may have ended up where he did?"

"In the ocean, you mean?"

I was trying to be delicate, but obviously Lahela liked to say it as it was. I nodded.

"No, not really. I know it wasn't Rita. She's the only nice nurse here."

Alani tut-tutted. "I'm sure that's not right. There are quite a few nice nurses here. Like that one, for instance," said Alani, nodding toward a nurse who sat talking to another resident.

"Kylie? Don't let her fool you."

"Really?" asked Alani, surprised.

I looked at Kylie. She appeared to be in her early forties, with long dark hair perfectly tied into a ponytail. Her emerald-colored eyes looked almost too green to be unenhanced by contacts, and judging by her body language and how tight she wore her uniform, she looked like she knew just how attractive she was. I amazed myself at how fast I judged people sometimes.

"Really. She normally has a stick up her bum about something, and on the gossip grapevine I heard she told the police that Rita's patients die more often than the other nurses' because she believes in euthanasia. If you ask me, she's just trying to get her into trouble. She doesn't like Rita very much, but then I don't think she likes anyone very much. Unless you're the manager, Tristan. Then she likes you *a lot*, if you get my drift."

I watched Kylie out of the corner of my eye. *Hmmm.*

"I've spoken to Rita about her beliefs," continued Lahela, "and I know how she feels, but I also know she would never kill anybody. Especially in the way that Albert died."

"Tutu, should I be worried about you staying here?" asked Alani, a frown appearing on her forehead.

"No, I'm okay. Tony loves us. He'll make sure nobody else is hurt."

I looked at Tony sitting in a chair and surveying the crowd, his double chin resting on his chest, and wondered how he could protect them.

"Should I be looking into him?" I asked.

"No. He's lovely. He wouldn't do anything wrong. He helps us by sneaking in some treats."

He probably needed to stop eating the treats himself.

"Who do you think did it?" I asked Lahela.

She sighed. "I don't know. I said earlier that Albert was an idiot, and he was. If he liked you, though, he was a sweetie pie, but he was also quite vocal about his political beliefs. A few people didn't like those opinions, and it's not what you know, but who you know. Some around here have the wrong kind of connections, if you know what I mean."

"No. I don't. Sorry."

"That man over there reading the paper…" I looked to the man Lahela was referring to. He sat hunched at a table, grey hair curling out of his ears, his glasses perched on the end of his nose.

"Yes."

"His brother is Barty the Butcher." I heard Alani's sharp intake of breath and turned to look at Lahela. I had no idea who Barty the Butcher was, but judging by Lahela's expression and Alani's reaction, I guessed he wasn't known for his pork cutlets.

Alani put her hand on Lahela's arm. "Why have you never mentioned this before?"

"Because there's nothing to worry about. Ernie," she said, nodding to the man reading the paper, "has a thing for me. He'd never hurt me."

Alani rolled her eyes so far into the top of her head that I thought she was passing out.

"You need to help Rita," continued Lahela, looking at me. "She shouldn't pay the price for someone else's bad karma."

I was contemplating that when a very official-looking man walked over to us, a purpose in his step.

"Lahela," he said, his smile forced as he looked around the table at us. "Got some visitors, I see."

"He's bright, this one," she whispered to me. She turned on her megawatt smile and beamed at him. "Tristan. You're so observant. No wonder you're such a good manager." Lahela winked at me.

"Yes, well… Hello, Alani," he said, turning to her, his cheeks turning pink. "I hope you didn't bring your grandmother any special treats today?"

Uh-oh, he was onto her. Alani didn't miss a beat though. She just batted her eyelashes at him a couple of times and sat back as his eyes glazed over. She knew the power she had over men.

Tristan looked to be in his early sixties. He was short and dumpy, and from what I could see sticking out of his open shirt collar, it appeared the hair on his head had moved to his chest. I looked at Nurse Kylie and shivered. Surely she couldn't be having an affair with him?

He turned to look at me, his shoulders hunching, his posture even more rigid than a moment before. I gave him a smile and a little wave. "I'm Sam, a friend of Alani's."

"You look familiar," he said. "Do I know you?"

You'd think I'd get sick of hearing that, wouldn't you?

"No, but you know my mum, Rita. She works here."

Recognition flashed. "Ah, yes. Of course. I'm sorry to say Rita no longer works here."

"What? Why?"

"I'm sure you can understand we can't have employees working for us who are being questioned for murdering one of our residents?"

"*Questioned* being the important word in that sentence," I added, feeling annoyed for Mum. "Whatever happened to innocent until proven guilty?"

"Yes, of course, it's more of a suspension than a definitive firing, and if it is proven she is innocent, then we will of course reinstate her immediately."

"I hope she's getting paid while she's stood down," added Lahela. "I mean, that would be the right thing to do, her being innocent and all."

"Now, Lahela, I need to follow procedure. I mean, do you know who killed Albert?" He opened and closed his fist and straightened his shoulders, his stance defensive.

"No," I answered. "But I intend to find out who did."

He returned my stare, then gave me a look that suggested I should mind my own business. "Well, I'll leave you ladies to it," he said through gritted teeth, turning on his heel, his smile tight.

I watched him walk away. As he passed Nurse Kylie, a look traveled between them, but he didn't stop. Instead, as soon as he reached the corridor and disappeared from sight, she stood and followed him. She glanced around the room to see who was watching, her body language casual.

"Do you mind if I just duck out to the toilet?" I asked, standing, feeling nosy.

"They're just down the corridor on the right."

I didn't really have a sudden urge to pee, but I did have a sudden urge to add "spy" to my résumé.

CHAPTER EIGHT

———

Turns out that all those teenage years I spent spying on Luke finally paid off. I was excellent at following someone without being noticed.

Tristan disappeared into an office. Seconds later, Kylie followed him and pushed the door closed. Unfortunately for her, but fortunately for me, she didn't click it shut. I moved to the side of it, leaned against the wall, and pretended I had something stuck in my shoe. Not real convincing when you were wearing sandals, but it was the best I could do on short notice.

I couldn't hear them as well as I would have liked, as their voices were low, but I got the gist. Lahela appeared to be correct in her assumptions about them having an affair.

"Are you still okay for tonight?" I heard Kylie say.

"Listen, it's not a good time, what with the murder and the investigation into Rita and all."

"Damn Rita!" Kylie exploded.

I jumped at her tone.

"I'm sick of hearing about her."

"Keep your voice down," I heard him say. "People may hear you. Look, you didn't even shut the door properly."

I heard footsteps start across the floor.

"Rita's all you're worried about! Do you even care about me? About everything I've done for you?"

"Of course I do," continued Tristan, his voice even lower, "but everyone knows that Rita reported you for…"

For what?

I wanted to hear his reply. Instead, all I heard was the click of the door closing. Argh!

I spun around and pressed my ear against it. I could hear Tristan's voice, but I couldn't make out the words.

"What are you doing?"

I heard a voice behind me. I turned quickly, my heart rate dramatically increasing, to find Tony staring at me, his expression quizzical.

"Umm, I was looking for the ladies' toilet, but I had something in my shoe," I said, smiling and hoping my voice sounded a lot more stable than I thought it did.

"You won't find the restroom in there. That's Tristan's office," he said, pointing to the door.

"Oh, really? Silly me!"

Tony stood studying me, his gaze forcing me backward into the door. Moisture broke out on my top lip as he stared. My knees started to knock, and I used the door for support. Thank God it was there.

Turned out, I thanked him a bit too quickly, as just then the door opened, and I fell backward, landing on my rear. Tristan and Kylie both stared down at me.

"What the…" spluttered Tristan.

"Oops," I said, my face burning from embarrassment.

"What are you doing?" demanded Kylie.

"Ummm, I was…umm." My thoughts didn't want to organize themselves.

"She was looking for the ladies' restroom," said Tony, stepping over to help me to my feet.

"In here?" asked Tristan.

"Well, no," I managed. "I was lost. You really need a sign on your door." I attempted to divert his attention.

"I have one," Tristan replied, waving at a nameplate approximately ten inches high.

"Oh, silly me," I mumbled, the temperature of my cheeks turning up to full heat.

"I was just about to show her where the restrooms are," said Tony, his smile making me feel a whole lot better. He turned to Tristan, and his smile froze. "She had something in her shoe and leaned against the door. I was going to say, 'Don't lean there because the door may open,' and guess what? It did!"

He beamed at Tristan and Kylie, yet there was something mechanical about it. If I had to take a guess, I'd say these two men were not friends. I wondered why.

"But you're okay, aren't you?" he asked me. "You're not intending to sue or anything like that, are you?"

With the word "sue," Tristan immediately started spluttering.

"No! Of course not," I said, surprised by his question.

"No harm has been done then," said Tristan. "Tony, show her where the restroom is, please."

Tony took hold of my elbow and led me further down the corridor.

"Why would you think I would sue?" I asked, once we were far enough away from Kylie, who stood in the corridor watching me suspiciously.

"I didn't, but Tristan is really scared of someone suing him, so just mention the word, and he'll do his best to get rid of you."

I smiled at Tony. I liked him already. "You remind me of someone," I said.

Tony stiffened. "Really? Who would that be?"

"I've been trying to figure that out, but I think it's my old neighbor. He was really sweet and kind and always helping me out whenever I needed it."

Tony rolled his shoulders, his smile spreading. "That's good. Young girls like yourself need someone watching out for them."

"Thanks, Tony."

We stopped outside two doors. One was clearly marked *Male* and the other *Female*.

"This is your stop," said Tony. "Do you want me to wait and show you back to the lounge room?"

"No thanks. I should be okay from here."

"Alright then. Take care. It was lovely to see you again, Samantha."

It was only as I was washing my hands that I wondered what he meant by "again."

* * *

"Did you get lost or something?" asked Alani when I made it back to the table.

I nodded. "Yeah. Tony helped me out though."

Alani beamed at me, shaking her head.

"Lahela," I said, sitting down in the chair I had earlier vacated. "Did Mum ever report Kylie for anything?"

Lahela's smile matched Alani's. "Yes," she said with great joy in her voice. The glint in her eye reminded me of a fifteen-year-old. "She did."

"What did she report her for?"

"Well, Rita didn't like the way Kylie treated one of the residents here. Her name was Valerie, and she had dementia. Val's case was pretty sad. She moved in here with her husband some years ago, but he died a few months back. She didn't always remember that though and often asked where he was. Kylie has no patience for things like that. If ever Rita was around, she would just tell Val that he'd gone to play bingo with the men and to carry on with what she was doing. He'd be back before she knew it. Of course he wasn't really coming back, but later Val would remember. Then she'd cry. I mean, of course she did. You see, he's either missing or dead. Not great for poor Val."

My heart broke just a little thinking of Valerie. How cruel could this world be?

"Anyway, Kylie wasn't that nice to Val. One day Val was having an episode, and she was getting really agitated. She kept asking Kylie where her husband was. I yelled out to her that he was at bingo, but for some reason this particular day, she didn't believe that. She got herself into a bit of a state actually. Kylie was being a real bitch, telling her over and over that he was dead. Val was screaming back at her that she was wrong— he couldn't be dead—and she was pacing backward and forward, all the while getting more and more agitated. Rita came onto the shift at that time and kind of took control of the situation, and got Val something to calm her down. But while she'd gone to get it, Kylie must have had enough, because she slapped Val right across the face."

I gave a sharp intake of breath.

"Oh my gosh!" cried Alani.

"Is that what Mum reported her for?" I asked.

Lahela nodded. "Rita came back just in time to see it all happen, and she reported Kylie immediately. I still believe if it had been any other nurse but Kylie, they would have been fired on the spot. As they should. But Miss Fancy Pants obviously worked her magic on Tristan and kept her job.

Alani fidgeted in her seat. "Tutu, why haven't you told me this before?"

"Because I'm not a gossip. And I'll only tell you what you need to know. Like now, for instance. You need to know that you should wear your hair tied back. I like to see your pretty face."

Alani flushed. "I'm worried about you, and all you can tell me to do is tie my hair back?"

"Yes, because it's all you need to worry about. I'm fine. Mallory here is fine. We're all fine, aren't we, Mallory?" she said, gently kicking Mallory under the table to wake her up.

Mallory snorted and jostled awake, startled. Lahela leaned over and handed her a napkin. "Wipe your chin. You're dribbling."

You'd think Mallory would be embarrassed by that, but no. She just accepted the napkin and did as she was told. I guessed that was the meaning of true friendship. You looked out for one another. That kind of friendship I'd yet to find. I looked at Alani and smiled. Maybe.

"Do you think Kylie would have anything to do with Albert's death?" I asked.

Lahela looked thoughtful. "I don't know. She hates Rita, but then she hates everyone. If you want my opinion, I'd leave it to the police to figure out. I wouldn't like to see you girls mixed up in something where you could get hurt."

Neither would I, but surely asking a few questions wouldn't hurt?

Alani nodded. "Okay, Tutu. Don't worry. We'll stay safe."

"Good. Now, last time you took me out to lunch at The Lava Pot, I got to see the good-looking bartender. Tell me—how's he looking these days?"

I smiled as Alani brought Lahela up to date on what Casey was looking like these days, but I was getting lost in my own thoughts.

If Kylie could hurt someone like Valerie, and she had a hatred for Mum, was she capable of killing a man and then setting Mum up to take the blame? But then, why not just kill Mum herself?

I didn't know, but at that moment, it seemed like the best lead I had.

* * *

That night I slept like crap, getting up at least four times. Earlier Lahela had recounted a few scary stories of island mythology, and to say I'd been freaked out was an understatement. Luke's snoring didn't help, and it was only after four a.m. rolled around and Luke's alarm went off that I actually managed to get some sleep. I rolled out of bed at nine and found Mum in the garden, pulling weeds.

I was torn. I wanted to grab a coffee and sit out on the deck enjoying the morning, but if Mum saw me, she'd get me to pull weeds with her. And that was one of the jobs I hated most in the world. Which is why, when living on my own, I lived in an apartment, my only plants being plastic.

I debated too long. Mum saw me standing at the screen door, watching her. She looked up and smiled.

"Don't worry—you're safe," she called out to me.

Phew. I smiled back. "Do you want a coffee?"

"Yes, please."

I poured two cups from the pot on the counter, grabbed the Tupperware container with the apple pie in it (hey, it's got fruit in it, so it's healthy and a good choice for breakfast, right?), and made my way out to the deck.

Mum pulled off her gardening gloves and moved to join me. "I decided since I had some time off, I would sort out this garden. It's been annoying me for so long, but I just haven't had time to fix it."

I looked at the garden. I had no idea what she was worried about.

"It looks great to me," I said, sitting down and handing Mum her coffee. I opened the Tupperware container and pulled out a piece of pie, devouring it in two mouthfuls. God, I loved Luke's cooking.

"Hommm cmmm—" I started.

"Don't talk with your mouth full," chastised Mum.

I swallowed and wiped the crumbs from my lips. "Sorry. How come Luke got all your cooking abilities and I got none? I can't even boil water without messing it up."

Mum sighed. "Samantha, everyone can boil water. You just fill a kettle and switch it on."

"Uh-uh. You're wrong. I know this because my old boss in Sydney told me I was useless at it."

"How can you be useless at that?" asked Mum incredulously.

"Apparently you have to empty the kettle every time and use fresh *cold* water. Not hot water, which I thought would speed up the whole boiling process. Then depending on what type of tea you are making, the water needs to be at different temperatures."

"Seriously?"

"Seriously. In the end she bought one of those kettles that has different settings on it so I couldn't mess it up."

"Well, at least she would have been happy."

I shook my head. "No. How you make the tea depends on whether it's black or green tea. She got a guy from the tea house to come and teach me. Still didn't help. In the end she gave up and got them to deliver it."

Mum was looking at me like I was making it up. I wasn't. My old boss was a cow. I'd like to say my new boss was better, but so far I'd hardly had an opportunity to find out.

"Samantha, I've been meaning to ask you—did you leave some money in the top drawer of the kitchen cabinet?"

I gave her a puzzled look. "No. Why would I do that?"

"I just found a few hundred dollars, and I don't remember leaving it there."

"You do tend to hide money and forget it," I commented, thinking this wouldn't be the first time Mum had done that.

"True," she said, shrugging. "I'll check with Luke though, just in case it's his." She smiled. "When do you go back to work?"

It was my turn to shrug. I stretched my legs out and rested my feet on the handrail surrounding the deck. "Whenever I get a call. It's good to still be getting paid, but I'm worried I'm going to be worked to the bone when I do go back in. How about you?"

Mum sighed. "I have to wait for this investigation to be over. Hopefully the police will figure it all out quickly, and I can get back. Albert's inheritance will help a lot once it comes through. In the meantime I have a small amount of savings, so I won't need to worry about money at least."

"Mum, do you think Kylie is capable of killing him?"

She looked thoughtful as a breeze blew up, wafting the fragrance of the frangipani our way. "Why would she do that? And how do you know Kylie?"

"Oh, Alani took me to Aloha Ohana yesterday. And by the way, what's with Tony the security guard?"

"What do you mean?"

"At first I thought he had a bit of a crush on you because his face kind of lit up at the mention of your name, but then he said he's never met you."

"As far as I know, we haven't ever met. I've heard the other nurses and residents talk about him, but to date I've never had the pleasure of meeting him. Which is a bit odd. I do a lot of extra shifts, but he never seems to be anywhere near where I am." That was strange, but not unheard of. I knew a lot of names of people on staff at my old job, but at least three of them I'd never met.

"Why do you think Kylie killed Albert?" asked Mum, her brow creasing with concern.

"I think maybe she did it to frame you. To get you in trouble for reporting her."

"Geez, how did you hear that I reported her?"

I quickly recounted how Lahela had told me what had happened.

"Listen, Samantha, Lahela is a gorgeous lady, but don't believe everything she tells you."

"Really?"

"Yes. She watches too much daytime television."

"But Kylie could have done it, couldn't she? I mean, she's a nurse, and she had access to the insulin. She could have given it to him. Then when you got the inheritance, it made it look like you did it. Rotting in jail would be a very big punishment for you."

"Kylie didn't know about the inheritance. No one did."

"Well, someone did. I heard Albert had no family here, so how did he change his will to add you?"

"If you're suggesting that Kylie drove Albert into town to change his will, then you're delusional. For starters, she's not that helpful. And second of all, even if she had been, she would have gotten him to name her, not me."

Hmmm. That actually made sense. "Okay. So she didn't know about the inheritance, but it doesn't mean she couldn't have done it."

"Any of the nurses could have done it."

"Do any of the other nurses dislike you enough to set you up?"

"Why do you think someone did it to set me up? Maybe they did it because they had a problem with Albert."

"Well…because…Lahela said Kylie hates you."

"She hates everyone."

"So maybe she hated Albert! You being accused was just a bonus."

"Look—let the police figure it out."

I sat quietly for a moment, thinking. "Detective Ray didn't seem too keen on looking into anyone else."

Mum sighed again. "I know, but what do you want me to do?"

"Nothing. I don't want you to do anything, but I intend to ask a few questions."

We sat in silence for a few minutes, both of us lost in thought.

"You know," said Mum. "I'm not sure if you're right about Kylie, but I've always been suspicious of her husband."

"Husband? I thought she was getting it on with Tristan?"

"Like I said, don't believe everything Lahela tells you."

My heart rate spiked as a thought struck me. I dropped my feet to the ground, excited by my idea. "But what if she *is* having an affair? Then maybe Albert told the husband about Tristan, and the husband got angry, and then Kylie turned on Albert and killed him. She could frame you for the murder. It's a win-win really!" Geez, I'd solved it already. How good was I?

Mum didn't look as convinced. "And I thought it was only cooking you were bad at."

"What?"

She looked at me and smiled. "I love you. You just don't make a very good detective."

"What's wrong with my theory?"

"For starters, if that were the case, I'm sure the police would have questioned her instead of me."

Humph. She had a point. Just not one I was going to admit.

CHAPTER NINE

Okay, I'd admit it. My detective skills sucked. I just wanted to talk to Kylie's husband and ask him a few questions. You know, all the questions I'd learned from watching many, many television shows, like "Where were you and Kylie on the night of the murder?" Anyway, it appeared that wasn't as easy as they made it look.

I'd asked Mum who Kylie's husband was and found out he owned a shop at the resort, so I grabbed the trusty old push bike and made my way there. His shop was a small touristy thing that sold all sorts of rubbish—actually, that little Hawaiian man made out of shells was kind of cute and would be a great addition to my bedroom. But the point was, it wasn't one of the high-end, expensive shops.

I slowly made my way around the store, pretending to check out the merchandise, but really I was looking over my shoulder the entire time, checking out the man behind the counter. It wasn't easy—he was constantly moving! I found a spot to stop and watch from behind a revolving rack of postcards. It was the perfect position. I blended into the shop perfectly, as the man hadn't noticed me yet, and I had a moment of thinking this was another skill I'd learnt as a teenager— sneaking around and listening in on Luke's conversations with his friends.

I spun the postcard rack and noticed the man serve a customer at the cash register. I got a good look at him when the rack was spinning, but when it was stopped, it blocked my view almost completely. I spun it again. And again.

To be honest, he wasn't what I was expecting at all. He was a lot younger than Tristan and was actually pretty good-looking. I guessed him to be close to six foot. He had a full head of hair, and judging by the way his T-shirt pulled tightly across his extremely muscled chest every time he moved, I figured he worked out.

I spun the rack, picking up a random postcard and waiting for the last customer to leave the shop so that I could approach him. The customer, however, was very chatty. Or maybe that was flirty. He *was* pretty cute. I had no idea why Kylie would be messing around with Tristan if she was married to this guy.

I spun the rack again, completely engrossed in what I was watching.

"What are you doing?" asked a deep voice from behind me. I jumped and let out a small scream, turning and coming face to face with a very grumpy looking man. *Where the heck had he come from?*

So much for me being the sneaky one.

"Sorry. I didn't see you. Been there long?" I asked, placing my hand on my chest, hoping it would slow my heart rate down.

"I've been standing here for the last few minutes, watching you."

"Really?" I guess I could cross *spy* off the résumé after all.

"Yes. Would you like to explain what exactly you're doing?"

No, not really. But judging by his stance, I didn't think it was optional.

"What makes you think I'm doing anything other than buying a postcard?" I asked, waving the postcard I was holding in the air.

The man took it from me and looked at it. "You're buying this card?" he asked, turning the card to face me. I blushed at the large-chested girl in the very wet T-shirt saying *Aloha*.

I snatched it from him and put it back on the rack, mumbling. "Well, not *that* one exactly…"

The man crossed his arms over his chest and glared down at me.

"Glenn," he said nodding toward the man behind the counter, "phoned me and said that there was a suspicious-looking woman in the store. He suspected shoplifting. Can you show me what's in your pockets please?"

I turned to look at Glenn accusingly.

"Well, I'm offended by that. Do I look like a shoplifter to you?" I demanded, placing my hands on my hips.

The man in front of me looked me up and down. "Yes."

Now maybe I shouldn't have worn the large jacket, baseball cap, and sunglasses, but I worked at this resort too, and I didn't really want him to know who I was. Too late for that now though. I sighed and opened the jacket to show him that I had nothing in my pockets after all.

"So what *are* you doing?"

"I was watching him," I blurted out, my heart still racing, sweat kicking up to maximum saturation.

"Why?"

"Because I'm investigating the murder of Albert Johnstone, and I want to know where he and his wife were on the night he died." Alright, I probably should have been slightly more diplomatic, but I hadn't really thought this through. I definitely didn't have a backup plan in case of capture.

"I don't have a wife!" shouted the man, looking shocked. The woman he was serving stood very still watching the whole scene unfold.

"Of course you have a wife," I stated. "Her name is…" It appeared that panic made me forget important pieces of information. "It's…ummm…K…Kyl…Kylie!" I blurted. Glenn looked taken aback.

"Kylie is not his wife. She's mine," said grumpy man. Now that made more sense. "Why do you want to know where we were?"

"I'm just asking, that's all."

Grumpy Man eyed me suspiciously and pulled himself up to his full height, which I wasn't exactly sure how tall that was, but it was a lot taller than me. "If you're with the police, show me your badge, or get out of my shop!" he demanded.

Well, as I didn't have a badge, I of course did exactly what he suggested. I pulled my shoulders back, held my head high, and exited the building, only to find Casey standing on the path out in front watching the entire show. Urgh! Could this get any worse?

Apparently, yes it could. I was just trying to explain myself to Casey in a way that didn't make me look like an idiot, when my phone rang. It was Luke.

"Hey, dude! What's up?" I asked, grateful for the distraction. Casey walked beside me, chuckling away.

"Hey." He sounded down.

"Are you okay?"

"No, I'm not."

My heart missed a beat, and I stopped walking, straining to hear every syllable he said.

"There's been another murder," he continued. "Here at Aloha Ohana. There are police everywhere. I don't know what's going on, but they've kicked us all out of the kitchen and are searching it."

"Are you sure?" I crossed my fingers that Luke had just misinterpreted things.

I heard his sigh. "Yes, I'm bloody sure!"

"Okay. Don't snap. I'm sure it's just procedure." I hoped.

Casey looked at me, his eyebrows raised. I mouthed *There's been another murder* to him, and I saw the appropriate amount of shock on his face.

"Who was it? What actually happened?" I asked breathlessly.

"One of the male patients died last night."

The nausea settled slightly, knowing that at least it wasn't Lahela or Mallory. "So? You work in an aged-care facility. I'm sure that's a common occurrence." Wasn't it?

"Yeah, but this guy didn't die from anything natural."

"How do they know that already?"

"His body was found early this morning in a dumpster downtown."

My stomach rolled with truly threatening nausea, and for a moment I looked around for a discreet place to throw up my lunch. Then I looked at Casey, took some deep breaths, and told myself not to do anything that embarrassing.

He must have seen the color I went, as he placed his arm around my shoulder and steered me to the nearest bench seat. The seat overlooked the grassy area near the pool, and the contrast of what Luke was telling me and what I was looking at felt surreal.

I sat heavily on the seat and waited for Luke to finish talking.

"But why are they searching the kitchen?" I asked.

"They're searching everywhere, but they seem to be spending extra time in there."

"Who died?" I asked, dread sitting heavily on my shoulders.

"His name was Jeremy. Jeremy Gibson."

I shouldn't have asked. Hearing about a murder was like watching a movie. It wasn't real until you put a name to it. Then it becomes a real person. One who'd had a life and a story and wasn't ready for that to end yet. I felt tears prick my eyelids.

"Do you want us to come up and be with you?"

"No, Mum's the last person who should be here at the moment."

"Oh, I'm not with Mum. I'm with Casey."

The line went silent for a moment. I pulled it away from my ear and checked that the call was still connected. "Luke? Are you still there?"

"Yeah, I'm here. Why are you with Casey?"

"I'm at the resort, and he was walking past."

Luke was going to go all "big brother" on me, wasn't he? I looked at Casey out of the corner of my eye. He was so good-looking that he could have any woman he wanted, so my chances were limited, but there was no bloody way I'd let Luke limit them even more.

"Okay. I'll keep you informed with what's happening," finished Luke, ending the call without even a good-bye. He was obviously annoyed as well as upset.

I turned to Casey and filled him in on what Luke had told me, leaving out the silent treatment I'd gotten. I'd make sure I had a chat with Luke about that before he could open his mouth and fill Casey's head with any unnecessary thoughts. Like *Leave*

Samantha alone—you don't hit on your friend's sister—you know, that kind of thought.

Casey looked worried. "There've been a lot of deaths around here lately."

"Yeah, I know. It's scary. I'll have to call Alani and make sure Lahela is okay. Maybe she should move her out for a while. She'll be safer at Alani's." I leaned forward, elbows on my knees, my hands cradling my chin. "At least they can't blame Mum for this one."

Casey turned to me, his eyes soft. I felt my breath hitch with the compassionate look he gave me as our eyes locked.

I wanted to sit like that for hours, totally lost in his eyes, but my phone rang again.

I sighed and pulled it from the pocket of my shorts. It was Human Resources. David Mahelona, to be exact.

"Hello," I said cheerily, even though my heart wasn't quite in it.

"Samantha, this is a call to let you know your classes will begin again in the morning. Start work at eight. Your roster will be emailed to you shortly." He hung up.

It must have been the day for no polite good-byes. I sighed and pushed my phone back into my shorts. Now I had two things to worry about. Proving Mum was innocent in the murder of Albert Johnstone and proving I could actually teach a bunch of kids to surf.

I once again placed my elbows on my knees, but this time I hung my head in my hands and sighed. A monster headache was starting right behind my eyes.

* * *

I should have made that three things to worry about. Pulling into Mum's driveway, I found my path blocked by Detective Ray's car. Dread weighed me down as I wheeled the bike to the back of the house and made my way inside.

I chastised myself for thinking the worst. I mean, they could be here to tell Mum they'd solved the first murder and she was no longer a suspect.

The second I opened the door and saw Mum and Mark sitting at the table, and Luke sitting in the lounge with the good detective, I knew my first impression had been right.

Detective Ray sat opposite Luke, a notebook open in his hand, scribbling notes, his expression grim. Luke sat answering his questions, his expression matching the detective's.

I moved to Mum and sat down. I whispered, "What's happening?"

She whispered back, "He's asking Luke questions about Jeremy Gibson."

Mark smiled at me, his way of a greeting. I gave him a tight smile back, straining to hear what the detective was asking Luke. I heard only snippets like, "Why keep it in the kitchen?" To which Luke replied, "I don't. I'm a cook," as if that explained everything.

I looked back at Mum.

"What's he talking about?" I whispered.

To which Mum whispered back, "Shut up and wait."

I sat back in my chair and folded my arms, sulking a little. I mean, I was part of this family too. I had a right to know what Luke was being asked.

Mark turned to me and whispered, "What were you doing at the resort today?"

To be honest, I was surprised he even knew I was at the resort.

I replied, "I work there, Mark. What do you think?"

"I thought you'd been suspended?"

"What?"

"I thought you'd been suspended?"

"Oh. Well, I start again tomorrow." What did Mark care what I was doing there?

Luke's raised voice floated up from the lounge toward us. Suddenly I understood why Mum had told me to shut up. I'd completely lost track of what the detective had been asking whilst I was distracted by Mark.

"Have you ever heard of evidence, Detective?" Luke asked, sarcasm dripping from every word. "It's generally what the police need to pin a crime on someone."

Mum instantly leaped up from her seat at the table and was across the room in less than a second.

"Luke," she said, cautioning him with one word.

He was red with anger, but his stare never faltered. "This is ridiculous. Come back with evidence, and then I'll answer more of your questions." He stormed from the room, slamming the front door behind him.

Detective Ray looked at Mum. "I could have taken him to the station to question him. I didn't have to do it here."

"I know. I appreciate that," she said, attempting to placate the detective, who was now fuming. "Do you know if Jeremy died the same way Albert did?"

"Not yet. We're waiting for his autopsy," he replied, his words clipped. "Don't think this puts you in the clear, Ms. Reynolds. Just because you're not working at Aloha Ohana at the moment doesn't mean I won't be asking you the same questions I asked your son."

I saw Mum suck her bottom lip in and knew she was biting it as hard as she could. Once she'd regained some composure, she asked, overly politely, "Would you like to ask me now?"

Detective Ray narrowed his eyes. "Where were you last night between midnight and three a.m.?"

Mum didn't miss a beat. "In bed. You can ask Mark to verify that. He was with me," she said, pointing to Mark.

All eyes turned to him. I held my breath and waited for Mark to back her up "Do you verify that?" asked the detective.

Mark's face went red. "Ummm…kind of. Yes. Yes."

"Are you saying that you were in bed with Ms. Reynolds between midnight and three a.m.?"

Mark stuttered, looking at his feet.

"Mark!" snapped Mum. "You were there. Tell him."

You could practically see the cogs in his mind working. "Yes. I was there with you. At midnight."

"What about the rest of the time period?"

Mark sighed. "Yes."

"Yes?"

I wanted to jump across the kitchen table and shake him. Mum needed him to give her an alibi, and he was stumbling.

What was the matter with him? Surely he could tell the truth? It wasn't hard—unless it wasn't the truth. And if it wasn't the truth—where was he?

"Yes, I can vouch for her. She was in bed with me. Here in this house!" He smiled charismatically at both Mum and the detective, but even from this side of the table I could see the sweat break out on his forehead.

Detective Ray frowned, his gaze moving from Mum to Mark. Eventually he scribbled in his notebook and slammed it shut. "That's enough for now. Call me if you change your mind," he said, his words directed at Mark.

At least Mark had the grace to blush. Once Detective Ray had gone, Mum turned to him.

"What was that about?"

"What do you mean?"

"You sounded like you were lying when you told him you were with me last night."

"I wasn't lying. I was with you."

"Then why did you act like that?"

"I just didn't like the way he put me on the spot," mumbled Mark, shifting uncomfortably under the stares both Mum and I were giving him. "Anyway, I've got to go."

"But you and I were having dinner together," said Mum, surprised.

"Sorry. I've got to take a rain check. I've received a message that I'm needed at work urgently." He moved to Mum and pulled her in for a hug, kissing her gently on the lips. "I'll make it up to you. I promise. Tomorrow night I'm taking you to Starlight on the Lagoon for dinner."

I felt the hair on the back of my neck rise as I watched him. Something was off. I just needed to put my finger on what.

* * *

I didn't know where Luke ended up. I had sent him several messages asking him if he was alright. He'd responded to one of them with a simple *yes*. I chose to ignore the tone I read into it, put my phone down, and watched a movie with Mum.

Halfway through it, I realized what it was about Mark that felt off to me.

"Mum, does Mark have a phone?"

"Yes, of course he does. You know that. He left his number on the fridge for you and Luke," she replied, helping herself to the homemade popcorn. It was, at present, sitting in a very large bowl balanced on my lap, mostly because I was eating the majority of it, and that felt like the most efficient place to keep it.

"I'm talking about a cell phone. He said he agrees with you about radiation and all that."

"Oh, no, he doesn't have a cell phone. Sorry, I thought you were referring to a house phone."

"Well, how did he get a message saying he was needed urgently at work if he doesn't have a cell phone?"

"He probably checked his home messages."

"But how did he do that?"

"It's easy. You can call your home messages from any phone."

"But I never saw him use the phone."

Mum sighed, giving me a warning look. "Don't read anything into it, Samantha."

"I'm not. I just thought it was odd." So odd I was going to ask him about it the next time I saw him. "Where does he work anyway?"

"At the nursery I get my plants from. That's how we met."

She smiled at the memory, her entire face lighting up for the first time tonight. Even Mr. Bean dancing across the television screen couldn't get that kind of a reaction out of her.

I guess I needed to lighten up on Mark a bit. Growing up, Mum had never had a man in her life. As an adult, I'd asked her about it, and she'd told me she never wanted to jeopardize our family unit. Our dad had done enough damage to that already. She deserved to have love again. I just hoped Mark was the right person for the job.

The niggly feeling in the pit of my stomach felt different about it though.

* * *

Surfing lessons had begun again. My confidence had definitely grown, as the practice seemed to have paid off, but that confidence dipped when I'd received a phone call from the resort's director of activities, Juls Kekoa, who was technically my immediate boss, requesting a quick meeting before my class began. I hoped it was all good news.

I'll admit to being just a little bit apprehensive about meeting Juls for the first time. Whenever I'd seen her around, she was either running or swimming or something equally energetic. I got exhausted just watching her.

Preparing for my class, I placed the last surfboard on the sand and stood surveying the water. I took a few deep breaths and allowed the salt air and water to calm me. I was just feeling quite zen-like when I heard a voice behind me.

"Samantha?"

I spun around and saw Juls speed walk over the sand toward me, her long, lean legs making it look effortless.

I plastered on a smile and hoped my nerves weren't showing. "Yes. You must be Juls."

She held out her hand for me to shake. "I'm so sorry that we haven't met yet. It's been pretty hectic around here, with Brad being unwell and then the death, so thank you for your patience."

I let out the breath I'd been holding, as she seemed quite friendly.

"No worries at all. The time off has given me more preparation time."

"That's good. We did throw you in the deep end expecting you to start the very day after you were hired."

I smiled and hoped I portrayed professionalism. You know what they say? Fake it till you make it!

"I know you're about to start teaching, so I won't take up too much of your time, but I just wanted to go over the roster with you." She pulled a folder from under her arm and opened it, showing me a very complicated looking spreadsheet. Geez, who knew there were so many things to do in a resort. I was glad I didn't have her job.

"We have suspended the adult lessons for now, waiting to find out what's happening with our usual instructor, Brad, but as you know, we're continuing with the children's lessons. Unfortunately, due to recent events, numbers for those classes have dropped. I've tried to condense those lessons so that you're not teaching just one child at a time." She handed me the roster. I took it from her, secretly wishing that I did only have one child to teach. "That's your copy. If you have any concerns about it, please let me know. My direct number is on the bottom, so feel free to call me anytime." She stood back from me and smiled, her dark eyes reflecting her islander heritage.

"Thank you. I'm sure it will all work perfectly."

"Okay. Well, I can see that you have students arriving, so I'll leave you to it. It was a pleasure meeting you, Samantha." She once again held out her hand for me to shake.

I accepted her hand and smiled. "You too, Juls," I said, thinking that was the fastest meeting I had ever attended.

* * *

It turned out I wasn't so bad at teaching after all. Don't know what I'd been worried about. Juls was correct when she'd told me that cancellations were pouring in since word had gotten around about the body washing up in the surf and a possible murderer running around Aloha Lagoon.

On the one hand, that was good for me, as it meant my audience wasn't so big. On the other, it meant I got through the lesson a lot faster than I wanted to, as I didn't have as many children to get through. I was happily making my way through YouTube videos of *Learning to Surf* lessons nicely, and I seemed to be remembering it all.

The kids were actually progressing a lot better than I expected them too, and I did wonder if I had a natural ability at teaching.

I gladly waved good-bye to the last of them, and even though I was exhausted, I gave myself a secret high five that I'd made it through my first full day as a surfing instructor. Yay me! I was even going to treat myself to a cocktail later.

My happiness disappeared as Luke walked toward me, his scowl visible from fifty meters away.

"Hey! What's up?" I asked as he approached me.

"What's up? I'll tell you what's bloody up. Bloody Tristan suspended me without pay until these murders have been solved, that's what's bloody up!"

It took me a moment for my brain to catch up with what he was saying. "What? Why?"

"Because apparently," he said, doing air quotes, "it's not a 'good look' for the Aloha Ohana when two of their residents are murdered and the suspects belong to the same family."

"Huh?"

"You heard me. The police are looking closely at me for the second murder." Luke ran his hands over his face, fatigue causing dark rings under his eyes.

"Why are they looking at you? That's ridiculous."

"I know. That's what I told them. Just not in those words. Jeremy Gibson's autopsy showed he was killed with rat poison. And they found rat poison with my fingerprints all over it."

"How were your fingerprints on it? Do you use rat poison as a cook?" My mind was starting to race. There had to be a good explanation.

Luke looked at me like I was an idiot. "No! Of course I don't use rat poison as a cook. But I did throw some out the day before last."

"Why? Where was it?"

"I found it behind the bin outside the kitchen and figured whoever threw it there must have missed the bin. So I picked it up and got rid of it."

Oh, well that was a good explanation.

"Anyway," continued Luke, "the autopsy also showed that the poison was injected, not ingested, but that's not what finished him off. Suffocation did that."

"So surely that would get you off the hook?" The knot in my stomach started to unravel. "You don't know one end of a needle from the other."

"Yeah, but Tristan thinks it doesn't look good."

Tristan was an idiot. "What about the police? What do they think?"

"They're still investigating and haven't made an arrest. '*Yet*' is what Detective Ray told me."

"They can't really believe you're a suspect, can they?"

"Apparently, yes. Mum is still number one suspect for the first murder. That puts me in the spotlight for this one, as maybe we were working together. Mum knows how to use a needle, and the rat poison had my fingerprints on it." Luke shook his head.

"That's ridiculous."

"Tell me about it. Anyway, enough of my bad news. What are you doing? Do you want to get a drink?"

I was surprised by his question. Luke and I hadn't hung out together for years. "Sure. I'd like to duck to the staff room though and have a quick shower first. I remembered to bring other clothes with me today."

Luke looked at me suspiciously. "Why? Don't you just put your uniform over your swimsuit and ride your bike home?"

"Well, yes, I did last time I worked, but I'm a quick learner."

Last time I'd been talking to Casey and stuck looking like crap. I wasn't letting that happen twice. I noted Luke's expression. "It's not very comfortable riding a bike with a swim suit full of sand," I added.

"Alright, alright. I don't need the details," said Luke, backing away from me very quickly. Maybe he was worried I'd show him or something. "Meet me in The Lava Pot when you're ready."

"Sure, I won't be long."

Luke turned and made his way to The Lava Pot whilst I made my way to the staff amenities for a shower. Actually, I was a bit longer than I had hoped. I was doing the best I could do without a hair dryer (I made a mental note to add *hair dryer* to staff requests next time I got the opportunity). I dusted my face with mineral powder, lined my eyes with brown eyeliner, and swiped on as much mascara as my lashes could cope with. I pulled on my skinny jeans and floaty top Alani had sold me at a hugely discounted price, and slipped into my sandals. I gave myself one last check over, scrunched my hair to hopefully give it some bounce, and made my way to the tiki bar.

I found Luke and Casey deep in conversation. I attempted to slide quietly onto the barstool next to Luke, but that didn't happen, as the second Casey noticed me, he smiled, which in turn made my knees go all rubbery, and then they didn't want to participate in the holding me up thing.

Seriously, I only had to move my backside onto the stool. You would think they could have held out long enough for me to do that gracefully? Instead, I hit the stool with my hip, knocking it over. It crashed to the floor, with me attempting to catch it before it hit the ground. All I managed to do though was knock Luke's drink out of his hand as he turned to see what the heck I was doing. Then all the hard work I had put into looking my best for Casey was destroyed as a full glass of beer dripped down my top. If someone could actually die from embarrassment, they would be zipping up my body bag about now.

Luke shook his head, his frown giving him a mono brow. Casey just turned the smile up even more. *Don't look at him, Sam. Don't look. It's the only way you'll survive!* This would become my mantra from now on.

I bent down to retrieve the stool as Casey handed me a pile of napkins to mop up my cleavage. Well, the positive was that he was at least looking at my cleavage. Maybe that was what I should have been doing all along. Covering myself in alcohol. No, the smell of it was starting to turn my stomach.

"You are so embarrassing," commented Luke.

"Yeah, I know, but you love me anyway," I said. I mean, what else could I say?

"Would you like a drink you can actually swallow?" asked Casey, the crinkles around his eyes making him look even more adorable.

I smiled back. I may be covered in beer, but that wasn't going to stop me. "Yes please. I'll have my usual."

Luke's mono brow disappeared somewhere around his hairline. "You have a usual?"

"Yes, I do."

I knew what he was thinking. And let him think it. I'd spend as much time with Casey as I could. Even if that meant spending my entire pay at the bar and becoming an alcoholic.

Actually, maybe I did need to review my plan. It probably wasn't the best one I could come up with.

"Maybe I should be working here," said Luke, giving me the evil eye.

"I can try to get you a job if you want one," said Casey, his expression turning serious as he looked at Luke.

"Really?"

"Yeah. If you're not getting paid from Aloha Ohana, then you'll need money. I just had someone quit, so I can talk to David Mahelona if you like."

Luke looked thoughtful for a second. As did I. This was probably a good thing for Luke, as he would still have some money coming in, but did I want Luke here every time I came to flirt with Casey? Yes, I knew it was hard to recognize, but that was my version of flirting.

"Alright. Sounds good. Unless of course I'm arrested. Then Mahelona may not want me hanging around the resort."

"It's all sweet. Don't worry about him. I'll sort it."

"Cool," said Luke, breaking out the first smile I'd seen from him today, his mono brow becoming two separate eyebrows once again.

"Are you alright?" Casey asked, turning his attention to me.

I caught my reflection in the mirror behind the bar and noticed that my mouth was very unattractively hanging open. I quickly shut it.

"I was just hoping to…ummm…get my drink!"

"Oh sure!" said Casey, his cheeks turning red. "Sorry."

I instantly felt bad for him. "It's okay. No hurry."

Actually, an alcoholic drink was exactly what I needed. Luke turned to me and smiled that smug smile he had whenever he'd gotten the better of me. I remembered it well from when we were kids.

"Luke, do you like Mark?" I asked, changing the subject before he could challenge me about Casey.

"He's alright. Why?"

"I think he's up to something?"

"Why do you think that?"

"Because I saw him in Mum's bedroom when she wasn't home, and he lied about a phone call. And I think he lied to the police about being with Mum."

Luke looked back at me, amazed. You'd think after twenty-eight years he'd know exactly how fast my mind worked, wouldn't you?

"Sam, he was probably in the bedroom because he stays over a lot. Maybe he left his tighty-whities in there."

I shuddered at the thought. "Why would he lie about a phone call though?"

"Okay, you're going to have to give me more information."

I gave him the fast version of events. When I got to the part about how Mark seemed reluctant to tell the police he was with Mum at the time of the murder, even Casey was frowning.

Luke scratched his head. "I don't know. He's always seemed good for her."

"You don't think he's connected to the murders, do you?" asked Casey, handing me my drink. Luckily, the bar was quiet tonight, as he didn't seem to be doing much other than talking to us.

I considered what he said. I hadn't actually thought of that. I just thought maybe Mark was up to something that would affect Mum. Like stealing her money or having an affair—that kind of thing.

I shrugged. I didn't know, but maybe I needed to add finding out to my To Do list.

CHAPTER TEN

The next day I finished work earlier than expected as class numbers had definitely dropped.

Those parents who had gone ahead with lessons had sat on the deck overlooking the sand and watched the entire thing, which was far worse than it actually sounded.

The wind had picked up a little more that day, which meant the waves had been slightly bigger, and I looked even worse than normal. It did help that I hadn't done any of my laundry, and the only clean swimsuit I owned was the bikini I'd got from Lahela's Surf on the first day I'd been employed.

This bikini was really a bit small for a surfing instructor to children, but the dads hadn't seemed to mind too much. In fact, I'd had quite a few requests for adult lessons too.

Thankfully, the lessons had been uneventful, and as I waved good-bye to the last of the kids, I put a surfboard under each arm and made my way up the sand to the trolley I used for carting them, starting my pack up for the day. I looked up and saw a woman smiling at me. We hadn't officially met yet, but I'd seen her around the resort.

"Hello," she called, stepping barefoot onto the sand. She carried a pair of gorgeous high heels in one hand.

I gave her a small wave. "Hi."

"You look like you're settling in really well," she said, smiling as she approached me. She was really pretty, with a slim face and a dark streak in her short blonde hair. Her blue eyes shone back at me. "Better than I did anyway."

"I'm getting there," I said, returning a smile. Something about her made me feel at ease.

"I'm Gabby, Gabby LeClair." I'd heard that she owned Gabby's Island Adventures. If you wanted to explore the island and see its many attractions, then she was the girl to see. I made a mental note to get a brochure from her later, as exploring the island was definitely on my To Do list.

"I'm Samantha, and I'm pleased to meet you, Gabby."

"Can I help you?" she asked. "I mean, that looks like a lot for you to handle."

"That's really kind of you, but I'm sort of balanced here," I replied. Boards weren't overly heavy, but they could be awkward when you were carrying two of them. Luckily, I'd figured out a way to balance them. "I've been meaning to come and see you, as I'd love to do one of your tours one day. I haven't seen very much of the island yet and thought it would be a great way to do it."

"Sure. That would be great. I can get you on anything you'd like. And I offer resort employees a discount."

A discount sounded good. Just then we both heard the distinct *whoop whoop* sound of a helicopter. We looked up to see Rick's Air Paradise fly over. It wasn't the first time today I'd seen him. He was obviously very busy.

"That's number one on my list of things to do," I said with a wistful sigh.

"I highly recommend it," said Gabby. Her accent was different than most I'd heard so far, and I wondered where in the States she was from. "You get to see so much of the island from his helicopter. It just takes your breath away."

"It sounds amazing." It also sounded pricey, so I figured I'd be waiting a while to do it.

We'd stopped in front of the trolley, and I placed my board on to it. Gabby set her shoes down and helped me.

"Word around the resort employees is that you're new to the island."

I nodded.

"We should grab a drink at The Lava Pot one night and get to know each other before you go all island on me," she said. "I haven't been here for that long either."

"That's so nice of you," I replied. "I'd love that."

I flipped its screen up and waited for it to light up. The laptop was pretty slow, but when prompted, I entered Mum's password (she only ever used one of three passwords for everything. It was either Luke, Samantha, or our old dog Rastas!). I got it right on the second attempt. A photo of the beach outside of the resort filled the screen. I moved the cursor to the top left of the task bar and clicked to see her browser history. The only page that had been opened today was her internet banking.

I couldn't guarantee that Mark had been the one who'd opened it, but I'd bet every cent I owned that it was.

* * *

I was contemplating what to make for dinner. Mum was staying out for the evening with Rebecca, and I had no idea where Luke was. I'd messaged him earlier and told him about Mr. Fathersham, and he'd messaged back that he would sort it out. Whatever *it* was. That left me to my own devices for dinner.

The fridge had no leftovers in it, as Mark had helped himself to those at lunchtime. In Sydney, I'd eaten a lot of takeout. Aloha Lagoon didn't have too many choices for takeout. It had a lot of restaurants, but I would have felt silly eating in on my own. I was just thinking *Bugger it, let me look silly*, when my phone rang. It was Alani.

"Hey!" I sang, happy to hear her voice.

"Hey you," she said back.

"What's up?"

"I'm going to see Tutu tomorrow and wondered if you wanted to come?"

"Oh, okay. That's cool. So long as it's in the morning. I don't have any classes booked until after lunch."

"Yeah, that suits. I just want some backup when I tell her I want her to move home with me for a few days. At least until they've caught the murderer." Alani's tone turned dark, and I could hear the concern in her voice.

"Do you think she'll resist?"

"Of course she'll resist. She's not known for doing what others tell her."

"I'm Gabby, Gabby LeClair." I'd heard that she owned Gabby's Island Adventures. If you wanted to explore the island and see its many attractions, then she was the girl to see. I made a mental note to get a brochure from her later, as exploring the island was definitely on my To Do list.

"I'm Samantha, and I'm pleased to meet you, Gabby."

"Can I help you?" she asked. "I mean, that looks like a lot for you to handle."

"That's really kind of you, but I'm sort of balanced here," I replied. Boards weren't overly heavy, but they could be awkward when you were carrying two of them. Luckily, I'd figured out a way to balance them. "I've been meaning to come and see you, as I'd love to do one of your tours one day. I haven't seen very much of the island yet and thought it would be a great way to do it."

"Sure. That would be great. I can get you on anything you'd like. And I offer resort employees a discount."

A discount sounded good. Just then we both heard the distinct *whoop whoop* sound of a helicopter. We looked up to see Rick's Air Paradise fly over. It wasn't the first time today I'd seen him. He was obviously very busy.

"That's number one on my list of things to do," I said with a wistful sigh.

"I highly recommend it," said Gabby. Her accent was different than most I'd heard so far, and I wondered where in the States she was from. "You get to see so much of the island from his helicopter. It just takes your breath away."

"It sounds amazing." It also sounded pricey, so I figured I'd be waiting a while to do it.

We'd stopped in front of the trolley, and I placed my board on to it. Gabby set her shoes down and helped me.

"Word around the resort employees is that you're new to the island."

I nodded.

"We should grab a drink at The Lava Pot one night and get to know each other before you go all island on me," she said. "I haven't been here for that long either."

"That's so nice of you," I replied. "I'd love that."

I had to give the guy the benefit of the doubt here. Maybe he was just awkward. "Alright, I'll keep it in mind. Thanks." I took a mouthful of my coffee to cover my discomfort and then spat it straight back out. Argh! "That's the worse coffee I've ever tasted!"

"Really? I thought it was delicious," said Mark, lifting his own cup to his lips. "It's just the way I like it."

I moved away into the lounge room in search of Mum's laptop computer. Two reasons: I wanted to check my bank balance and see if my first pay had gone in, and I wanted to get out of Mark's zone.

"What are you looking for?" he asked, watching me as I walked. "Maybe I can help."

"Do you know where Mum's laptop is?" I knelt down and looked under the sofa.

"The laptop?"

"Yes. Mum's laptop."

"She doesn't own a laptop."

"Yes, she does. Luke was using it the other day." Maybe I should be looking in his room for it.

"Ahh, I know the one now." Mark shifted uncomfortably, shuffling the papers on the table as he spoke. "Sorry, I haven't seen it."

As he moved, I caught a view of a sliver of silver the same color as Mum's Apple MacBook.

"Is that it under your newspaper?" I asked.

"What?" Mark's cheeks turned a bright crimson color.

I moved to him and lifted his arm, moving a newspaper aside. And sure enough, there was Mum's laptop, the underside of it warm, as though it had just been used.

Mark fidgeted, adjusting his paper unnecessarily. "I'll be damned. Had no idea it was there." He beamed at me charismatically.

I figured it was a tactic he used often and probably got away with when used on a woman Mum's age. Me? It gave me the creeps. I was about to question how a laptop—a whole laptop—could be under your newspaper and you didn't even know it, when the doorbell rang. I sighed, placing the laptop on

"I'm Gabby, Gabby LeClair." I'd heard that she owned Gabby's Island Adventures. If you wanted to explore the island and see its many attractions, then she was the girl to see. I made a mental note to get a brochure from her later, as exploring the island was definitely on my To Do list.

"I'm Samantha, and I'm pleased to meet you, Gabby."

"Can I help you?" she asked. "I mean, that looks like a lot for you to handle."

"That's really kind of you, but I'm sort of balanced here," I replied. Boards weren't overly heavy, but they could be awkward when you were carrying two of them. Luckily, I'd figured out a way to balance them. "I've been meaning to come and see you, as I'd love to do one of your tours one day. I haven't seen very much of the island yet and thought it would be a great way to do it."

"Sure. That would be great. I can get you on anything you'd like. And I offer resort employees a discount."

A discount sounded good. Just then we both heard the distinct *whoop whoop* sound of a helicopter. We looked up to see Rick's Air Paradise fly over. It wasn't the first time today I'd seen him. He was obviously very busy.

"That's number one on my list of things to do," I said with a wistful sigh.

"I highly recommend it," said Gabby. Her accent was different than most I'd heard so far, and I wondered where in the States she was from. "You get to see so much of the island from his helicopter. It just takes your breath away."

"It sounds amazing." It also sounded pricey, so I figured I'd be waiting a while to do it.

We'd stopped in front of the trolley, and I placed my board on to it. Gabby set her shoes down and helped me.

"Word around the resort employees is that you're new to the island."

I nodded.

"We should grab a drink at The Lava Pot one night and get to know each other before you go all island on me," she said. "I haven't been here for that long either."

"That's so nice of you," I replied. "I'd love that."

"Cool. Well, here's my card with my number on it." She pulled a business card from her shirt pocket and handed it to me. "Give me a call, and we'll organize it. And in the meantime, if any parents ask me for a recommendation for a surf instructor, I'll point them your way."

* * *

On my way home, I decided that as I'd had no luck with Kylie's husband, I would change tactics and watch Mark for a while. (I know. I know. I should focus a little bit more. And I will. I promise. Right after I find out what Mark is up to.)

It so happened that Mark was in the house when I got home from work the next day.

"Where's Mum?" I asked him, pouring myself a cup of coffee from the pot that was always brewing. Mark sat reading a newspaper. Looking at the three others in a pile under his elbow, I thought he must love current affairs.

"She's gone to visit her friend Rebecca," he said, turning the page of the *Aloha Sun* but watching me. "They're starting a gardening project at her house. Rita thinks it will give her a purpose until this investigation is over."

I didn't know why Mark was watching me. I was only opening the refrigerator, which was hardly riveting stuff.

"Has anybody ever told you how much you look like your mother?" he asked.

"Yes. All the time." I poured milk into my coffee, wondering what was coming next.

"You're a very beautiful girl, Samantha."

I stopped pouring and looked at him. "Thank you?" I said. Really, it came out as a question, which wasn't my intention at all.

"I watched one of your lessons today. You have quite a bit of talent, but you really do need to focus a bit more."

Yeah, I knew it. Focus! *But hang on...* "You were watching my lesson?" I asked, a creepy feeling running down my spine.

"Yes, if you sit on the deck outside The Lava Pot, you get a very good view of the beach. I wasn't the only one watching."

Okay, now I felt the heat creep up my neck. I crossed my fingers and hoped that Mr. Mahelona hadn't been one of those watching. Or Casey. I didn't mind if Casey watched me. In fact, quite the contrary. I just didn't want him watching me while I floundered, attempting to teach kids something I was totally underqualified to teach.

"Why?" was all I could come up with.

"Why what?"

"Why were you all watching me?"

"I was watching because I want to know what you're actually doing here. I can't vouch for the woman though."

"What do you mean?"

"Hmmm?" He put the newspaper down on the table and looked closer at me.

"What do you mean you want to know what I'm doing here?"

"Oh that. Well, you've been happily living in Sydney all these years, and suddenly you want to get back in with the family." He said all this with a smile on his face, but I felt the undertone like ice down my back.

"I've been living in Sydney because that's where I grew up. And I've moved because I lost my job and Mum asked me to move here."

Mark eyed me suspiciously. "Okay. If that's your story, then you stick to it."

I gave him my serious face and narrowed my eyes at him. "What do you mean?"

Mark picked up the paper again and turned the page. "Samantha, are you sure you're not here to find your father?" He said this looking at the paper, not at me.

"*What*? Oh my God! I haven't thought of Dad in years. And why would I come here to look for him? As far as I know, he's still somewhere in Australia."

"Forget I said anything. I'm just being jealous. I'd just…well, if you'd like to look at me as your dad, then I would be okay with that."

I had to give the guy the benefit of the doubt here. Maybe he was just awkward. "Alright, I'll keep it in mind. Thanks." I took a mouthful of my coffee to cover my discomfort and then spat it straight back out. Argh! "That's the worse coffee I've ever tasted!"

"Really? I thought it was delicious," said Mark, lifting his own cup to his lips. "It's just the way I like it."

I moved away into the lounge room in search of Mum's laptop computer. Two reasons: I wanted to check my bank balance and see if my first pay had gone in, and I wanted to get out of Mark's zone.

"What are you looking for?" he asked, watching me as I walked. "Maybe I can help."

"Do you know where Mum's laptop is?" I knelt down and looked under the sofa.

"The laptop?"

"Yes. Mum's laptop."

"She doesn't own a laptop."

"Yes, she does. Luke was using it the other day." Maybe I should be looking in his room for it.

"Ahh, I know the one now." Mark shifted uncomfortably, shuffling the papers on the table as he spoke. "Sorry, I haven't seen it."

As he moved, I caught a view of a sliver of silver the same color as Mum's Apple MacBook.

"Is that it under your newspaper?" I asked.

"What?" Mark's cheeks turned a bright crimson color.

I moved to him and lifted his arm, moving a newspaper aside. And sure enough, there was Mum's laptop, the underside of it warm, as though it had just been used.

Mark fidgeted, adjusting his paper unnecessarily. "I'll be damned. Had no idea it was there." He beamed at me charismatically.

I figured it was a tactic he used often and probably got away with when used on a woman Mum's age. Me? It gave me the creeps. I was about to question how a laptop—a whole laptop—could be under your newspaper and you didn't even know it, when the doorbell rang. I sighed, placing the laptop on the kitchen bench, and moved through the house. Mark followed me.

On the outside of the fly screen door, I could once again see an elderly man dressed in a cream-colored suit two sizes too big, his beady eyes framed by his tortoiseshell glasses. He pushed them up the bridge of his hawklike nose as he shuffled his feet. Edward Fathersham, Estate Lawyer.

"Hello, Mr. Fathersham," I said politely, wondering what he wanted. Maybe there was a problem with Mum's inheritance. I figured Mark thought the same thing as he moved close behind me, his big ears flapping. "Mum's not here. Sorry."

"Oh, I'm not here for your mother. I'm looking for Luke. Would he be around, by any chance?"

"Luke? No, sorry. You should have called and saved yourself the trouble."

"Yes, but my secretary forgot to get the home phone number last time Rita visited."

"What do you want Luke for?"

"Well, it's a private matter, and I'm sure you can understand that I can't discuss that with you."

"Can you at least give me an idea? That way I can tell Luke what you're chasing him for."

"If you could just please tell him to call me at his earliest convenience, that would be appreciated."

"I will, but he has a cell phone you can contact him on if you want." I patiently rattled off Luke's number three times before Mr. Fathersham got it right, but he happily left, telling us to forget we ever saw him. He'd call Luke as soon as he got back to the office.

As if I was going to forget. I immediately pulled my phone from the pocket of my shorts and sent Luke a text message. As I was typing, I heard Mark shout out that he was going and heard the back door slam shut.

As soon as I heard his car pull out of the driveway, I went back to the laptop. I now had a third reason for wanting it. I wanted to check the browser history to see what he'd been up to. I didn't believe, for one single second, that he didn't know it was under the newspaper. Add the fact that it was warm, as if it had been running, and my suspicions just doubled.

I flipped its screen up and waited for it to light up. The laptop was pretty slow, but when prompted, I entered Mum's password (she only ever used one of three passwords for everything. It was either Luke, Samantha, or our old dog Rastas!). I got it right on the second attempt. A photo of the beach outside of the resort filled the screen. I moved the cursor to the top left of the task bar and clicked to see her browser history. The only page that had been opened today was her internet banking.

I couldn't guarantee that Mark had been the one who'd opened it, but I'd bet every cent I owned that it was.

* * *

I was contemplating what to make for dinner. Mum was staying out for the evening with Rebecca, and I had no idea where Luke was. I'd messaged him earlier and told him about Mr. Fathersham, and he'd messaged back that he would sort it out. Whatever *it* was. That left me to my own devices for dinner.

The fridge had no leftovers in it, as Mark had helped himself to those at lunchtime. In Sydney, I'd eaten a lot of takeout. Aloha Lagoon didn't have too many choices for takeout. It had a lot of restaurants, but I would have felt silly eating in on my own. I was just thinking *Bugger it, let me look silly*, when my phone rang. It was Alani.

"Hey!" I sang, happy to hear her voice.

"Hey you," she said back.

"What's up?"

"I'm going to see Tutu tomorrow and wondered if you wanted to come?"

"Oh, okay. That's cool. So long as it's in the morning. I don't have any classes booked until after lunch."

"Yeah, that suits. I just want some backup when I tell her I want her to move home with me for a few days. At least until they've caught the murderer." Alani's tone turned dark, and I could hear the concern in her voice.

"Do you think she'll resist?"

"Of course she'll resist. She's not known for doing what others tell her."

"But she could be in danger."

"I know. Try telling her that though."

"Alright. I will. Right after you've told her."

"You don't want to say it first? She might listen to you."

"Ummm...maybe." Of course I didn't want to say it first, but what could I do? "Hey, do you think she'll listen to Mum? I could get her to come with us."

"Hasn't Rita been asked to stay away from Aloha Ohana until the investigation is over?"

"Yeah, true. Maybe I could get her to call Lahela and tell her she needs a vacation for a while."

"How about that can be our backup plan? If Tutu resists us, then we'll ask Rita to call her."

Good. That sounded like a plan.

"What are you doing for dinner?" she continued.

"Looking in the fridge, willing it to miraculously fill with Luke's cooking."

"Do you want to do something?"

No need to ask me twice. I was about to say *hell, yes*, when I heard the beeping of my phone alerting me to another call coming in. I looked at the display.

It was Casey.

My heart did a little happy dance as I put Alani on hold and answered him.

My happy dance thing didn't last long when he informed me that Luke was at the bar, he was extraordinarily drunk, and would I come and pick him up? I sighed. What exactly did he think I was going to pick him up with? My push bike?

I told him I'd be there as soon as I could and went back to my call with Alani, explaining to her that I'd have to take a rain check, as Luke needed saving.

"I'll come and get you," she said, happily, "and we'll bring Luke home in my car."

"You wouldn't mind?"

"Of course not. You're helping me tomorrow with Tutu."

I smiled. You just never knew when a good deed would come back to you.

Alani didn't take too long. I heard her beep her car horn and ran out to meet her, pulling the front door locked behind me.

"Thanks," I said, smiling at her in the glow of the car's interior light.

"No worries at all. I'm always happy to help Luke." Did I just hear a hitch in her voice? "And you. I'm always happy to help you."

On the short drive to the resort, Alani embellished Lahela's stories of Island traditions and folklores. Some of the stories freaked me out a little, especially the one about the faceless creature known as the Mijuna. He was known to roam the dark roads at night, asking travelers for water or tea. I made a vow to myself to never ride my bike alone after dark ever again.

I stuck close to her as she locked the car in the resort parking lot, and we made our way toward The Lava Pot. It didn't take long for the resort to ease my anxiety. It was such a beautiful place that I figured nothing bad could ever happen there. *Hang on a second—a body washing up on the beach was pretty bad.*

The wind gently blew the fronds of the palms, and the flames danced on the torches as we passed the fishpond. I made a mental note to stop by here in the daytime and see if I could spot Harold the Turtle (he'd been named by the resort guests).

A few of the guests were enjoying the night air, still sitting around the pool, some watching the kids swim, whilst others lay on the loungers, enjoying a cocktail or two. Candles burned on the restaurant tables at the Loco Moco Café as we passed, and the sound of laughter floated our way. As did the aroma of all the delicious food, making my stomach growl, as I still hadn't eaten. Maybe I'd be able to control Luke long enough to grab something to eat at The Lava Pot.

Casey had put Luke on a barstool at the far end of the bar, away from the rest of the patrons. Luckily, tonight was another quiet night, and only a few tables were filled. Alani and I made our way toward him.

Casey winked. My pulse picked up, and my hormones raced the moment he looked my way.

Alani got to Luke before I did, sitting on the stool alongside him. Her motherly instinct took over, and within seconds she was *oohing* and *ahhing* at him, as if being this drunk in a public place was acceptable.

Not me. I death-stared him and asked him what the heck he thought he was doing.

His slurred response was a bit hard to understand at first, but I got the gist of it.

"I hash a baaaad one. No…no…not baaad. Yesh it wash…" He dropped his head, laying it on the bar.

"You poor thing," said Alani, lifting his head from the bar and propping him up.

"Was it, or wasn't it?" I snapped.

Luke turned to face Alani, his crooked smile beaming at her with affection.

"Luke!" I snapped again.

He jumped. "Whaaaat?"

"Your day. Was it bad, or wasn't it?"

"Oh," he replied, sitting up straight. "Where's my driiink? Casey! Where'sh my drink?"

"You drank it, mate," Casey called.

"I did?" Luke looked around, completely bewildered. "Then get me another!" Luke almost cheered, slamming his hand on to the bar.

Casey smiled and moved closer to him, leaning on the bar. "I'm pulling the pin, mate. I think you've had enough already."

"But how can I shelebrate with…without a drink?"

Celebrate? "What? You just said your day was bad."

Luke turned to me and grinned. "I got an inheritansh," he slurred.

My mind flicked back to Mr. Fathersham's visit this morning.

"Who from?" I asked. Casey handed Luke a glass of water.

"Jeremy. He was my mate, but I didn't know that! Why didn't I know that?"

Luke's eyes filled with tears, and my attitude with him dissolved.

"Jeremy Gibson?" I asked, just to clarify. "The last guy murdered at Aloha Ohana?"

"Ahuh!"

Alani rubbed Luke's back, encouraging him to drink some of the water.

"Does Detective Ray know about it?" I asked.

"Ahuh!"

That couldn't be good.

"Did he question you about it?"

"Ahuh!"

"Am I going to get any other words from you tonight?"

"Ahuh!" He then shook his head. "Nuh-uh!"

Okay, job number one for the morning was to find out what the good detective was thinking. In the meantime, I wondered if The Lava Pot kitchen was still open for business.

* * *

Detective Ray was a very busy man. I couldn't see him until almost ten. That didn't give me a whole lot of time, as I'd promised I'd visit Lahela and still had to be at work by one thirty.

Luckily, Detective Ray was very efficient and didn't like to waste time on small talk. As I sat at his desk, waiting for him to arrive, I looked around me to see if a window was open, as the mess on his desk suggested a windstorm had come through recently.

"Miss Reynolds," he said, approaching the desk and making me jump. "To what do I owe the pleasure?"

It sounded like a nice way to greet me, but the scowl he was wearing told me differently. He pulled out his chair and sat down. I blinked against the glare from his very bright shirt.

"Hello, Detective," I replied, determined not to let him intimidate me. Well, okay, just sitting there had already done that, but I wasn't going to show him that. "I was hoping to speak to you about my brother, Luke."

"Yes." His tone was clipped, and I wondered how a man who wore such bright, happy shirts could actually look so grumpy all the time. I guessed it was the job.

"Oh, well, Luke said you questioned him about the inheritance Jeremy Gibson left him."

"Yes. I did."

"Great. Can I ask, is Luke a suspect in his murder?"

"Everyone is a suspect until I rule them out."

"Really?"

"Really."

"Oh. Okay. Why? Why is Luke being questioned? He didn't know Jeremy that well."

"Listen, Ms. Reynolds, I am continually looking at evidence. At the moment the facts state that your brother worked in the same facility Mr. Gibson lived in. He had access to the murder weapon, and we found his fingerprints all over it. Add that to the fact that Mr. Gibson changed his will to name Luke as the sole beneficiary, Luke is the son of my number one suspect for the murder of another resident of Aloha Ohana who also strangely changed his will, and the facts are looking like your family is involved in something very sinister."

Anxiety swirled in my stomach. When you looked at it like that, it didn't sound good at all.

"But it couldn't have been Luke."

"Why? Can you give him an alibi for the time of the murder?"

"What time was that exactly?

Detective Ray shuffled through a stack of papers, locating a file. For such a mess, he obviously knew where everything was.

"Twelve forty-five a.m. on the morning of the twenty-first."

I thought back to that night. It was the night after I had visited Lahela, and I'd slept like crap, my mind going over Lahela's stories and what Kylie had done to Valerie.

"Yes!" I yelled, a bit louder than I meant to. The detective jumped. "Sorry. Yes. He was at home asleep. I know that because his snoring kept me awake for most of the night."

Detective Ray scribbled some notes. "But you didn't see him?" he asked.

"No. Not with my eyes. But he was there. He snores loudly enough to keep the neighbors awake."

"Don't worry. I'll be talking to them as well."

I gulped.

"Are you going to arrest him?" I asked quietly.

Detective Ray sighed, his shoulders dropping slightly. "Not at this stage. I'm still gathering evidence. But rest assured that once I have it all, I will be arresting whoever is responsible for the death of Jeremy Gibson. Now, Ms. Reynolds, if you'll excuse me, I have a murderer to catch. If you find anything that is relevant to this case, bring it to me. In the meantime, good day to you." He stood, signaling to a uniformed officer to show me to the door.

* * *

I rode my bike through town, past the town square, a church, under the canopy of trees covering the road, and stopped outside the solicitor's office. I'd had an idea. I needed to find out why those men named Mum and Luke in their wills. I also didn't know if it was a coincidence or not, but I found it interesting that both of the murdered men had used the same estate lawyer.

Hopping off, I looked around me. The town was reasonably busy for the time of day. Cars were parked in the street, locals were going about their daily business, and a few tourists were laughing and taking happy snaps.

I leaned the bike against a palm tree, enjoying the relaxed atmosphere. In Sydney I would have had to lock up the bike, but here in Aloha Lagoon, I knew that it was safe. Still it felt odd, like I'd forgotten to do something. Oh, who was I kidding? As if I would have ridden a bike in Sydney.

I straightened my T-shirt and looked at the outside of the building I was about to enter. It was a two-storey, painted dark green with white trim, and it had a reddish-brown tin roof. It was old but still in good condition.

I stepped up to the door and noted the brass nameplate— *Fathersham Estate Lawyers*. I wondered who worked there other than Edward Fathersham.

Pushing the door open, I heard the faint tinkle of a bell alerting whomever that they had a visitor. A blast of welcome cold air hit me as I stepped inside.

The reception area was empty of people, so I took the opportunity to have a good look around. Not that I was looking for anything out of the ordinary—quite the contrary. I was just here to ask Mr. Fathersham for some information. The area was light, the furniture dark, and the walls bare. I was just about to sit in one of the worn leather seats when a woman, I'd guess to be in her forties, wandered down the hallway, carrying a cup of coffee and a biscuit.

She looked surprised to see me. "I'm so sorry," she said, hurrying to her desk. "I didn't hear the bell. Have you been waiting long?"

"No. I only just walked in," I replied, smiling in an attempt to convey that I was friendly. "I was hoping to see Mr. Fathersham."

"Do you have an appointment?"

"No. I'm sorry. I don't."

"He's a very busy man, but I'll see what I can do." I looked around the empty room and figured Mr. Fathersham wasn't as busy as she was making him out to be. I figured it to be more like his nap time.

She flicked through a schedule that lay open on her desk. I was a bit surprised. I thought everyone in this century used a computer. Showed you what I knew.

"Can I ask what it's in reference to?" she asked.

"Ummm…yes. I wanted to make a will."

"Oh!" She looked surprised. "Well, that's very good. Mr. Fathersham can definitely help you with that. In fact, he's available at the moment, if you'd like to do it now?"

"Definitely. No time like the present." I gave her my biggest smile.

I'd actually planned on him seeing me right away, which was probably a silly thing to have done. For all I knew, he could have been extremely busy, and I'd have had to wait weeks to see him. Looking around me once more, I figured I was safe in my first assumption.

"What was your name, please?" asked the lady.

"Samantha."

She tilted her head, suggesting I give her more information.

"Samantha Reynolds."

If she questioned my motive for being there, she didn't show it. "Please take a seat, Samantha. I'll let Mr. Fathersham know that you're here."

"Thank you."

It didn't take long, and she was back, smiling once again. "He'll see you now, if you'd like to follow me?"

I did as asked and followed her down a relatively long hallway, our footsteps echoing on the timber floor. She showed me into an office, where Mr. Fathersham stood behind a large oak desk, rubbing his eyes as if I'd just woken him. He quickly pushed his glasses back on and stood.

"Hello again, Samantha," he said, extending his hand.

"Hello. Thank you for seeing me on such short notice."

"My pleasure. Cathy tells me you wish to make a last will and testament."

"Ummm…sure. I mean yes, definitely."

He narrowed his eyes at me as he indicated that I take the seat opposite him. It didn't make him look intimidating. It just made him look like he'd had a stroke.

He seemed to be moving fine as he took his seat, so I figured he was okay. He pulled a legal pad from the top drawer of his desk and picked up a very expensive-looking pen.

"Have you ever written a will before?" he asked.

I shook my head.

"Okay. First of all, I need your personal details."

I rattled off my name, date of birth, and address, then answered his questions involving my next of kin and told him how I wanted Mum and Luke to get equal shares in my estate.

He nodded knowledgeably. "Now I need the details of your estate. Your bank accounts, savings, property portfolio, investments like shares, term deposits, and of course any insurance you have."

I looked at him blankly. "Well…I have…" What did I have? Not a lot.

"What about money? Bank accounts?"

"Oh, yes, I have a bank account. Here at the local bank. Mum had insisted that I open it as soon as I arrived in Aloha Lagoon."

"Very good. I'll need the account details, of course."

I had a good memory for numbers, so I rattled off what he needed.

"Savings? Investments?"

"I have about $10 in my savings account at the moment, and no, I don't have any investments. But I will! I just need some time."

I was starting to sweat actually. This was worse than being interrogated by Mum. And not even the reason I was here. This was simply an excuse. Maybe I needed to get the conversation going in the direction I needed it to. "Ummm, Mr. Fathersham, if I change my mind about my beneficiary, how do I change my will?"

"Any solicitor can do that for you. It's quite simple. We either write a new will or a codicil, which is an addition or amendment to this will. I have a smaller fee for amendments."

I gulped at the word *fee*. "Exactly how much is a will going to cost?" I asked quietly, scared to hear his response.

"I bill by time. At the moment this isn't going to be more than a few hundred dollars."

A few hundred dollars?

"Amendments are popular at the moment," he said, placing his pen carefully on his legal pad and looking at me through his tortoiseshell glasses. "Why do you want to know all of this?"

"Well…" *Come on, Samantha. Ask him what you came to ask him.* "My mother, Rita, and my brother, Luke, have both been named in the wills of the two men who were murdered. I was wondering who changed the wills to add their names."

Mr. Fathersham sat back in his chair, placing his fingers together, steepling them under his nose.

"In Hawaii a will must be signed by the testator and be witnessed by two people."

"Yes. And?"

"Unless a representative has been appointed by the testator for reasons being that they are physically unable to sign it themselves, then only the testator can change it."

"Okay. So did they sign the changes themselves?"

"Samantha, this is a police investigation of not one, but two murders."

"I understand that. I'm not trying to interfere—I'm just trying to help Mum and Luke, Mr. Fathersham. That's all. I'm scared that Detective Ray is trying to pin the murders on them."

I felt the tears prick my eyelids. I'd thought I was handling all this well, but I guess it was all bottling up inside. Now wasn't the right time to let it out though.

Mr. Fathersham shifted in his chair. "Rita is a special lady. I know many of the residents of Aloha Ohana she helps. My mother was one of them. She had nothing but good to say about Rita. I too would hate to see her convicted for something so awful, but I'm bound by the law, Samantha."

I felt the weight of his words stick in my throat. He couldn't help me.

"I'll tell you what I told the detective though. Those men both came in here voluntarily."

I nodded, defeat weighing me down.

"Can you tell me why they both used the same estate lawyer to make those changes, though?" I secretly crossed my fingers that he could at least tell me that much.

"I'm the only estate lawyer in town. Now, should I write up this will for you?"

I shook my head. "No, sorry. I can't afford it."

"How about I do this one for you as a gift?"

I looked at him surprised. "Oh, you don't need to do that."

He waved his hand, dismissing me before I could launch into why. "It would be my pleasure. Now, I can have this written up by tomorrow afternoon for you. You'll need to come in and sign it, but please bring a witness. My secretary, Cathy, witnesses everything for me, but a will, or a *change* to a will, needs *two* witnesses, so please bring another person with you." I wondered about the inflection he put on the word "change" and "two." Then it hit me—Cathy was one witness, but who was the second?

"Mr. Fathersham, did those men who died bring a witness with them?"

He smiled back at me. "Like I said, Samantha, all wills and changes need two witnesses. It's the law."

"So who were their witnesses?" Maybe I could ask them why the wills were changed. Surely if they were willing to accompany the men to the solicitor to witness their wills, you would have an idea of why they were changing them? I wasn't one hundred percent sure why, but I felt like it was an important piece of information to find out.

"Any beneficiary can see the will at any time."

Mum and Luke. They could see it.

I stood, a new purpose driving me. "Thank you, Mr. Fathersham. You've been amazing."

He stood and extended his hand. "You're welcome, Samantha. Good luck, and I'll see you tomorrow for the signing of your will."

I moved to walk out the door, when a thought hit me. "Can you tell me how long ago those men changed their wills?"

"Samantha, if you need to make any changes to your will, I would suggest no longer than two weeks." He winked as he said it.

I beamed at him.

"Oh, one last thing. Have any other residents of Aloha Ohana got appointments to see you about changing their will in the near future?"

"Not at this stage, but I intend to alert Detective Ray if anybody makes one."

CHAPTER ELEVEN

I needed to talk to Mum and Luke and ask them who'd witnessed the wills they were named in, but first I needed to see Alani. I'd told her I would go with her to visit Lahela.

The bike was exactly where I'd left it, leaning against the trunk of the palm tree. Without paying it any real attention, I threw my leg over it, ready to ride to the surf shop. It wasn't that far from where I was—just on the other side of town—which should only take me a few minutes. I checked my watch. It was eleven thirty, and the humidity was making my hair stick to my face.

I pushed off on the pedal, thinking how the first thing I was saving for was a car, when instead of moving quickly, the bike felt slow and sluggish. I stopped pedaling, looked down, and noticed that my back tire was flat.

I sighed and got off. I must have gotten a puncture on the way there and hadn't noticed. Upon closer inspection though, I could see a big gash in the rubber. Whatever I'd hit was sharp, because the cut was deep and about an inch long. How had I not noticed that when I'd ridden to the lawyer's office?

Wondering where I could get a tire fixed, I pushed the bike back to the tree. Alani's was probably a ten-minute walk or a two-minute drive. Maybe I could get her to drive by and pick me up. We could throw the bike into the trunk of her car, and I could get it fixed later. I pulled my phone from my pocket and dialed her number. It went to voicemail, so I quickly filled her in on my predicament and asked if she could pick me up.

Now I had two choices. I could walk part of the way, pushing the bike, or I could buy myself an iced coffee, sit under the palm tree in the nearby park, and wait for Alani to pick me up. I was going with option number two—iced coffee under the tree.

Walking to the nearest convenience store, I bought my coffee (okay, I may also have bought a chocolate bar) and made my way to the park. It wasn't a large park—in fact it didn't even contain a kids' swing set—but it was filled with lush green grass and a selection of palms to lean against.

I made the good choice of a palm tree that gave me a view of the town as I waited for Alani and sat back to people-watch.

I waved to the postman as he walked up the street, delivering mail to businesses. I admired a ukulele street performer, and I giggled at a few of the tourists getting tongue-tied with Hawaiian place names. I understood how they felt.

Working at the resort, I'd quickly realized people expected you to know those kinds of things and often asked me for help. I'd been living in Aloha Lagoon for a couple of weeks now, but my pronunciation wasn't any better than it was the day I'd arrived. More than once I'd directed them to Malie, the lifeguard.

I wanted to relax, but my mind was going over and over my conversation with Mr. Fathersham and how a will needed two witnesses. Who had accompanied those two men to his office?

If Mum or Luke could tell me who'd signed the will, then I could ask the signers if they knew why Albert Johnstone and Jeremy Gibson had made the changes. Mum had always told me that understanding a problem was the key to solving it. Without understanding, you would know nothing.

I took it from the way Mr. Fathersham had winked at me that the changes had only been made in the two weeks before their deaths. And I was relieved to know that no other resident had any appointments set up with him in the near future.

I was thinking of Lahela when a man walked past the park and caught my eye. It was Mark. He was wearing dark sunglasses and a baseball cap, and he was talking on a cell phone. Wait a minute! He'd told me he didn't have a phone! And Mum had verified that. I stood and ran toward him, ready to ask him about it.

"Mark!" I called, dodging a tourist as I made my way to him. "Mark!"

He heard his name and stopped, turning to face me. His face paled slightly, and he abruptly ended his call. He then turned on the charismatic smile.

"Samantha! How nice to see you!"

Liar. "Hi," I replied, wondering how the heck I was going to ask him about the phone.

"What are you doing here? Shouldn't you be at work?"

"I only have afternoon lessons booked today. Ummm...did I just see you on a cell phone?"

"Yes. Do you need to use it?"

"Well, I actually thought you didn't like cell phones. You know...radiation and all that." I laughed lightly, catching him off guard. I reckon he'd forgotten about that conversation.

"No. No. You're mistaken. It's your mother who doesn't use a cell phone."

I might have believed that if the tips of his ears hadn't turned red. I nodded. "Yes, but you said that you didn't either. I remember."

He laughed. "You are attractive, Samantha, but you're not the most focused girl I've ever met."

I should have been insulted by that, but he did have a point. This time I knew I was right though. So why was he lying?

"Ummm, actually would you mind if I borrowed it? I need to call Alani. My bike's got a flat tire."

"Of course. Call whoever you need to," he replied, handing me the phone.

"Thanks." I accepted the iPhone and swiped the screen to open it. "Oh, Mark, it's locked."

"Of course it is. Sorry," he said, taking the phone back and entering his four-digit code. I watched his every move and saw that his code was 3017, the same code Mum used for her bank ATM card. Was that a coincidence? I'd bet it wasn't. My suspicions of him checking Mum's bank balances just doubled.

I didn't really need to call Alani, but instead I discreetly checked who his last caller was. It didn't list a number. Instead it read *Patrick*.

"You know what? I actually don't remember her number. Silly me."

He eyed me suspiciously but never offered to help me with the bike.

"Look," he said, pushing the phone into one of the many pockets of his cargo shorts. "Can we keep the phone between us? It's a sticking point for Rita, who really doesn't like me to have one, and we'd get into an argument if she knew I did. I love your mother, and I hate arguing with her."

That sounded reasonable enough. "Sure, it'll be our secret," I replied, smiling. What I didn't understand though was that Mum didn't care about Luke and I having one.

"Good. Well, I'll see you later. For dinner maybe."

I watched him walk away, my thoughts traveling around my mind at a million miles an hour. Mark lied about too many things. Sure, we all tell little lies every now and then, but his seemed to be big fat whoppers. Why?

* * *

I sat back on the grass and attempted to dial Alani again. Still no answer. Okay, what options did I have? I could try Luke, but as he'd successfully gotten the job at The Lava Pot, and today was his first shift, he wouldn't be available to rescue me. Mum had no cell phone, and she was out on a nature walk to a nearby volcano with her friend Rebecca, getting inspiration for her new gardening project. And Mark hadn't offered. Even though at the time I would have turned him down, now I might just change my mind. I sighed and pushed my phone back into my pocket. It seemed like I had no other option than to get the bike and start pushing.

Getting up, I threw my empty iced coffee container and chocolate wrapper in the bin and pulled the bike to standing. The upside was that I might just burn off all the calories from my snack. The downside was that it was hot. And Lahela's Surf was on the other side of the hill.

Five minutes in, the sweat was pouring down my back, making my shirt stick to me, my hair was a frizzy mess, and I'm sure my makeup had run just enough for me to look hideous.

Thankfully, a knight in shining armor drove by and stopped to offer me a lift. But that knight was Casey. Now don't get me wrong—seeing Casey was actually a highlight of my day, but why, oh why, could he have not seen me *before* I got all hot, sweaty, and stinky?

He pulled his car alongside me and wound down the window.

"Hey," he almost sang. "Is there a reason you're taking your bike for a walk?" His smile dazzled me, and I took a second to enjoy it before answering.

"Yes, well, Mum wouldn't let me have a dog."

He laughed, all deep and throaty, making the hair on my arms dance in a good way.

"I have a flat tire," I continued, my own voice sounding a bit croaky all of a sudden. Didn't know why. Must be something to do with the air. Not lust or anything to do with Casey. No, definitely the air affecting my vocal chords.

"Hang on," he replied, moving his car forward and pulling to a stop on the roadside ahead of me. He got out and jogged back to me.

I used the minute to pull myself together. It was amazing how much I could accomplish in a very short space of time. Leaning the bike against my body, I coughed to clear my throat of any emotion that sat there. I quickly smoothed my hair and wiped under my eyes to clear any stray mascara. With my other hand, I wiped away the sweat running down my temples and straightened my clothing. Not great, but it would have to do.

I looked up at Casey as he took the bike from me, his fingers skimming my hip as he did so. Despite the hot day, goose bumps broke out at his touch. Oh boy.

"Wow, what did you hit?" he asked. He was dressed in shorts and a T-shirt that showed his physique off perfectly. I tried not to drool as he looked over my tire.

"I have no idea."

"Whatever it was, it was sharp. And not that big." Casey sighed and straightened up to look at me.

Honestly, I was really trying to listen to what he was saying, but my senses were overtaken by the scent of his aftershave.

"I'm not sure if it's repairable or not, but my place isn't far away. I can take it there and see if I can fix it."

"Huh?"

I blushed. I'd been so caught up in his smell and his presence that I hadn't heard a word he'd said. He smiled, his eyes twinkling down at me. It didn't help. All it did was cause blood to rush to areas it shouldn't have been going. Oh well, at least it was leaving my ears.

"I can take the bike to my place and give you a lift to wherever you need to go."

That sounded like a great offer. "Yes please. I'm supposed to be meeting Alani, but I can't seem to contact her."

"Alright then, hop in. We'll make a quick stop at mine, and then I'll take you to Alani's."

I watched, mesmerized, as he effortlessly lifted the bike and secured it in the trunk of his car, half in and half hanging out, and tied it down with some rope. We then both got in the car and made our way to his house.

I was secretly excited about this. I loved looking through people's houses. Not to be nosy or anything, but I just liked to see how other people lived. Oh, who was I kidding? Of course it was because I was nosy!

Casey wasn't lying when he'd said his house wasn't far away. He followed the road up the hill, made a right turn, and pulled into a small street lined with beach huts overlooking the ocean.

He stopped in his driveway, and I wasn't sure what I wanted to look at first. His house or the view.

Remembering that the seat belt stuck, he unclicked my belt for me, and we got out of the car. He moved to the trunk, and I moved to the road, the ocean drawing me to it. He followed my gaze.

"It's amazing, isn't it?" he said, stopping what he was doing and standing next to me.

I nodded and crossed the road to stand on the grass. Casey followed me. He was spot-on with his description. The sight of aqua blue water crashing against white sand was amazing. The sound of the waves roared through the salt-filled air, and I took a deep breath, filling my lungs then letting it out on a blissful sigh. My soul felt recharged already.

"Come with me," said Casey, grabbing my hand and pulling me along. "I want to show you something."

My hand tingled under his touch as I followed him a few meters up the road to a well-worn path that led to the beach.

It wasn't a big drop, but the path was reasonably steep. Casey held my hand tightly and kept me safe on the numerous occasions I slipped on the grass. Making it to the bottom, we crossed the sand dunes and walked farther up the beach, coming to a small island.

I called it a small island, but really it was an extremely large rock jutting out into the water. Casey helped me climb the few meters to the top and then led me to the end that rose from the water. Nature had seen to it that high tide had carved a seat, so Casey and I sat shoulder to shoulder and looked.

It was fricking awesome. The water surrounded us on three sides, the waves crashing up to the rock face in front of us, splashing our faces with sea spray. The smell of the salt air and the water filled my lungs, and all my worries disappeared.

I turned to see Casey looking at me, his eyes soft and a smile playing on his lips. It wasn't his dazzling smile. This one felt a lot more intimate. All the air I had breathed into my lungs disappeared as my stomach somersaulted and my heart rate picked up.

"It suits you," said Casey quietly. "The ocean…"

"Really?" I managed to say.

"Yeah, you're different when you're looking at it. Peaceful."

"It has that effect on me." I smiled. I couldn't help it. Right at that moment I was as close to heaven as I'd ever get.

"Me too. You should see it at sunset. It's spectacular."

He turned to face the ocean, his features relaxing. I watched, mesmerized, as he closed his eyes and took some deep breaths. "Whenever life gets too hard," he said, opening his eyes again, "this is where you'll find me.

"Wow." I wasn't sure whether I was saying that in response to the magic of this spot or to Casey. Both were pretty magnificent.

"I've hardly seen any of Aloha Lagoon since I've been here. I really need to spend more time exploring it," I continued.

"I can show you the most amazing things," said Casey, his voice animated with excitement.

I'd bet he could.

"The walks around the volcanoes will take your breath away. And there are so many channels to explore with a kayak." His eyes danced, and the color deepened. "Have you been kayaking?"

I shook my head.

"What about a *luau*? Have you been to one of those yet?"

I shook my head again, his excitement making me want to go to one right now.

"They're heaps of fun. The one at the resort has the best Hawaiian music. Nani plays traditional ukulele right before the fire dancers come on."

Fire dancers? That did sound amazing.

"I'll take you to one, if you like. When I have my next night off."

I smiled, my insides all warm and fuzzy. "That would be great. So long as I'm not stopping you from doing anything else." I had my fingers crossed he wasn't.

"Are you kidding me? All I do on my nights off at the moment is watch movies."

"That doesn't sound so bad?" Especially if I had him for company.

"On my last night off I watched *Toy Story 3*."

I laughed. "That was a very sad movie. And scary. I took my boss's kids to see it, and it gave them nightmares for weeks."

"*Toy Story* 1 is my favorite," said Casey, his enthusiasm contagious.

"Mine too!"

"To infinity and beyond!" he called loudly.

I joined Casey in doing our best Buzz and Woody impersonations.

I completely lost track of time sitting there with him, laughing at his bad jokes and telling him about my life in Australia. Listening to his stories, I wondered how we had never met before. We must have crossed paths a thousand times in Sydney.

The ringing of my phone brought me back to reality. I didn't want this moment to end, but I guessed reality would always bring us crashing back to earth. Looking at the display, I saw it was Alani calling me. Probably a call I needed to take, considering I was supposed to be at the shop by now.

"Hi," I said, my voice croaky once again.

"Hi," she said, very obviously stressed. "I'm so sorry I missed your calls. Are you okay? I thought you'd be here by now."

"Sorry. I had a flat tire on my bike."

"Oh no. Do you need me to come and get you?"

"No, it's okay. Casey's helping me."

"That's good. I can't come anyway. I'm stuck and annoyed," she continued. "Hani was supposed to be doing a stock take, but she's a complete idiot at times. She didn't even show up for her shift, so I've been stuck here doing her job for the last two hours."

"That sucks. Are you still going to see Lahela today?"

I had a dilemma on how I felt about this. On the one hand, getting Lahela to move to Alani's for a few days would give me peace of mind knowing she would be safe, but going to visit her today meant my time with Casey would probably end sooner.

"Yes, I am," said Alani, breaking my thoughts. "I'm just going to go a bit later this afternoon. Does that still suit you?"

It suited me perfectly. "Yeah, no worries. Whenever you want to go," I almost sang. "I should be finished with work by four thirty."

"Okay. How about I give you a call later and work out a time? I'm still waiting for Hani to get her backside here!"

"Don't stress. It's all good."

Once I'd hung up from Alani, Casey stood.

"We probably should get back and look at your bike tire," he said. Sadness overwhelmed me.

"Definitely," I said with fake cheeriness, standing.

I loved it here. I loved spending time with him, and I didn't want to leave just yet. Getting back wasn't all that bad though. Casey held my hand and almost pulled me up the grass path back to the road, which went a long way to helping my mood get back on track. Happily, I was behind him for the climb. This had two benefits. One, he couldn't see my backside, and two, I *could* see his.

* * *

It didn't take Casey long to unload my bike from his car and move it into his garage.

"Before I start, I just need to change into some old clothes that won't matter if I get grease on them," he said, leading the way into his house. "Come on in. I'll make you a drink."

"I'll come in, but I don't want a drink, thanks. It's too early for me to start on alcohol." Plus, who knew what I'd do if I had a few drinks under my belt. I might completely embarrass myself by dragging him to the floor and kissing him. No, I'd never actually do that, but it was fun to think about.

Casey smiled. Geez, I hoped he couldn't read my thoughts.

"I meant a coffee or something like that. I can make drinks other than alcoholic ones."

He said it in good humor, but it didn't stop the heat from creeping up my neck. Argh! I was such a moron.

"Oh…of course…duh!" I said, thumping my forehead.

Casey slung his arm over my shoulder and pulled me inside. I didn't know what I'd expected his house to look like, but what I saw was exactly it. It was a small, two-story beach hut, the main room containing a sofa, a TV, and a coffee table. At the back of the room was a kitchen, also small, with just one counter running along the back wall and a dining table with three chairs. A set of stairs were on the left of the room.

"Sorry about the mess," he said, blushing, quickly throwing a pile of surfing magazines under the coffee table in the middle of the room and turning to straighten the cushions on the sofa.

"It's not messy," I quickly replied, hoping to put him at ease. "It's lovely."

"I don't get a lot of company here, so I don't really tidy up as often as I should."

"Really, it's fine. I love it!" And I did. It looked, smelled, and felt like Casey. In fact, I wanted to curl up on that sofa and stay there. Forever.

Casey picked up the PlayStation controller and pushed it into the cabinet under the TV.

"Leave it. It's not messy. I live with Luke, remember."

Casey smiled. "True. Well, make yourself at home. I won't be long." He ran his fingers through his hair, uncomfortably.

"Actually, do you mind if I use the bathroom?" I asked, the iced coffee making its way through my system.

"Yeah sure, of course. I should have offered. Follow me."

I did as asked and followed him up the stairs into a small hallway. Three doors opened off of it.

"It's that door right there," he said, pointing to the door closest to me.

"Thanks."

I entered the room and closed the door behind me. I heard Casey move over the timber boards and a door creak open and then close. Good, he shouldn't be able to hear me tinkle.

The bathroom was pretty basic. A toilet, a freestanding bathtub, and a pedestal basin. It was clean, considering a man lived there. I resisted the urge to open his cabinet and check out what type of toothpaste he used and instead moved to the toilet and did what I had to do.

Thoughts that Casey was only a few meters away from me, probably half-naked about now, had my hormones racing in a way that could win a Grand Prix, but I fanned myself, finished my business, and moved to the sink to throw some cold water over my face.

I looked in the mirror and groaned. My reflection was worse than I'd imagined. Washing my face was probably my best option, so I turned the water to high and used my hands to splash my face, rubbing under my eyes to try to remove the mascara that had pooled there. Water wasn't doing the trick, so I pumped some liquid soap into my hands and rubbed. Within seconds my eyes were stinging.

I turned the water up as high as it would go and almost put my head under the tap, hoping to get the water flushing my eyes as quickly as possible. Thankfully, it worked, but it also soaked my T-shirt in the process. Grabbing at a towel, I dried myself as best I could and then looked back in the mirror. The mascara had disappeared, but now my eyes were bloodshot and stinging. Geez Louise, I couldn't take me anywhere.

I gave up trying to make myself look better and headed downstairs. I'd heard Casey making his way back down there a few minutes ago.

He was standing in the kitchen when I walked in, now wearing an old black V-necked T-shirt and torn shorts. Upon seeing me, he broke out into a full-on smile. It stopped me in my tracks.

"You could have had a shower if you'd wanted one," he said, his smile almost contagious. Almost. The heat once again racing up my neck stopped any smiling I might have been doing.

"Sorry" was all I could say. I moved closer to him and sat on one of the chairs at the dining table. Casey looked closer, and his expression changed.

"Are you okay?" he asked.

I nodded. "Yes."

"Have you…have you been crying?" he asked, concern causing those adorable creases on his forehead to deepen as he moved to sit next to me. "Your eyes look really red."

"Oh, no. I washed my face and got soap in them. They're just stinging."

"Ah, hence the wet shirt. I had a look at your bike while you were in the bathroom."

Geez, had I been in there that long?

"And the bad news is I can't fix it. You need a new tire," he continued.

I sighed.

"I can easily pick one up for you this afternoon if you like. Would you like that drink now?" he asked.

I smiled. "Yes, please."

He stood and moved to the fridge. "I have beer, cola, or juice?"

"Juice would be lovely, thanks."

He poured two glasses. Instead of handing one to me, he picked them up and looked at me. "Follow me," he said, smiling. "I want to show you something else."

I stood and followed him back up the stairs. This time we passed the bathroom and made our way to the door on the far end of the hall. The one at the front of the house.

Casey used his elbow and pushed the handle down, opening the door with his hip, his smile at full wattage.

The door swung open, and he entered, revealing his bedroom to me. *His bedroom!* I looked at the smile he was giving me and wondered what vibes I was putting out.

"Come on," he said. "You won't regret it."

I'd bet I wouldn't. But this was a bit quick, wasn't it? I mean, I definitely did not look my best. If Casey and I were going to be doing this, then I at least wanted to be looking my best. Crap, did I have time for a quick shower?

"Ummm…"

"I promise you'll love it," he said, jerking his head and indicating I should come in.

His T-shirt rode up his side slightly as he moved, showing me his smooth, golden skin. I gulped, my eyes skimming his body. Man, he looked good. *Oh, you know what? You only live once, right?*

I moved silently into the room, having a quick look around me, my heart racing. The bed sat opposite us, the sheets messily straightened, and I felt slightly awkward wondering how this was going to happen. Was he going to put the drinks down? Would he kiss my neck? I really hoped so. I liked having my neck kissed.

Casey smiled, and suddenly I didn't care how we did this. I just wanted to do it. Right now. On the floor if I had to.

Casey handed me my glass, and I accepted it, smiling back at him. It was my goddess smile, but one look at myself in the mirror behind him, and I vowed never to smile like that again. Casey frowned but then continued to smile anyway.

"This way," he said, leading the way to the opposite side of the room and opening a glass sliding door that led out onto a timber deck. He moved through it, placed his glass on the little table, and leaned against the railing.

What?

I slowly made my way across the room and outside onto the deck, the vast ocean in front of me.

"Awesome, isn't it?" he said, nodding toward the view. "It's my second-favorite place in the world."

Ohhhh, he was showing me the view! Well, I was…disappointed. As hard as I tried, I couldn't stop the heat from racing up my neck again. I didn't know what Casey was thinking, but whatever it was, he didn't comment. I moved to stand next to him.

He wasn't wrong in his opinion of this being awesome. I could imagine waking up to that view every day.

"I've sent photos to my family in England, but photos don't do it justice."

It took me a few moments to gather my thoughts onto the path they were meant to be on, but when I managed to get words to form once again, I said, "Have they ever been here to visit?"

"One of my sisters has. She loved it, but not enough to move here."

"How many siblings do you have?"

"Five sisters. They're all married and scattered about the UK. I also have six nieces."

"Any boys in your family?"

"Only me and Dad."

"Geez, no wonder you moved across the world."

Casey laughed. "I miss them though."

"Would you ever move back there?" That thought actually made my stomach cramp.

"I'd always intended to, but lately, I love it here more than ever, so I think I'll stick around for a while."

"Yeah, what's not to love?"

Casey's eyes looked directly into mine. "Exactly," he said. I gulped, feeling far more vulnerable than I had a few minutes ago when I'd thought… (You know what I'd thought).

"What about you?" he asked. "Do you regret leaving Sydney?"

"No. There was nothing left there for me. Sure, I miss my friends, but family is all that counts, right?"

"True, but we make new family all the time. They don't have to be blood relatives, you know. Look at Luke. He's like the brother I never had."

I really hoped Casey didn't think of me as another sister then. I didn't know what to say to that, so I changed the subject.

"Am I stopping you from doing something else? I mean, you didn't plan on rescuing me from a flat tire today."

"No, I was on my way home for a surf, but I can do that later. Unless you'd like to join me?"

"I'd love to, but I have to work and then meet Alani later."

"Oh, that's right. What are you ladies up to today?"

I quickly filled him in on Alani's plan to move Lahela for a couple of days. He laughed.

"Good luck," he said.

I laughed. We were going to need it. "I hope Lahela agrees to move for a while. I hate the idea of her being at Aloha Ohana with these murders happening."

"Do you have any theories about the murders? Who's behind them?" Casey asked.

"I'm working on it." I filled him in on my visit to Mr. Fathersham. "I think if I can find out who accompanied those men to the lawyer's office, then maybe they can give me some insight into why the murdered men changed their wills. Surely it can't be a coincidence."

"But I don't get it."

"I don't get it either."

"Two men change their wills to name Luke and Rita in them, and then they're murdered. Do you think there will be a third who names you in a will?" I had already wondered about that myself, and the idea really scared me.

"I hope not," I replied quietly. If a third will was changed, it felt like a reasonable assumption that the owner of that will would be in danger. And as much as some extra money would come in handy, I definitely didn't want to be the recipient if it meant someone had to die.

Casey frowned. "Should I be worried about you?"

I shook my head. "I asked Mr. Fathersham if anybody else had appointments with him to change their wills, and he said no. He's the only estate lawyer in town."

"Any theories as to who it could be?"

I thought for a moment. "I have my suspicions about Mum's boyfriend, Mark. He tells a lot of lies, and I caught him in her bedroom when she wasn't home. I know he sleeps over at times, but it felt wrong. And he lied about not seeing her laptop when it was under his newspaper all the time. Why would he do that? Plus, he knows her ATM pin. If he got his hands on her card, then he could withdraw whatever money he wanted."

"So what are you thinking?"

"Maybe he got those men to change the beneficiaries in their wills to name Mum and Luke, and then he killed them."

"Why didn't he get them to name him in the will instead?"

"Because with Mum in jail for murder, he's free to take her money without him being a suspect."

"Yes, but how will he take her money?"

"Like I said—he knows her ATM pin and could easily get her card out of her purse."

"How do you know that he knows her pin?"

"I used his phone, and his lock screen code is the same as Mum's ATM pin."

"Doesn't mean he knows it's the same."

I shrugged. "I guess not. It just seems like a big coincidence though."

"It wouldn't matter even if he did though. Here in Hawaii he can only get a few hundred dollars out of an ATM at one time. It would take him forever to get the inheritance, if that's what you're thinking."

I thought about what Casey had just said. That would make it harder for Mark to get the money but probably not hard enough to stop him. If Mum was in jail long enough, he could eventually drain the bank account.

"There are rumors going around town that he has a money problem though," Casey mused.

"There are?"

"Yeah, and I had to call security one night to get two men out of the bar who were talking to him, demanding money."

There was information I didn't know.

"But what about Luke? How does he fit into this?" asked Casey.

"I don't know about Luke yet. If it's not Mark behind it, I still think it could be Kylie," I continued, naming suspects. I suddenly realized how hard a detective's job was. My head hurt just thinking about all the possibilities. "She hates Mum, and I'm sure that she would love to see Mum rot in jail for a crime she didn't commit. Plus I have doubts about Tristan too. I think Lahela's right in saying that he's having an affair with Kylie."

"And?"

"Well, I did wonder if those men found out and threatened to tell her husband. At the time I thought that was a good motive for Kylie. But it's just as good a motive for Tristan."

"But whoever did it, you think that these murders were planned a while ago, with all the pieces put into place before anyone got killed?"

"Yes, I just need to figure out how and who, and then prove it."

"That sounds dangerous."

"I'll be careful. At the moment, I'm only asking questions."

Casey looked thoughtful for a moment. "Maybe you're asking the right questions."

"What do you mean?"

"I didn't want to say it before, but I'd bet your bike tire was slashed."

I was surprised by his words.

He continued, "The cut's really clean and precise. If you'd gotten a puncture by riding over something or against something, it would be much more jagged and irregular."

I stood looking over the ocean, thinking about what Casey had just said. "But nobody knows I'm looking into it."

"Are you sure?"

"Yes." I thought for a second. "You, Alani, Luke, Mum, Mark, Lahela, Mr. Fathersham, Tony the security guard at Aloha Ohana, maybe Tristan, and Kylie's husband are the only people who know. Oh, and Mum's lawyer, Mr. Chatsworth, may know too."

Actually, now that I'd said it out loud, that was quite a few.

CHAPTER TWELVE

It was five thirty by the time Alani and I got to Aloha Ohana. The woman at reception was no friendlier to me this time than she had been the last time, but Tony, the security guard, seemed very happy to see me.

"Samantha!" He beamed. Geez, I'd obviously impressed him last time I was here.

"Hi, Tony," I replied, noticing the bruise and stitches on his forehead.

"Staying out of trouble?"

"Always," I replied. "You?" I nodded toward his head.

"Yes, I'm okay. Just had a little fall. Nothing serious. Now, I'm sorry to hear about Luke. He's a good guy and didn't deserve what Tristan did to him."

I raised my eyebrows.

Tony continued. "Suspending him until the investigation is over."

"Oh, yeah. Terrible. I bet Tristan yelled at you all."

"Huh?"

"Well, you being security and all. Shouldn't you be keeping the residents safe?"

Tony prickled slightly, rolling his eyes upward, a habit he seemed to have. "We're doing our best. And anyway, none of this happened on my shift. No, it was Patrick who was in charge on both nights."

"Patrick?" Maybe I should be talking to him. Could this be the same Patrick that Mark had in his caller list?

"Yeah. Patrick. Big guy, red hair. He's usually on day shift, and I do the nights, but lately the roster has changed to swap us around."

"So he's not here at the moment?"

"Maybe. His shift starts at six, so he should be around soon."

I made a mental note to find a big redheaded man and ask him a few questions. But what would I ask? I racked my brain and thought back to all the cop shows I'd ever watched.

"Hey, Tony," I called, suddenly remembering an episode of *CSI*. "Did Jeremy Gibson and Albert Johnstone know each other? I mean, Aloha Ohana isn't that big that they could have never seen each other. Is it?"

Tony grabbed hold of his belt and jiggled it uncomfortably, once again rolling his eyes around. "Well...I can't really say. It's not like I ever questioned them about who their friends were."

"No. But you see things. You hear things."

Tony nodded knowledgably, puffing his chest out. "Yes, but I like to be a bit discreet about what I see."

"You can trust me. I'm not going to tell anyone."

Tony let go of his belt and straightened his shirt. He obviously protected the privacy of the residents because, if his body language was anything to go by, my questions sure made him uncomfortable.

"Most people here know each other. Unless you're in the Bamboo Orchid Wing, that is. That wing is for the high-care patients who can't really communicate anymore."

I wasn't sure what this new piece of information told me, but I filed it in my mental filing cabinet for future review.

"Samantha, don't ask too many questions," warned Tony. "It's best to let the police figure this mess out."

Whilst I'd been talking to Tony, Alani had walked ahead of me, and I found her in the large room with the awesome view, talking to a very stern-looking Lahela. Alani's brows were knitted together, and she stood with her hands on her hips. I watched as Lahela stood and matched her pose.

I figured I'd hang back until needed. Hopefully, they'd forget I was even there. Taking the nearest seat, I sat quietly checking Facebook. My view of the corridor was obstructed by two potted palms, but a voice I recognized drifted my way, getting my attention.

It was Mark, and he was talking on his cell phone. To say I was surprised to see him here was an understatement. I added *ask him why* to my list. Happily for me though, he'd stopped on the opposite side of the palms and continued his conversation in hushed tones.

"Listen, I told you I would get you the damned money, and I will," said Mark. "I just need more time."

The person on the other end of the call was obviously talking, as Mark went quiet.

"I'm here now, waiting," said Mark.

What was he waiting for?

"No, I won't. So far I've done everything you asked. Now I'm asking for more time." His voice dropped, and it became difficult to hear what he was saying.

For the first time in my life, I wished my ears were bigger. That way I might have been able to hear the rest of what he said, because what he'd said so far had caught my attention.

It confirmed what Casey had told me about Mark having money problems.

"Alright!" snapped Mark, almost making me jump. "Tonight. I'll be there. Yes, on the beach, the usual spot."

I couldn't believe my luck in overhearing this much of his conversation. I didn't know what beach he was referring to though. Hmmm, how would I find out? Yes, I had every intention of following him. He was definitely up to something.

I heard Mark sigh as he ended his call. Just as he did, a large redheaded man in a security guard uniform walked past. That had to be Patrick. I wanted to talk to him, but I didn't want Mark to know I was here. Bugger. A memory stirred of the night on the beach when I'd nearly been knocked over by a tall redheaded man. I peeked through the palm fronds to see where Patrick was going, and as I did, I noticed a look pass from Patrick to Mark. Patrick dagger-stared him and nodded. Mark paled and nodded back.

I sucked in my breath. I had so many questions that needed to be asked, I figured I needed a notebook. Instead I opened my phone, pulled up notes, and started to write down everything I knew.

Turned out, I didn't know much, but I did have a long list of questions, including what the heck Mark was doing here and was he the guy Patrick met on the beach? Mark had moved away from the palm and down the corridor, so I jumped out of my seat and followed him, pretending I was looking for the toilets again. When I got close enough, I yelled, "Mark?"

He turned at his name and scowled. He was obviously having a bad afternoon.

"Samantha! What are you doing here?"

"Looking for the restroom," I said quickly. Probably a bit too quickly actually. It sounded rehearsed, which of course it was. I'd been saying it over and over in my head whilst following him along the corridor. "What are you doing here?"

"I help with the residents sometimes. Take them to do their errands and such."

Now he really had my attention. "I didn't know that you did that. Mum never mentioned to me that you work here."

"I don't work here. I volunteer."

"You volunteer here?" I asked, surprised.

"Yes. Rita told me how badly they need volunteers, and I offered my help. I've been doing it for a couple of months now." That information just pushed him up the list of suspects. I now knew that he had access to the murdered men.

"What are *you* doing here, Samantha?" he asked irritably.

"Visiting Lahela. Alani is trying to convince her to move home for a few days until these murders are solved."

He nodded but never flinched. "Probably a good call."

"What are you doing tonight?" I asked, thinking on my feet. Not a strong suit of mine, but I was giving it a go.

"Why do you want to know that?" he asked, his posture stiffening.

"I was going to try to organize a family dinner. My treat."

"That...that would have been lovely. I do have a prior engagement, but maybe we could work around it?"

"Sure, I was thinking of going to The Lava Pot. Is that anywhere near where you need to be?" (See what I was doing there? Was I clever or what?)

"Yes. I can probably work that out. The Lava Pot isn't too far from where I need to be."

Great. I could follow him.

"What time though?" he asked.

"What time works for you?"

"Say seven?"

I nodded. That didn't give me much time. "I'll check with Mum and Luke and let you know. What's your cell phone number?"

Once again Mark's posture stiffened, but he gave me his cell phone number and made excuses to leave. Fine by me. I didn't really want to talk to him anyway.

I turned to make my way back to Alani and walked straight into Tristan, who was leaving his office in a great hurry.

I squealed. "Sorry," I said, more out of habit than the fact I was sorry.

"Are you okay?" he asked, putting his hand out to steady me. At the speed he'd left his office, the bump had propelled me backward slightly.

"Yes. I'm fine, thank you." Tristan looked at me quizzically.

"You're…Rita's daughter, aren't you? Samantha?"

I nodded. "That's me."

"But…what are you doing *here*?" He no longer seemed concerned for my well-being after nearly knocking me over.

I sighed. Personally, I really wished everyone would stop asking me what I was doing here. Couldn't a girl just visit once in a while without all the questions?

"Visiting Lahela. Why?"

"Well…it's not the best place for your family to be seen, is it?"

"What do you mean by that?"

"I'm sure I don't need to remind you that both your mother and brother are suspects in murder investigations." Tristan seemed irritated.

Not sure if that was entirely my fault or not. "Yes, and they are both innocent."

"That's for Detective Ray to decide."

"It's not up to him to *decide*! It's the truth."

"I'm sorry. I phrased that wrong. It's up to him to prove it."

As I stood there, my thoughts flicked back to a conversation I'd had with Casey.

"Tristan, did you know that those men had changed their wills to name Mum and Luke?"

The inheritances were bothering me the most. All my theories about the murders worked except for the small fact of the money. I could believe one will being changed to name my family was a coincidence, but not two.

He narrowed his eyes at me. "What are you doing?"

"Asking you a question." He moved in close and stood over me.

"It's disruptive enough that the police are annoying the staff and residents with questions. If you're snooping around here, bothering anybody, I will have to ask you to leave."

"I'm not bothering anyone." Except him obviously. He'd certainly got defensive once I'd started to question him. Maybe I shouldn't ask him where he was on the night of the murders then? "I'm just here assisting Alani."

"Where is Alani?" he asked, looking around as if she would just miraculously appear.

"In the lounge room. I needed to go to the restroom."

Tristan narrowed his eyes at me again. If he didn't stop that, he was going to need Botox. "Someone as young as you shouldn't be having bladder problems, Samantha. If I was you, I'd get that checked."

I felt the heat creep up my neck and stop at my ears. I really didn't know how to respond to that.

"A word of advice," he continued, his tone menacing. "This place already has enough people sticking their noses in where they don't belong. We certainly don't need another one." He gave me a warning stare and walked off in the opposite direction.

I opened my notes and added Tristan's name to my list of people with weird behavior.

* * *

I did try to make plans with my family, but it turned out that Luke had to work. David Mahelona had started Luke as a waiter-slash-barman, but when The Lava Pot's cook had gotten caught smoking something he wasn't supposed to be smoking, Mr. Mahelona had relieved him of his duties and given the job to Luke. Which suited Luke perfectly, as apparently his waitering skills weren't much better than mine.

Still, it meant that Luke couldn't join us. Mum agreed to come along, as did Mark. The upside was that Casey also had to work, so I got to look at him a lot.

"This is lovely," said Mark, putting down his knife and fork. He seemed uncomfortable, fidgeting more often than normal, not really meaning what he was saying.

"You can't be finished already," said Mum. "You've hardly eaten anything."

"I had a big lunch," he said in way of explanation.

I knew the truth. His meeting time was getting closer.

"You never told me Mark volunteers at Aloha Ohana," I said to Mum, enjoying the big fat chips served with my fish.

"Really?"

"Ahuh," I said, my mouth full of food.

"Oh. Well, he does. Don't you, Mark?"

He nodded. "Yes. I saw Samantha there today."

"What were you doing there today?" asked Mum, looking at me.

I quickly filled her in on Alani's plan.

"Did it work? Did Lahela agree to move?" she asked.

"No. She's too stubborn for her own good."

"That she is."

"Do you think she's safe though?" I asked, looking at Mum, genuine concern churning my stomach. I put the chip back on my plate, my appetite slowing.

"I don't know. Two weeks ago I would have said a definite yes, but I never would have thought we would have one murder, let alone two."

"Do you know why Albert Johnstone changed his will?"

"He never mentioned to me that he was going to or that he had."

"Mark," I said turning to him, "you said you take the residents on errands at times. Did you take Albert Johnstone or Jeremy Gibson to the solicitor to change their wills?"

He shifted in his seat, nerves starting to show.

"No, I didn't."

Did I believe him? And would he give me an honest answer if he had?

"But I only volunteer on Mondays."

"Hey, Mum, when you visited Mr. Fathersham, did you get to see the will, or did he just read it to you?"

I watched Mark for his reaction. So far he held the poker face. I did notice a small bead of sweat on his top lip, but then it was hot in the restaurant, with only the overhead fans blowing.

"He read it to me. Why?"

"I was wondering if you saw who had witnessed it."

She shook her head. "Is that important?"

"Maybe. I just wondered who drove those men to the solicitor. They may know why the wills were changed to name you and Luke."

"Samantha, leave it alone," warned Mark. "Don't get involved in things that don't concern you."

"But this does concern me. Mum and Luke are suspects, Mark. Suspects! Doesn't that bother you enough to try to find out why?"

"Of course it does, but you don't know what you're dealing with."

Was that a warning? Mum continued to eat her dinner, not even batting an eyelid at Mark's tone.

"I won't leave it alone. They're my family, and I will do whatever's needed to prove they didn't hurt those men."

"All you're going to do is get more people hurt!" said Mark, his voice agitated even more.

"How? How is me asking a few questions going to get people hurt?"

"What if whoever did it comes after your mother? What if they come after you to shut you up?"

"How do you know I'll even find anything?"

"Exactly! You're not a detective, Samantha. You are an intelligent young woman who needs to focus more and get a job she is actually qualified to do. You need to mind your own business!" He stood so fast his chair fell back. He didn't even pick it up before storming out.

"Now look what you've done!" said Mum. "It'll take him days before he comes around again."

"What?" I said, standing and picking up his chair.

Everyone in the bar had turned to look, and I hated being the center of attention like that. I felt my face burn.

"Listen, Samantha. I know you have good intentions, but you need to stay out of it, like Mark said."

"Mum, I think he's up to something," I said, taking my seat once more.

Mum's brow creased, and she sucked in her bottom lip. Carefully considering her words, she said, "Mark is a good man. He's never been married, has no children, and has no real concept of what any of that is like. He sulks when he's angry and often disappears for days without me seeing him, but he treats me well, and I like that. It's been a very long time since I've had any attention from a man."

My heart sank for her. Placing my hand over hers, I said, "I'm sorry. I just think he's not being honest with you."

"Honest?" she said, snatching her hand away. "Do you have any idea what a real relationship is like? Of course we all have our secrets. I have them, you have them, and Mark has them. We just need to ask ourselves if we can live with them. A very long time ago I felt I couldn't live with the secrets your father had, so I ended it. To this day I wish I'd kept my mouth shut."

I felt a jolt to my chest at her words. Mum never spoke about Dad. Never. "Why?"

"Because then you and Luke would have had a family to grow up in."

"But, Mum, we did great. You did great. We were happy."

Her eyes filled with tears. "Really?"

"Yes, really. We had an amazing childhood."

She nodded and wiped her eyes. "Okay then."

I wanted to say more about Mark, but the look of vulnerability I saw in her dark eyes blew the wind out of my sails. If I was going to break Mum's heart with the news that Mark was up to something, I needed proof.

Which was exactly what I was going to get. I'd organized for Alani to accompany me so that I wasn't alone whilst following Mark, and as only a true friend would, she was standing at the door, eyeing me to hurry up. Mark had already left The Lava Pot, and while I knew she'd been watching where he was going, he'd be out of her sight if I didn't speed things up.

"I'm sorry, but I've got to go," I said, standing. "Casey's going to make you a cocktail, and I'll be back before you know it."

"Don't worry about me," said Mum. "I told Rebecca what we were doing tonight, so she was coming down to join me for karaoke. No one else will sing with me."

Yeah, there was a reason for that. Mum couldn't sing. I didn't mean just that she was out of tune. I meant it sounded like someone was killing the cat.

I smiled and kissed her cheek, waving to Casey as I went. Earlier I'd filled him in on what Alani and I were going to do. He hadn't liked it and had wanted to come with us, but he had to work. He even offered to call in sick for the night, but I told him we'd be fine. We were only going to follow Mark and not get involved in anything else. I'd even pinkie promised.

CHAPTER THIRTEEN

———

Okay. Following someone was harder than it looked. Mark had made his way down to the sand, turned right, and headed up the beach. Alani and I had been following him for a good couple of kilometers, trying our best to stay close to the dunes and the scrub. The moon was past being full and was working its way around again, only giving us minimal light to see by. I had no idea how Mark could see where he was going. He obviously ate more carrots than I did.

"Ouch," cursed Alani.

"Sorry," I replied. "I can't see where the heck I'm going."

"Haven't your eyes adjusted yet?"

"Yours have?"

"Sure. I can see just fine."

Humph. She obviously ate her carrots too.

"Surely he can't be going too much farther?" I said in a whisper. Even though Mark was a good twenty meters or so ahead of us, and the waves were crashing loudly, we didn't want to risk him hearing us.

"Ssh," said Alani, leading the way. "I think there's someone there."

Alani stopped moving, and I nearly walked into the back of her. I still couldn't see a thing.

"Be quiet, and we'll see how much closer we can get," she said.

I gave up trying to see what was going on and followed her, trusting her completely.

As we moved farther into the scrub, I heard the distinct sound of a branch snapping behind us. I spun around to see who was there.

"Stop moving," said Alani. "He's met someone."

I was suddenly more concerned about what was behind us. The stories Lahela and Alani had told me about island folklore suddenly came rushing back. The only problem was, I couldn't quite remember them correctly. Was I supposed to give gin to Mijuna the faceless lady, or was that the green lady? Hang on a minute—that legend was the green lady of Wahiawa, so surely that couldn't be the one. Maybe I was supposed to give gin to the Menehune, the little people of Hawaii? Or was that pork I was supposed to give them? Oh, what did it matter anyway? I didn't have any gin or pork, so we were pretty much stuffed if it was one of them. I made a mental note to ask Alani for another lesson in Hawaiian mythology. And this time I'd actually try to remember it.

Another branch snapped.

"Alani, Alani," I whispered, pulling on her shirt.

"Shush, I'm trying to listen."

"You heard it too? What do you think it was? Should we be worried, or are we safe because you're Hawaiian?"

"What are you talking about?"

"The noise. The one we both heard!"

"Mark just met someone. I'm trying to hear what they're doing."

I took a deep breath, did my best to ignore the noises from behind me, and strained to see where Mark was. After a minute or so, I could just make out the silhouette of two people. One was Mark, and judging by the size of the other one, I figured it to be a man. A very big man. But what were they doing meeting half a mile down a beach at nine o'clock at night?

"They're on the move," whispered Alani. "Come on."

Staying at a safe distance and hidden amongst the dunes, we managed to follow them. They moved along a sandy pathway through the trees, which made it much more difficult to not lose them, but their voices kept us in touch. I guessed they thought they were alone and didn't need to whisper, like Alani and me. However, we couldn't make out what they were saying clearly, only getting snippets here and there.

We heard, "It's in the car."

Then, "You'd better have the cash next time," and, "I'll break your kneecaps if you don't."

Okay, that all sounded pretty serious. I'd give Mark his due though. He stood strong and didn't back down to this guy, who was seriously a good six foot five. My mind flicked to Patrick.

They eventually made their way to a road where a car was parked on the grass. Alani and I stayed back, hidden on the path, and watched. The big guy opened the trunk, and their voices became muffled. I wondered what was in there and desperately wanted to have a look, but I knew that would be foolish. I definitely didn't want my kneecaps broken.

When Mark was satisfied with whatever it was, he seemed happy and said, "Alright. I'll have the cash tomorrow."

This seemed to satisfy the big guy, who then offered Mark a ride into town. I'm not sure I would have accepted that ride, and I had a moment of wondering if I would ever see Mark again. I made a quick note of what the car looked like just in case I didn't.

Once they'd driven away, I heard Alani let out a sigh.

"That was interesting."

"Yeah. What do you reckon was in the trunk?" I asked.

"Nothing good, I would guess."

"It wasn't a complete waste of time following him. We did find out that he *is* up to something. Maybe I need to watch him a bit more closely when he goes to Aloha Ohana."

"Maybe."

Alani turned to make her way back the way we'd come. Without the purpose and focus of watching Mark, it seemed so much creepier walking through the tree-lined path back to the beach, but the upside was we could at least use our phones for some light this time.

Movement ahead of us, just outside of the beam of our lights, made us stop dead.

I grabbed Alani's arm.

"Hello?" she called.

We stood silently waiting for a response. None came. Alani flipped off her light and told me to do the same. *Really?* I honestly felt safer with the light on.

"Turn it off," she whispered to me. Okay, she was the local expert out of the two of us. I'd let her take the lead on this one. I flipped my phone off.

We strained to listen. In Australia, walking through bush like this at night, you'd probably get taken out by a kangaroo, but I figured Aloha Lagoon didn't have any of those. For all I knew though, it could have been something equally as big.

After what felt like an eternity of standing still in the dark waiting for something to hit me, I whispered to Alani. "What are we doing?"

"Listening."

Okay, that I understood. "Do you hear anything?" My heart rate was slightly higher than normal, but definitely not in the danger zone.

"Yes."

Alright, my heart rate just entered the danger zone.

"What?"

"I'm not sure. It isn't an animal. It's too heavy," she whispered

"What's heavier than an animal?"

"A human."

My anxiety settled slightly. "Maybe it's a couple making out."

"It's only one. If it was two, I would have heard the first snap of the branch followed by a second quieter one."

That made sense I guessed, but it did nothing for my blood pressure.

"So what should we do?"

Alani thought for a minute. "How fit are you? Can you run in soft sand?"

A good question. The sand on this path was definitely soft in a lot of places. So much so it had been hard to walk through, but if someone was chasing me, I'd run through quicksand.

"Fit enough." I hoped.

"Okay. On three we run for it. Ready? One, two…"

She took off at a run. I didn't even hear her say "three."

I quickly ran after her. Two seconds in, I realized Alani was a lot more skilled at running on sand than I was. It didn't take long for her to lose me.

The path felt like it went on forever, like one of those dreams where you're running as fast as you can but getting nowhere. I could hear Alani ahead of me, but without light, I was running on instinct and sound as to where the path actually went. My legs burned with the strain, and my breathing became more ragged.

Unreasonable fear gripped me as I ran, but eventually I could see the small amount of moonlight glinting on the ocean, and knew I had nearly made it. Only when I caught up with Alani standing along the water's edge did I stop and double at the waist. I was so unfit. As a surf instructor, that was something I needed to work on.

"What do you think it was?" I asked when I finally got my breathing under control.

"I dunno. Probably nothing."

I stood, my hands on my hips. "Really?"

"Uh-huh. No one jumped out at us, so maybe it was just our imagination."

The hysterical giggle started in my throat. How stupid had we been, thinking someone had been in the scrub, watching us. And if they had, they would be having a very big laugh at our expense right now.

* * *

The beach was a beautiful place at night. Even though the air had slightly cooled, and I wished I'd brought a sweater with me, it was peaceful and serene.

Our scare with our imaginary stalker had given us a good laugh, but we were making our way back to the resort in companionable silence. I was thinking about Mark and how I would tell Mum what I'd seen, when up ahead of us we saw lights heading our way.

I felt Alani stiffen next to me. Oh no, what now? She turned to me and grabbed my arm.

"What is it?" I asked, the jitters starting once again. I didn't know how much more of this I could handle, to be honest.

"Do you hear that?"

"No. What? Is someone there? Are they following us? It wasn't our imaginations, was it?" I was rambling, but I couldn't seem to stop it.

"The chants. Do you hear the chants? And the drums!"

"No." I couldn't hear any chanting over the blood pounding in my ears. "There's chanting? And drums?"

She turned back to the lights heading toward us. "I think it's the Night Marchers," she said.

Okay, what on earth was she talking about? I was about to ask, when she grabbed my arm and pulled me to the sand, the lights moving closer.

"Lay on your stomach!" she demanded. "And whatever you do, don't look at them. If you make eye contact with them, you'll die and be forced to march with them for eternity."

That didn't sound like any fun at all. "What are Night Marchers?" I asked, totally freaked out by Alani's reaction.

"They're the ghosts of ancient Hawaiian warriors."

"But surely they're just a myth."

"No. They're real. Tutu has seen them. She told me all about it when I was young. I think I'm an ancestor, but I'm a bit unclear about that, so it's best not to risk it," finished Alani. The wobble in her voice betrayed her true emotions.

"What does being an ancestor mean?"

"It means they won't hurt me. But you, well, you're screwed, so just don't look at them!" *Was she serious?* As she put her head to the sand, I figured she was. My blood pressure entered the stroke zone. A headache started, and tears welled. I didn't want to spend eternity marching with *anyone*.

I could hear the chants Alani was talking about. It was distant, far more distant than the lights, but what did I know? I lay next to her, put my fingers in my ears, closed my eyes, and put my face on the sand. When you were faced with death and marching for eternity, who cared if you got sand up your nose?

It didn't take long to feel the movement around me. Ghosts obviously moved fast. When Alani had told me about the

Night Marchers, I'd figured they would be a group, but it felt like only a couple. Would they just ignore me and keep walking?

I closed my eyes even tighter and pushed my fingers farther into my ears, blocking any sound, except the blood pounding.

I screamed when something prodded me on the shoulder. It was difficult to do with my head literally in the sand, but I managed it anyway.

I then felt the hand on my back. Tears escaped, as fear like I had never known shot through me, spiking my adrenalin. I wanted to run. Run as far away from here as I could get, but I remembered Alani's warning to keep my head down.

Hands were placed under my shoulders, and I felt myself being lifted in the air. *Oh God!* Alani hadn't told me about this!

A sob escaped my lips as I tried to keep my eyes closed. *What sort of ghosts were these?* The movement pulled my fingers from my ears, and I heard laughing. *Hang on a minute.* That laugh sounded awfully familiar.

I snapped my eyes open and saw in front of me—Luke, laughing harder than I had ever seen him laugh. I was placed on my feet as I spun to see who was holding me. It was Casey. And even in the dim light from the moon, I could see his smile. Did I feel like an idiot or what? Alani stood next to Luke, and from the light of his torch, I could see she was looking sheepish. Well, at least I wasn't alone.

"W-what d-did you think...you were doing?" asked Luke, almost bending at the waist with laughter.

"We...we just thought that...you know..." My face burned with embarrassment. Thank goodness it was dark enough so Casey wouldn't be able to see that.

"Who did you think was coming?" he asked, his voice a lot more caring than Luke's.

"We thought you were the Night Marchers," I mumbled, looking at Alani for support. I mean, it was her idea. She was the one who'd freaked me out!

"Night Marchers!" cried Luke.

"Why would you think that?" asked Casey, gently wiping sand from my face.

All thoughts fled my mind the second his soft fingers skimmed my lip. My pulse, which had only just started to settle, picked up again, but this time for a completely different reason.

"Ummm…"

"It was my fault," said Alani. "I saw the lights and heard the chants and drums."

"The chants and drums were from the resort," explained Luke, his tone softening as he spoke to Alani.

Well, that was interesting.

"I didn't know that," she continued.

I didn't hear what she said after that, as Casey had been ever so helpful brushing sand from me, and as he did, his arm accidentally brushed my breast. The world around me ceased to exist as all the air in my lungs disappeared.

I heard his sharp intake of breath. "I'm so sorry," he stuttered, removing his hands immediately. "I'm sorry."

I wasn't sorry at all. I wanted to respond and tell him that it was fine, no problem, but my brain was scrambled, and words would not form properly. Instead I stood there awkwardly, tears still skimming my lashes as the adrenalin started to settle, leaving my knees rubbery. Or that could have been from running in the sand before.

"What are you doing out here?" asked Alani.

"Looking for you," replied Luke.

Casey remained quiet, standing close but not touching me. I could feel his presence, smell his musky scent, and in the dark evening air, it was the most intense feeling I had ever felt. I wanted to lean into him, to take his hand and walk along the edge of the water back to the resort, but I didn't have the courage. Instead I followed Luke and Alani as they led the way.

"You've been gone for a long time," said Casey, his step falling in with mine.

"Really? How long?" I asked, my voice croaky.

"A good hour and a half."

"We were worried," continued Luke. "So when Casey suggested we come and look for you, I left the kitchen for the busboy to clean up and came straight down here. Why didn't you tell me about your suspicions involving Mark?"

"I did, but you didn't really listen. Anyway, they were just that. Suspicions. I needed to find out more." I brought everybody up to date with what we'd seen. "I'm not sure I'm cut out for this investigating business. It's a lot scarier than I thought it would be."

"Why? What happened?" asked Casey.

"Nothing," said Alani, a warning tone in her voice. I wondered about her tone, but then maybe she didn't like the idea of the guys thinking we were silly little girls scared of our own shadows. "We just thought someone was watching us or following us or something, but it was just our imaginations," she explained.

"Are you sure?" Luke asked. I thought for a second.

"No. I'm not." Even I was surprised by my answer. Earlier I'd been positive it was my imagination. "I thought someone was behind us as we walked up the beach, but all I could think of was the stories that Alani and Lahela had told me about island mythology. My imagination went into overdrive, which is probably why I overreacted before, but I know I didn't imagine the noises."

"So what do you think it could have been?"

"I don't think it was an animal. Unless the wildlife around here stalks people. It obviously wasn't Mark, as we were following him." I shivered, the evening air suddenly feeling cooler than a second before. "Who else would be following us?"

"Maybe they were also following Mark," added Alani. Hmmm, I hadn't thought of that.

"Do you think Mark is involved with the murders?" asked Luke.

"Yes. I think he got those men to change their wills to name you and Mum, and then he killed them. He's going to try to take the money once Mum is in jail. I just haven't figured out if my theory is correct yet."

"But that doesn't explain why I was named in the will."

"No it doesn't. Hey, Luke, when that will was read, did you see who witnessed it?"

"No. Did I need to?"

I nodded in the dark. "Yes. If Mark was the one who took them to change the wills, and he's named as a witness, I can take my theory to Detective Ray."

"Okay. Tomorrow I'll go and ask to see the will."

I felt something settle in my stomach. "Thanks."

Tomorrow this could all be over.

CHAPTER FOURTEEN

It was another day in paradise. The sun was shining, the birds were singing, and the waves were rolling in. I tried to concentrate on the six kids in my last class. I tried, but all I could think about was Luke visiting Mr. Fathersham and finding out who'd witnessed the will. And how I would have to tell Mum what Mark was doing.

Last night we'd decided not to tell her anything until we knew more. Luke wanted to tell her before we visited Detective Ray, but I was worried that she would confront Mark and something bad would happen. I'd have to cross that bridge when I came to it.

Luke had the day off work, as did Casey. I had no idea what either of them was doing after Luke visited the solicitor, or even if they were spending the day together. It felt different around the resort without Casey. Lonelier and not as much fun. I really needed to sit down and have a good chat with myself about him. I knew my feelings went beyond hormones. I was starting to get past the rush I felt when he smiled at me. Oh, who was I kidding? I didn't think I'd ever get past that! But the point was it felt like this was more than a crush. I felt a connection with Casey that I had never felt with anyone before. He made me laugh, he truly cared about people, he was compassionate when I was worried or scared, and even though I'd seen him flirt with just about every patron at The Lava Pot, I knew that he was loyal. I'd never met a man like him.

I was happy to report that my skills as a surf instructor were getting better. I think I actually taught the kids something that day. Yes, I even surprised myself. Plus, I saw David

Mahelona smiling when he was watching me teach. That had to be good, right?

My pay had started to roll in, but I still hadn't earned enough to buy myself a car, so after I locked the surf shed, I worked my way through the resort to the staff parking lot to get the bike. I passed the pond where Harold the Turtle was and took a minute to watch him. He had a pretty good life, as far as I was concerned. He got to wake up every morning in the world's most beautiful place, food was literally handed to him, he had no worries, and he got to swim all day or laze in the sun. I thought in my next life I wanted to be Harold.

I heard the distinct *whoop whoop* sound of a helicopter and looked up. Rick's Air Paradise helicopter tours were busy. I'd lost count of the number of times he'd flown over that day. I remembered what Gabby had said about his tours. I'd love to do it one day, but as I swung my leg over the bike, which thanks to Casey was now complete with shiny new back tire, I knew I had other priorities to consider first. Still, it was definitely on the list.

The upside to riding a bike was that my fitness was getting better. I could now easily make my way up the hill to home. Okay, maybe *easily* was a bit generous, but at least I didn't collapse in a heap at the top anymore.

The house was empty when I walked in, so I took advantage of that, turned the radio up to loud, and made my way straight to the bathroom.

I took the time to pamper myself. I shaved my legs, washed my hair, used one of Mum's moisture treatments, and then exfoliated everywhere that needed exfoliating. By the time I turned the shower off, I felt amazing. I hung my wet towel over the towel rail and realized that I'd left my clean clothes in my bedroom. No one was home, so a quick dash across the hall wouldn't hurt. I grabbed my towel and tied it around my body. It was on the small side and barely covered my backside, but that didn't matter. It wasn't like I was about to entertain company. The radio was blaring a hit from the sixties, which was really catchy, so I flung the bathroom door open and danced into the hall. And directly into Luke.

I screamed. Luke screamed. In fact, I didn't know who screamed the loudest. Hmmm, actually, I think that was probably Luke.

I quickly used my hands to pull the towel over my backside as much as I could and yelled at him.

"Where the hell did you come from?"

"I just got home. Where are your clothes?" he yelled, turning his back to me.

"I had a shower. No one was home!" I ducked across the hall to my room. As I did, I looked over Luke's shoulder and saw Casey—his grin the largest I had ever seen it.

If a person could self-combust from overheating, I would have. I had never been so embarrassed in my life—even the time I'd been caught photocopying my boobs as a dare. I flung myself onto my bed.

My life sucked. I hated living with my brother. I hated it. All the memories I had of living with him as a kid came flooding back. Soon anger started to replace the tears, but then I settled down and figured it wasn't his fault. He didn't know I would be walking around half naked. And really, it wasn't Luke that I was embarrassed about. It was Casey.

I stood and moved to my mirror and checked just how much of my flesh that Casey would have seen. The towel had been tied low across my chest, showing quite a bit of cleavage, and I hoped like anything that I hadn't been bending at the waist when Casey saw me. If I had, I would have been showing him areas where the sun didn't shine.

Argh!

I found some clothes and applied some makeup. My hair was drying naturally, which was something I was getting used to. Using my fingers, I fluffed it to give it some bounce and then flopped myself on the bed. It didn't take long lying there for me to fall asleep.

I woke to the sound of someone tapping on my door. Darkness had fallen outside, so I must have been out for quite a while. Feeling groggy from sleep, I stood and opened my door. Casey grinned back at me. And the events of the afternoon suddenly came rushing back.

Now I didn't know what to do. Instinct made me want to slam the door in his face and hide, but adulthood told me that would be rude. I needed to face him and pretend nothing had happened. Or pretend like it was a common occurrence for me to get caught half naked.

No, that wasn't right. I didn't want him to think that. Maybe I'd just go for nonchalance. It didn't bother me. Yeah, that was the one I'd try.

"Hey!" I sang, leaning against the door as if I didn't have a care in the world.

Casey's grin kicked up a notch, and I felt the door slip. Or was that me? He put out his hand and caught me before I slid into the hallway. Argh! I might as well just show him that the real me was a klutz who often gets caught doing stupid things. He'd probably figured that out by now anyway.

"Hi," I said, embarrassment once again burning my ears.

"Luke's made pizza, if you want some," said Casey, his voice deep and gravelly, his hand still holding my arm.

I plucked up courage and looked him in the eyes. They looked back at me, deep blue like the ocean, holding an expression I couldn't explain. I moved my eyes to his lips and saw the hint of a smile, but his look was intense. Normally this was the moment when I couldn't handle it anymore and would look away. But I didn't want to. I wanted to meet his gaze head on and see where it led.

Luke's loud, stomping footsteps echoed up the hall, interrupting anything that might be about to happen. Actually, maybe nothing was about to happen. Maybe that was my imagination. Whatever it was, I was no longer embarrassed about being caught showing more of myself than I had wished. And anyway, I had the bike riding and surfing to thank for the fact that my thighs were no longer as wobbly as they used to be and that my body was close to the best it had ever been. I wasn't saying it was supermodel status or anything, but everything was where it was meant to be—not hanging or jiggling or anything.

"What's going on?" asked Luke.

I could feel him going big brother on me and wondered if he'd spoken to Casey about it. I never did have the conversation with him to tell him to back off.

"Sam was just coming for pizza, and I was about to use the toilet," replied Casey, winking at me before facing Luke.

"Oh. Well, it's ready." Luke turned back down the hall, his shoulders hunched. Casey turned and entered the bathroom. I followed Luke.

Reaching the living room, I heard the doorbell chime. I raised my eyebrows as I looked at Luke.

"I invited Alani," he said. "Hope you don't mind."

No, I didn't mind. In fact, I had a very good idea that there was something happening between Alani and Luke, and it gave me the perfect reason to tell him to back off where Casey was concerned.

Alani looked extra beautiful tonight. Her hair was tied in a high ponytail, she was wearing a short, flowy lemon-colored dress that showed off her perfect skin, and she'd applied just enough makeup to accentuate her big brown eyes and still make it look like she wasn't wearing any.

The TV was on in the lounge, and a midevening weather update was being read. The Hawaiian weather reporter in the very bright shirt was announcing how tomorrow was going to be one of the few wet days we would see. Not great when you rode a bike.

I moved to the remote and turned the volume down as Luke placed the pizza on the center of the table.

"Where's Mum?" I asked, noting the places set at the table and how we were a place too short.

"She's out with Rebecca. There's a show on at the resort that they wanted to see."

"Good for her," I said, thinking how she needed more fun in her life.

I pulled out a chair and sat down between Casey and Luke, helping myself to a piece of pizza as I did so.

"Hey, Luke, did you go to see Mr. Fathersham today?" I asked before taking a bite.

"Yeah."

"And?"

"And I saw the will. It wasn't Mark who witnessed it."

I felt disappointment sink in my stomach.

"Who did?" asked Casey.

Luke wiped his mouth with a napkin. "It was actually a bit of a disappointment."

Okay. He had everyone's attention.

"The first witness was Mr. Fathersham's secretary, and the second was April Clements. I know April. She's a caregiver at Aloha Ohana."

"There goes your theory about Mark," said Alani quietly.

She was right. Without Mark being the witness to the will change, my theory about him coercing Albert Johnstone and Jeremy Gibson had nothing to support it.

"Unless," I continued, "he talked the men into making the changes, and then the caregivers were just the ones to take them for the drive. Assuming that Mark didn't witness Jeremy Gibson's will either. I'll have to ask Mum to check on that for me."

"Maybe," said Alani, not entirely convinced.

"I still need to talk to April. I'll ask her if she knows why Luke was named."

"I'd ask her for you," said Luke. "But I've been told to stay away from the Aloha Ohana."

I took a bite of pizza and shrugged. "It's okay. I'm happy to chase it up," I said.

"I was going to tell you about a guy in the bar last night," said Casey, speaking up for the first time since he'd winked at me in the hallway. "He was really big, red hair, and he was talking to another guy who's known around here as not being the best kind of person. If you want drugs, you go to him. Anyway, I overheard their conversation. It was along the lines of the red-haired guy moving here because he got fired from his last job for taking drugs."

"And?" asked Luke.

"The red-haired guy is a security guard up at Aloha Ohana, and he moved here just before the murders. I wondered if he's involved."

I immediately thought of Patrick.

"If it is him, then how did he get the job? Wasn't a security check done on him prior to being employed?"

"Who does the hiring and firing up there?" asked Casey.

"When I was employed," said Luke, "it was Tristan who was in charge."

"So is he incompetent and hired a criminal without knowing it?"

"Maybe he knew exactly what he was doing."

"If that's true, then I suggest you pass your concerns to Detective Ray and stay away from it. The guy from the bar is trouble." Casey looked at me, those adorable creases on his forehead deep with concern.

"Maybe the red-haired guy is stealing drugs here, and the victims caught him. Maybe he blackmailed them into changing their wills," said Alani, going along with Casey's theory.

"Yes, but why were Mum and Luke named as beneficiary in those wills?"

"Does he have any connection to them?" asked Casey.

"Not that I know of," said Luke.

"I still think it's Mark," I said.

"But what if you're wrong?"

"I've seen the red-haired guy at Aloha Ohana," said Alani.

So had I.

"Alani, how many people around here are as tall as he is?" I asked.

"The red-haired man?"

I nodded.

"Not many. He'd have to be around six foot five."

"Do you think he was the guy Mark met on the beach?"

She thought for a moment and then nodded. "He could have been. That guy's silhouette was pretty big."

"So hang on a minute," said Luke. "Do you think that Mark is involved with this red-haired man, who is involved with the bad guy, who is involved with drugs?"

That pretty much summed it up.

"I'm not working tomorrow, so I think I'll visit Aloha Ohana in the morning and talk to April," I said. "Can anyone give me a lift?"

"Not enjoying the bike?" asked Luke humorously.

"The weatherman said it's going to rain."

"It is? It hardly ever rains."

"I have to work. Sorry," said Alani.

"Me too," said Luke.

"I can take you," said Casey. "I have tomorrow off."

Even better. "That'd be awesome. Thanks."

I couldn't wipe the smile off my face for the rest of the night. Luke, on the other hand, looked like you'd killed his cat.

* * *

I got up early the next morning and put extra effort into my appearance. I even found my flat iron and straightened my hair. I studied it in the mirror and decided I liked it better natural, so I stuck my head back under the shower and wet it again, this time just fluffing it with my fingers and applying some product to help with the humidity.

So far the rain had held off. Personally, I would have liked it to stay away until tonight, when I could fall asleep to the sound of the rain pattering against the windows. Looking at the clouds, I didn't like my chances.

I pulled on a little skirt that stopped about midthigh, found a tank that accentuated the color of my eyes, and swiped on an extra layer of mascara. I even added lip gloss. Was I going all out or what?

Casey pulled into the driveway at nine fifteen. Locking the house door behind me, I ran out to meet him.

The plan was to go to Aloha Ohana and ask for April Clements. I'd already checked with Mum, and she confirmed that April did indeed witness Albert's will and that April did work at Aloha Ohana as a caregiver. She just didn't work every day. Hopefully, I'd find her there today. If I had any problems, I was going to ask Lahela for tips. Surely she'd know the comings and goings of the place.

Opening the car door, Casey's scent overwhelmed me. It was a subtle mix of aftershave and soap. His hair was still wet from his shower.

"Sorry. I'm a bit later than we planned," he said, giving me a coy smile. "I went surfing this morning and ended up at the rock. I lost track of time."

"Don't worry about it. I can understand losing time sitting there." I gave him a big smile, pulling my seat belt over my shoulder and locking it into place.

Putting the car into gear, he reversed out of the drive and headed to Aloha Ohana. Casey's mood was different this morning. He wasn't his usual exuberant self.

"Are you okay?" I asked after a few minutes of silence.

"Yeah. Why do you ask?"

"You just seem quiet."

"Sorry. I don't mean to be."

"I hope you didn't mind giving me a lift? It hasn't started to rain yet, so I could have ridden my bike. I'm probably wasting your time today."

"You're not wasting my time. I'm happy to help," he said, his eyes firmly on the road ahead.

"Okay, so long as we're good."

He turned look at me. "We're good," he said, giving me his dazzling smile.

I took a deep, shuddery breath and tried to stop my heart from doing its trippy thing.

"I spent a lot of time sitting on the rock thinking this morning," he said. "I had a lot to think about," he continued, in way of explanation. "Maybe that's affected my mood. Sorry."

"Really, it's okay. I didn't mention it to be awkward. I was just concerned, that's all."

Casey turned back to concentrate on the road, and silence filled the car once more. I looked out the window at the volcanoes in the distance, the clouds hanging low over them.

"Lahela told me that Hawaiians believe the sky to be sacred," I said. "They think it protects us. I like that."

Casey looked up through the windscreen at the sky. "What does it protect us from?"

I thought for a moment. I really didn't know. I shrugged and looked back out the window, deciding I really needed to study Hawaiian culture just a little bit more before opening my mouth.

Casey pulled the car into the parking lot of Aloha Ohana and killed the engine. He turned to unlatch my seat belt. Before he did though, he stopped and looked at me, his expression sad. Oh no. What was he about to say?

"Luke had a chat with me last night," he said quietly.

I instantly felt a flash of irritation. I knew what was coming.

"He said he thought there was something going on between us."

I certainly hoped there was.

"Did he just?" I replied, anger simmering in my voice. Luke really needed to let go of the big-brother routine.

"Don't worry though. I told him he was wrong. We're just friends."

"Really?" I whispered.

Casey nodded. "Yeah, a mate doesn't hit on his mate's little sister."

His words felt like a punch to my stomach. Casey didn't feel anything for me other than me being his mate's sister.

"Well, you can tell Luke that I'm only his little sister by six minutes. It hardly makes him an authority."

I pushed Casey's hand aside and attempted to undo the seat belt myself. Tears stung my lashes, and I needed to get out into the fresh air before I embarrassed myself once more.

Casey's scent surrounded me in this car, and I couldn't cope, having admitted to myself that my feelings for him were more than a crush. I'd never met a man like him. He was funny, caring, thoughtful, understanding, and downright sexy. He was my perfect man. One I felt I could be best friends with and whom I could spend a very long time sitting on a rock overlooking the ocean with. Right now, I hated Luke. For the first time in my life, I didn't want to be his sister.

Damn this seat belt! No matter how hard I tried, I couldn't get it to unlatch. Casey gently took my hand and placed it on my lap. I could hear his breathing, uneven and fast, as he performed his magic trick and unclicked the belt. I didn't look at him. The second the belt released, I opened my door and almost leaped into the cooler air outside the car.

My knees felt rubbery, and my hands shook, but I had to get a grip before Casey saw my reaction. It was humiliating enough that I had these feelings for him. If he knew how I felt, he would feel bad for me, and then things between us would be awkward because he was so kind.

I heard his door close. His footsteps were heavy on the driveway. I didn't turn to look. I made a beeline for the entrance into Aloha Ohana, desperately trying to pull myself together. By the time Casey followed me in, I'd already signed the visitors' book.

I stepped over to the desk where the receptionist, Ania, glared at me. "Hello," I said, going for cheery. Even I heard the wobble in my voice. "I'm looking for April Clements. Would she be available at all?"

"What do you need April for?" she asked me suspiciously.

"I just wanted a chat, that's all."

I knew my face was flushed, and I was grateful that Casey had kept his distance and was standing closer to the door than to me.

"If she's here, she'll be around the lounge room, but she may have left already."

"Thank you," I said before she had the chance to interrogate me anymore.

I made my way around to the lounge room. I had no idea what April looked like. Fortunately, I spotted Lahela. She'd be able to help me.

As we approached, Lahela sucked in her breath. My first instinct was that I hoped I hadn't done anything wrong, but when I saw her quickly adjust the flower behind her ear, I knew her reaction was for Casey's sake.

"Hello!" she called, standing to kiss my cheek. She'd never done that before. She then moved to Casey. "*Hello*," she said, reaching up to kiss him as well.

I looked at him for the first time since the car and noticed how her kiss almost made his lips. Almost. I didn't think it was from lack of trying. Casey blushed. It made him even more irresistible. I groaned. I had to stop thinking like that. I had to. It wasn't any good for my emotions.

"Sit down," Lahela ordered.

We both did as asked, sitting at the square table Lahela had been reading the paper on. Casey sat on my left, his leg brushing mine as he moved. I groaned again.

"Are you okay?" asked Lahela.

"Yes, thanks."

I wanted to say no. I wasn't fine. I wanted to put my head on her shoulder and cry, but I didn't. I plastered a smile on my lips and told her why we were there.

"Do you know April Clements?" I asked her.

"Yes. I know April. She sometimes takes me to the hairdresser." Lahela smoothed her hair. "It's all natural color, you know. No dye in this."

Impressive. Not too many greys in sight, which was remarkable for a woman of her age. I guess a life surfing didn't hold too much stress.

"Is she around today so I can ask her a few questions?"

"Ummm...I'm not sure, but if she's still here, she'll be in with Bill. He's over in the Oleander wing. Just go down that hall to the right, and you'll find him in room six."

"Thanks, Lahela. You're a star." I stood to follow her directions.

Casey stood too.

"Would you mind sitting with me for a while?" Lahela said, grabbing his hand. "I'm feeling a bit low today, and some company would cheer me up."

I saw the glint in her eye from here. Casey looked trapped, but the gentleman in him came to the surface, and he smiled and sat back down.

"Sure. I'll be waiting here for you," he said to me. "Call me if you need me."

"Thanks."

I turned and walked away. *Call me if you need me!* Well, of course I bloody well needed him. Just not in the way he was referring to. *Oh, cut it out, Samantha! It's not going to happen. He doesn't want you.* Tears stung once again, but I brushed them away with determination and made my way to the Oleander wing.

It turned out I had missed April. She'd been there early that day, had taken Bill to his dentist appointment, and had the rest of the day off. I was just making my way back to the lounge room when I bumped into Tony.

"Hello, lovely lady," he sang, waddling toward me, rolling his eyes upward. I realized this was a habit of his, one I wished he would stop. "What are you doing in this neck of the woods?"

I smiled. "Hi, Tony. I was looking for April, but apparently I've already missed her."

"Yeah, she left early today. Her daughter bought her a voucher for a massage at the resort spa, so that's where she's headed. Why do you need April?"

I looked around me, hoping Tristan wouldn't pop out of nowhere. Though, I wouldn't mind asking him a few more questions. "I just wanted to chat with her about the men who were murdered."

"Really? Samantha, why don't you stay out of it? Detective Ray seems to have this all under control."

"If it's up to Detective Ray, then Mum will rot in jail for a crime she didn't commit."

Tony shifted uncomfortably, his brow wrinkling. "I see what you mean, but I can't see how he can find the evidence he needs to arrest her."

"Yeah, well, I like your way of thinking. I just don't trust him to get it right. And April witnessed the changes to the wills. If I can prove that Mum and Luke knew nothing about it, then I'm hoping that Detective Ray will back off and look for someone else to pin it on."

Tony adjusted his belt uncomfortably. "I wouldn't bother if I was you. My money's on Detective Ray proving it couldn't have been either Rita or Luke. He's been talking to me about this, you know." Tony looked over his shoulder and moved his head closer to mine. "I'm a bit of an insider for them, alerting them to anything out of the ordinary around here."

This got my attention. "Tony, you know the security guard, Patrick?"

"Yes, yes, I know him."

"Have you heard the rumors about how he was sacked from his last job?"

Tony looked even more uncomfortable, pulling me into a nearby alcove. When he was sure nobody could overhear us, he whispered, "Yes, I heard. But as far as I could find out, they were only rumors. There was no evidence to support it."

"Do you think he could have murdered those men?"

"Samantha, go home. Let the detective do his job."

I ignored Tony's warning. "My friend Casey saw Patrick at the bar with a man known to the locals for his involvement with drugs. What do you think?"

"I think you should keep out of it! Men like that are dangerous."

I was getting tired of people telling me to stay out of it. Mum and Luke needed to be cleared of any wrongdoing.

Tony gave me a look filled with compassion. "I can imagine it's difficult for you. You're a lovely girl, Samantha. One I'm sure your father would be proud of."

"Thanks, but I don't know my father. He left when Luke and I were four."

"Well, that's his loss, and something I'm sure he regrets."

"Probably not. I was twenty-eight last birthday. Not once has he tried to contact me. He could be dead for all I know."

"I can only speak for myself. I wasn't involved with my children, and I regret it. I'd do almost anything to put it right now." Sadness sat heavily in Tony's eyes.

"Then contact them. It's never too late."

I didn't know what it was, but something about Tony pulled at my heartstrings. I thought about my dad and what I would do if he contacted me today. I honestly didn't know, but I'd always figured he had his reasons for staying away.

"I wish it was that easy, but what do you say after so long?"

"You could start with hello."

Tony smiled, and his eyes crinkled at the corners. Weight and age had not been kind to him, but I thought that once upon a time he was probably quite good-looking.

"You're a special girl, Samantha. Please stay out of this investigation. Imagine how your mum would feel if anything happened to you."

I hadn't thought of it like that, but what could happen to me? I was only asking questions, and I was being careful.

I nodded. "Okay. Thanks, Tony. I appreciate your help."

I touched his arm and squeezed. He surprised me as his eyes filled with tears. He shook it off pretty quickly though when we both looked up to see Patrick glaring at us. I gulped. His expression was menacing. On second glance, I figured maybe that was just his look.

From where I stood, I could see his sheer bulk, I could see the scar that ran down his left cheek, stopping at his lip, and I could see how dark his eyes were. "Everything okay?" he asked, his eyes darting from Tony to me.

"Yep. Everything's fine," snapped Tony.

I was actually a bit surprised by his tone. I didn't think I would have been game to speak to Patrick in that way.

Patrick eyed us suspiciously. "Alright. So long as everything is fine." He sauntered off, occasionally looking back over his shoulder at us.

I sighed in relief once he was out of sight.

"I'm surprised that Patrick is here today," I said, more to myself than Tony.

"Really?"

"Is it normal for two security guards to work the same shift?"

"Nah. Tristan's doubled the security throughout the day to make it look good to visitors."

"I hope it helps."

"I'd better get going," said Tony. "Got work to do. I'm pulling a double shift today."

"Oh, sure. Sorry. I didn't mean to hold you up."

"You didn't. I just need to go. Now."

"Okay. Thanks for the chat."

"No, thank you, Samantha." Tony looked at me sadly and left.

As I watched him walk away, I wondered about his emotion. Maybe I reminded him of the child he left behind and all the regrets he had. Tony seemed like a nice guy. I didn't like the idea that I'd made him sad.

I moved to make my way back to the lounge room and bumped straight into Kylie. I squealed. "Sorry. I didn't see you there."

But seriously, how had I not? She must have been standing against the wall, listening to my conversation with Tony. Why?

"What are you doing here?" she asked, her face flushed.

"I could ask you the same thing."

"I work here!"

"Well, yes, of course you do. I actually meant, what were you doing right here?" I pointed to the wall I believed she'd been leaning against.

"I don't know what you're talking about. I just walked around the corner, and there you were, right in my way."

"Alright. Sorry!" I stepped around her to continue on my way, but she blocked me with her body.

"What did you want with Tony?"

"How do you know I was with Tony if you only just walked around the corner?" I asked. She made my skin prickle, and I could understand why the residents didn't really like her.

"Because I saw him walking away."

"So?"

"So what were you doing?" She was a strange woman.

"That's none of your business."

"Listen," she said, getting in close to my face, "I know you questioned my husband about the first murder. I'd appreciate you staying out of my business. Got it?"

Oh, I got it alright. "Sure. Whatever. No problem." This time I did actually step around her.

She called after me. "I'm onto you!"

Whatever that meant.

CHAPTER FIFTEEN

It was becoming a long, exhausting day. I'd left Aloha Ohana with Casey, and we'd visited the resort. I even went to the spa to try to find April Clements. Casey was very patient waiting for me in the reception area whilst I looked for her. I did eventually find her, but that was after I'd lied to the spa manager about having an appointment for a massage. She was so nice about it, apologizing profusely about them making a mistake and double-booking, and then she showed me into a room, where I was asked to remove all my clothes and wrap myself in a towel. Someone would be with me shortly.

I wasn't a hundred percent comfortable with a stranger touching my body, but I did my best to relax. Easier said than done. I'd never actually had a professional massage before, and I didn't think I ever would again. It turned out that I wasn't very good at lying still. I kept thinking of April lying in one of these rooms and how I wanted to talk to her before she slipped away. Eventually, I gave up and told my masseur that I'd had enough. She was a bit upset at first, asking me if I didn't like the treatment. I assured her it was fine, just not for me. Once she'd left, I tucked my towel around me and snuck out of my room and to the one next door. In hindsight I should have gotten dressed first, but I thought I would blend in better if I was wearing the spa towel.

I had my excuse ready in case any staff members questioned what I was doing wandering around. I was just going to say that I was lost and couldn't find the bathroom. I added *come up with a better excuse* to my mental To Do list. Aloha Lagoon wasn't that big of a place, and if I didn't find another excuse, word would soon get around that I had an incontinence problem. That wasn't a rumor I wanted spread.

I gently knocked on the door, then opened it to find a lady lying facedown on a similar table to the one I'd been lying on.

"Excuse me," I said, quietly.

She looked up sleepily from the little hole that her face lay in.

"Are you April Clements?" I asked once I knew the room was clear of any staff.

"No, sorry."

Oops. My bad.

I apologized for my intrusion and moved to the next room. No luck there either. It was empty.

This part of the spa was huge but luckily pretty quiet. I smiled at a staff member as she passed me. She stopped and asked if I was lost. I quickly gave her my excuse, and she directed me to the bathroom. She was watching me, so I felt like I needed to go through with it. Even though, sneaking around did seem to be having an effect on my bladder, so maybe it wasn't such a bad idea. And the upside was I walked past the steam room, peeked through the little glass window, and noticed a lady sitting alone. I turned to see the staff member had gone and then swung open the door. The lady was sitting on the edge of the timber bench, her eyes closed, her posture rigid.

"Excuse me. Are you April Clements?" I asked quietly.

She opened her eyes and looked at me, surprised.

"Yes. I'm April." Her body language didn't appear very relaxed. In fact, I got the distinct impression she didn't like the intrusion.

It didn't deter me. I stood at the open door and quickly filled her in on who I was. "I tried to get you at Aloha Ohana, but unfortunately I missed you. Anyway, I believe that you took Albert Johnstone and Jeremy Gibson to the lawyer to change their wills. Could you tell me why they changed them? Please." It all came out in a rush, but I was nervous, and it seemed I really did need the bathroom now. Confusion crossed her face.

"What?"

"Albert Johnstone and Jeremy Gibson. They're the two men from Aloha Ohana who have been murdered."

"I know who they are," she snapped. Geez, she needed to turn the steam up a bit more. Maybe that would help her relax. "Why are you asking me about them?"

"I was hoping that you could tell me why they changed their wills. It's really important that I know."

"Listen, couldn't this wait?" She sat forward and glared at me. "This is really inappropriate!"

She could have a point there, but I wasn't going to admit that.

"Well, yes, but..."

"But nothing!" she yelled, her voice reverberating around the small room. "I came here today to relax! In fact, my daughter paid a lot of money for this! It's supposed to be my time-out!"

"Yes, I'm sorry, but..." I tried to explain my situation. Only she didn't seem interested in listening. She stood and tightened her towel around her, irritated that I'd interrupted her time. I got that. I wouldn't be happy if someone was asking me this when I was trying to relax. But I needed answers.

"I don't appreciate being interrogated."

"I'm not interrogating you. I just asked a question. That's all." April really needed a chill pill.

"If you don't leave me alone, I will file a complaint."

"Of course. Sorry!" I quickly chose a different tactic. "I won't bother you," I said, moving in and closing the door behind me. I sat on the bench as the steam filled the room once more, filling my lungs and making me feel like I couldn't breathe. April sighed heavily, opened the door, and left.

Bugger!

I jumped up and followed her, appreciating the cool air in the corridor.

She stomped toward the bathroom, and I followed her in. The spa must have been having a quiet day, as we were the only people in the room that I could see. April spun on her heels and glared at me.

"What are you doing?" she demanded.

"Using the facilities," I replied weakly.

She narrowed her eyes but allowed me to do what I needed to do.

I really didn't want to let her out of my sight until I'd gotten the answers I'd come for, but nature really was calling. I quickly answered that call, listening the entire time to what she was doing.

After, I moved to wash my hands and then wandered to see what had happened to her. Walking around a wall of some very upmarket lockers, I came face-to-face with April, standing in her underwear, pulling her shirt over her head. Geez, did she not know about the lockable cubicles you could use to get dressed in?

She looked up, saw me watching her, and let out a small scream.

"What are you doing?" she yelled. "I could have been undressed then."

Yes, well, I would have regretted that immensely. April seemed to be in her early sixties, and from the flesh that I could see, I thought that she probably should have used her daughter's money for waxing more than anything else. She was particularly hairy for a woman.

"Sorry, but if you could just tell me why they changed their wills, I'll leave you alone. I promise!"

April rubbed her temples, suggesting her head was hurting. "I just drove them there and witnessed their signatures," she snapped.

"Oh. Really? They didn't mention anything to you about their motivation?"

"It was none of my business. But if you must know, they both gave me almost the same reason. They were doing it to help a friend."

I opened my mouth to ask something else, when she narrowed her eyes and said, "Now, leave me alone, or I'm filing a complaint to the spa."

I thought about what she had previously said. "But who were they helping?"

"I don't know!" she snapped.

"You didn't ask? Weren't you even the little bit curious?"

She pulled on her shorts, pushed past me, and stomped out the door, muttering something about having enough. In hindsight that was the part where I should have quickly revisited my room, grabbed my clothes, and left. But no, not me. I rushed after her as she marched to reception.

"Ummm…did they mention any names to you? Any at all?" I called, attempting to keep up with her. My towel wasn't staying put, and I had to stop to readjust it, or everyone would get to see far more of me than I wanted them to.

I tucked my towel tighter around my body and quickly followed her. She stopped in front of the reception desk, her cheeks red with anger. Now Lahela had told me that April was a lovely woman. I guess Lahela had never accompanied her to a spa.

"I cannot believe this!" she shouted to the young girl behind the counter. The three women in the waiting room turned to look at her. Casey turned to look at me. My cheeks heated up and matched the color of April's, but for a whole different reason.

The girl paled. "Is there a problem?" she asked.

"Yes. This woman came barging into the steam room when I was in there relaxing, demanding that I answer her questions. She then followed me to the locker room, whereby she *watched* while I got dressed. I answered her questions, hoping that would get rid of her, but no. She still won't leave me alone! Does this spa not enforce the rules that you made me sign when I came in? Aren't we supposed to respect others' privacy?"

The girl turned to look at me. "Umm…yes. Of course. We ask all our clients to do that!" she stated, rather vehemently. I cringed.

"Look," I said. "There's been a misunderstanding. I didn't barge into the steam room."

"No. First you stood with the door open letting all the steam out!" shouted April.

She actually had a point there. "Sorry," I said, remorsefully. "But I just needed to ask you some questions."

"In regards to murder, no less!"

I could see heads of the clients in the waiting room moving from April to myself.

"But I didn't accuse you. I just wanted to know why those men changed their wills. That's all."

"And I answered you!"

"Yes, and I appreciate that. I just wondered…"

"Enough!" yelled April. "Leave me alone!"

"Okay. No need to yell." Geez, this woman was uptight. At that moment another staff member arrived and escorted me back to my room to get dressed, whilst the spa manager was called and April filed her complaint.

After that Casey took me home with the promise that I would never go to the spa again. As if I would.

* * *

It was four o'clock by the time I got home. My head was pounding, and Casey only added to that. He'd been so close to me all day, filling my senses bloody everywhere I turned. His deep blue eyes filled my mind when I closed my eyes. He overwhelmed my sense of smell, and my fingers tingled from when we'd accidentally touched hands over lunch. I had this desperate urge to kiss his soft, full lips, and all I could think of was how his whiskers would feel against my cheek. Emotions bubbled up in me everywhere, and I wasn't sure how much longer I'd be able to hold it all in.

He pulled the car into the driveway and cut the engine. The weatherman had been right in his prediction. It was pouring rain. Large drops of water soaked the windscreen as the wipers worked overtime, attempting to clear them away.

"Luke's home," I commented, thinking another reason for my headache was about to kick in. I was annoyed with Luke, and he was going to hear about it. "Are you coming in to see him?" I asked Casey.

He shook his head. "No, I'll catch up with him another day."

Good. It meant I wouldn't have to hold my temper for too long. "Okay, would you mind undoing my seatbelt, please?"

"Sure." Casey swiveled in his seat but stopped before unclicking me. I heard his sigh as he took a deep breath. "Sam, I wanted to say that I…"

He stopped what he was saying as the front door opened and Luke stepped onto the deck. He stood and crossed his arms over his chest.

"What? What did you want to say?" I asked Casey, glaring at Luke.

It probably would have been more effective if Luke could actually see my face through the pounding rain hitting the windscreen.

He let out the breath. "Nothing. It doesn't matter," he said, watching Luke through the glass.

Argh! (See what I have to put up with?) No wonder my head was pounding!

"Okay. Whatever," I snapped. "Can you undo me please?"

I saw the regret in his eyes as he unclicked the belt, releasing me. I opened the car door and stepped into the rain, slamming it behind me. I stomped all the way toward Luke.

"Bastard!" I snapped at him as I passed, tears of anger simmering behind my lashes.

"What?" he snapped back. "What have I done?"

"You know what!" I yelled, working myself up.

I heard Casey's car start back up and move out of the driveway. The tears spilled over my lashes as I flung the front door open and stomped inside. Luke followed, slamming the door behind him.

I turned on him, my eyes blazing. "You're a hypocrite!" I yelled.

"Keep your voice down! I think Mum's in bed sleeping," snapped Luke. "And what did I do?"

"You told Casey to stay away from me, didn't you? And what's Mum doing in bed at this time of day?" I snarled in a much quieter voice, hoping I didn't wake her. She'd just be angry with both of us if I did.

"How would I know? Probably a woman thing. And of course I told Casey to stay away from you!"

"Why?" I was having trouble standing still, adrenalin and anger mixing into a nervous tension that was about to explode.

"Because he's my friend. We talk about women. How is that going to sit if it's you he's talking about?"

"Stop talking about things like that!"

"It's not just that. What happens if you two get together and it doesn't work out? He's the best mate I've ever had. I don't want you to stuff that up like you did with James."

That wasn't fair. James had been a friend of Luke's in high school. He'd been my first true love. "James cheated on me, remember?" Thinking of James took some of the wind out of my sails.

"I know. And if he'd cheated on anyone else, I could have been angry with him but still been his friend."

"But what about you and Alani? If it doesn't work out with the two of you, then that could affect me."

"There's nothing between me and Alani."

"Yet. I've seen the looks. The way she dresses up extra nice when you're around."

"She does?" Luke gave me a cheeky smile. The one that usually got him out of trouble.

"Don't start, Luke! I'm angry with you. You're being hypocritical saying I can't have a relationship with your friend, but you clearly want one with mine."

"I'm sorry, Sam. I don't mean it that way. It just took me a long time to settle here and make friends. I…I don't want some things to change."

I let out a big breath. "It doesn't matter anyway. Casey only wants to be my friend."

Luke nodded. "Yeah. That's what he told me too."

I had a feeling Luke wanted to say more, but as he opened his mouth to speak again, my phone rang. I pulled it from my bag and looked at the screen. It was Alani.

"Speak of the devil," I said, showing Luke the screen. He tried not to smile. I scowled at him.

"Hello," I said, answering it.

"Hi, Sam." Alani's happy voice floated down the phone, alleviating some of the tension I was feeling.

"How's things?" I dropped my bag at the door and moved through the house.

"Not bad. Hey, I want to show you something. Do you want to grab a drink at The Lava Pot?"

A drink sounded exactly like what I needed. "Sure. I'll see if I can get Luke to drop me down there."

"He can join us if he likes."

"I'll tell him."

He'd be thrilled, I'm sure. I ended the call and scowled at the unfairness of it all. But then again, if my new best friend and my brother were to have something special, then who was I to stand in the way? It wasn't Luke's fault Casey only saw me as a friend.

How did I really feel about that? Could I just be Casey's friend, being happy for him when he did find someone special? Jealousy rolled in my belly, and I felt the green-eyed monster lurk on my shoulder, ready to pounce. I had to stop it. If the only part of Casey I could get was his friendship, then that was what I would to have to learn to deal with, because I really didn't like the idea of him not being part of my new life.

* * *

It was after six when Luke and I walked into The Lava Pot. Alani was already sitting at a table. Spotting us, she waved enthusiastically. I couldn't help but leave some of the day's tension at the door. She looked extra pretty tonight, I'm guessing for Luke's benefit.

"Hi," she sang, leaning in for a hug.

She didn't normally hug me. When she greeted Luke the same way, I suddenly understood why.

"Hi," we both responded.

I told Luke I wanted a cocktail. Alani already had her drink.

"Are you okay?" she asked me as soon as Luke left for the bar.

My eyes stung as I recounted my day and how Luke had told Casey to stay away from me. Alani was just building up steam on my behalf when I said, "It doesn't matter. He only likes me as a friend."

She placed her hand over mine. "I'm sorry, Sam."

She looked like she wanted to say more, but Luke came back to the table. He handed me my drink and sat smiling at Alani, his crooked grin doing its best to woo her. It seemed to be working.

I groaned. Don't get me wrong—I was happy for them. I just couldn't seem to get the jealousy monster to go back into his hole.

"Hey, Alani," I said, breaking their eye contact moment. "You said you had something to show me."

"Oh, yes, I do," she said, retrieving her phone from her handbag. We watched patiently as she swiped and scrolled, stopping when she found the right thing. "Hani sent this to me. I thought you'd find it interesting."

We leaned forward over her smartphone as she pressed Play on a video. "It was taken on the beach the day the dead guy washed in. Hani's friend Jess took it."

The screen filled with Casey putting up the beach umbrellas. Geez, he looked good. A lump formed in my throat, but I did my best to swallow it down. In the picture Casey looked up, his expression quizzical. Jess turned the phone to see what he was looking at. It came back into focus with me in the surf, waving at one of the kids to come on in. Behind me I could see something large looming into the frame. I knew now that it was Albert's body, and I waited for it to hit me in the back, knocking me off my board. Jess's scream could be heard through the speaker, and she spun the camera around the beach, videoing the lifeguard, Malie, running toward me. Alani pressed Pause on the picture, zooming in to a man standing in the background. Unmistakably it was Tony, the security guard from Aloha Ohana.

Now my first instinct was, *so what?* It was probably a coincidence he'd been there at the same time I'd been conducting my first surf lesson, but when Alani pressed play on the video again, my breath caught in my throat. Tony was holding a video camera of his own, and it appeared he was filming me in the water.

What the...

"That's creepy," said Luke, his jaw flexing as he thought about what he'd just seen.

"Do you think it was a coincidence?" I asked as Alani pressed Pause on the video. "I mean, maybe he was just out for a stroll, filming the wildlife, and he saw the dead guy wash in."

"Maybe," said Alani. "It doesn't look like it though. Keep watching."

She pressed Play again. This time we kept our focus on Tony. He'd pushed himself back into the sand dunes, his cap pulled down over his eyes. There was no mistaking who he was though. Not too many people were his size. Why hadn't I noticed him? Probably because I was focused intently on the kids in front of me.

As Malie pulled Albert's body from the surf, I watched Tony's body language change. He straightened up, almost as surprised as everyone else that a body had washed up in the water, but then he grabbed his camera and instead of running to help like several others around me had, he ran back through the dunes and disappeared.

"What do you think he was doing?" I asked, goose bumps breaking out all over me.

"Maybe he knew you'd be teaching and he has a thing for you," she said.

Luke tensed next to me. He really needed to settle down. At some point he was going to have to be okay with a man looking at me again. Even though, I got his point with Tony.

"I'd never met Tony at that point," I stated.

"Why do you think he ran off like that?" asked Luke.

I shook my head. "Maybe dead bodies freak him out."

"He works at an aged-care facility. Dead bodies happen there all the time."

"Maybe he recognized this one."

"Then why didn't he run toward the ocean?"

I honestly had no idea. The day had already been too long, and the alcohol was doing nothing for my headache. In fact, if anything, it was making it worse.

I opened my own phone and added to my list of weird and wonderful things to do with my investigation, thinking that this one was a job to worry about tomorrow.

Half an hour later, I asked Luke to take me home. I wanted a shower and to go to bed, where I could dream of Casey all night long. I might not be able to have him in my waking life, but in my dreams I was damn well making the most of him.

* * *

It turned out Alani's car wouldn't start, so Luke, being the Good Samaritan he was, offered to drop me off and then take Alani home. Tomorrow he'd go back and try to find out what was wrong with her car. As if he'd have any idea.

I didn't check on Mum. When she had her lady thing, it was best to let her sleep peacefully, so I tiptoed past her bedroom and quietly put myself to bed.

I tried to sleep, but my mind kept going over my day—or more specifically, Casey. For some stupid reason it wanted to torture me with images of him holding my hand, kissing my neck, touching my...well, you got where it was going, right?

"Argh!" I said to no one.

This wasn't helping me at all. I rolled over and fluffed my pillow, hoping that would help. My stomach grumbled. I was hungry, which probably explained why I was so restless. I needed to eat. Yeah, eating before sleep wasn't recommended, but what the heck—if the stomach wanted food, then the stomach would get food.

I swung my legs over the edge of my bed and flipped on my bedside lamp. Luke hadn't made it home yet, and I wondered what was happening between him and Alani. It would be kind of cool if she became my sister-in-law. I could be a bridesmaid at their wedding. Oooh, a Hawaiian wedding would be so beautiful. And Alani would look gorgeous in white, her hair filled with flowers. Yeah, I had to admit that Luke didn't scrub up too badly either.

I was lost in my imagination, getting carried away on an idea, when I flipped on the kitchen light. I opened the refrigerator door and looked for leftovers. Yes! Pizza.

Zapping a piece in the microwave, I leaned against the kitchen counter, watching the timer countdown. As I stood there I noticed a piece of paper on the floor, almost completely under the fridge.

I bent down to retrieve it. Turning it in my hands, I could see someone had scrawled all over it in a black marker pen. The words were hard to make out. I looked closer, studying it and wondering who had written it.

My stomach plummeted and nausea swirled as I made out the words:

Bring me the inheritance before midnight, or she dies! Don't bring the police either, or she'll die also!

My hands shook as I turned the paper over, wondering what the hell it was about and simultaneously looking for a location of where I was supposed to go. There were no instructions. I looked at the clock ticking away on the kitchen wall. It was eleven fifteen.

Oh my God! Someone had taken Mum? What was I supposed to do? I had exactly forty-five minutes to get an inheritance that Mum hadn't even received yet and give it to whoever had left this note! *What the...*

Hang on. What if this was a hoax? I mean, this paper could have been there for ages.

I ran to Mum's room, hoping to see her tucked up asleep in bed. Flinging the door open, I hit the light switch, hoping that she would yell at me for waking her. Instead I found her bed empty. Unexplainably I ran to it, lifting the covers. I didn't know why. I knew Mum wasn't there, but I did find some evidence that she'd been taken. Blood drops on the floor. A sob escaped my lips. This was real.

Don't cry, Samantha. Hold this together. Mum needs you.

I sank to the bed, put my head in my shaking hands, and thought it through. Who would have done this? Who knew about the money?

This town wasn't that big. Almost everyone knew about the money.

Hang on. It had to be from Mark. It had to be. He knew Mum's schedule, and he knew about the money. But why would he kidnap her? I had no idea, but it was the best I had. I ran back to my room and grabbed my phone. With trembling fingers, I dialed his cell phone. He didn't answer. Okay, where did he live? Maybe he'd taken her there.

I didn't know where he lived. I had never asked him. I'd never had a reason too.

Shit, shit, shit! My heart pounded, and my thoughts became erratic.

I phoned Luke, but when I heard it ringing in his bedroom, I knew that he'd forgotten it. I tried Alani, but she didn't answer either, so I left a message telling her I needed help and what was happening. And if she was still with Luke, to please tell him.

I sunk to the floor and attempted to stop the shaking that had taken over my body. Panic was starting to bubble. I felt my pulse become erratic, my breathing become tight, and tears start to sting my eyes.

With fumbling fingers, I tried Casey. I needed help and advice on what to do. The note said not to call the police, but my instincts told me I should. But then I'd never been in this situation before, and fear was definitely messing with my thinking processes. I listened for the call to connect, but instead, it immediately went to message bank. Maybe Casey switched his phone off when he slept.

Okay. I needed a plan, and I couldn't risk calling the police just yet. I made sure that I had Detective Ray's number in my phone for when I needed him though. The ransom note said I had until midnight. It was now eleven twenty. Damn! Why didn't kidnappers allow for you not getting the note on time? I mean, it was only thanks to my urge for a late-night snack that I'd even found the bloody note. What if I hadn't found it until the morning? Then what?

My thoughts flipped to Patrick. Maybe Mark and Patrick were in this together. I did find Patrick's phone number in Marks' phone, after all. And it would be just like Mark to be stupid enough to not leave me any contact details.

Alright. Where would I find Patrick? The only place I knew of was Aloha Ohana.

Okay, that would have to be the first place I tried. After I got some money. How would I get that?

Think, *think*!

A memory stirred of Mum hiding money around the house in case of an emergency. I figured this was an emergency.

I jumped up and ran to her dresser. Growing up, Luke and I both knew exactly where Mum hid her secret stash of cash. It would be tucked safely under the pretty paper she used to line her undies drawer.

I felt guilty as I emptied the drawer, lifted the paper, and removed the cash that Mum had neatly hidden. I did a quick count.

There was three thousand dollars. A lot of money to have lying around the house, but hardly the entire inheritance. However, I wondered if it would buy me some more time. Hopefully the kidnapper, aka Mark, would know I could give him the rest of it later.

Riding up the hill to Aloha Ohana was the hardest ride I had ever done. My lungs burned, and my legs ached, but I didn't notice any of it. I just knew that I had to get there. God, I hoped I didn't meet the Night Marchers now. The only upside was that the rain had stopped. I probably wasn't going to find Mum in time, but I had my fingers crossed that the kidnapper would call me before doing anything rash. My phone was tucked safely in the elastic of my undies. Why the elastic of my undies? Well, I was wearing a nightshirt, and it didn't have a pocket, so the undies were the only thing that was secure. Sure, I should have taken the time to get dressed, but I already didn't have enough of that, so I definitely didn't want to waste any more of it. I had thrown a sweater over my nightshirt and slipped my flip-flops on, and I was sure the kidnappers wouldn't care what I was wearing.

I cried as I made it to the parking lot of Aloha Ohana, threw my bike on the ground, and ran to the door. I banged the glass in the hope that someone would hear me. I found the phone on the wall that told me to press nine if calling after six when the doors were locked.

Tony, the security guard, answered the door.

"Oh, thank goodness," I cried as he opened the door for me.

"Samantha! What's wrong?" he asked, pulling me inside, tears streaming down my cheeks.

"It's Mum. She's…she's been kid…kidnapped," I blubbered.

Tony looked shocked. I didn't blame him.

"Calm down, and tell me what's going on?"

I took some deep, shuddery breaths and brought him up to date with the events of the last hour.

He paled as I told him about the blood and that Mum was gone.

"I don't know what to do," I cried. "I think it's Mark, but I don't know where to take the money." It too was hidden in my knickers. Not the most comfortable place to keep it, but you do what you have to, right?

"Why did you come here?"

"Because I think Mark and Patrick are involved, and I was hoping to find Patrick, or at least where Patrick might be."

"I'm covering his shift. Why do you think Mark's involved?"

Oh geez. I didn't have time for this. The grandfather clock sitting proudly in the reception donged that it was already twelve o'clock. My time was up.

No! It couldn't be! *I had to have more time!*

As silence filled the room, the clock finishing its sequence, my phone started to ring. Tony looked at me, confused, obviously wondering where the noise was coming from.

"Excuse me," I said, turning my back to him and retrieving the phone. The call was from an unknown number.

I swiped to answer it. "Hello," I said, my voice shaking.

"I told you you had till midnight," said a muffled male voice.

"I know! I'm sorry. I didn't get your note in time."

I heard a growled response.

"But…but I have it! I have the money! Please don't hurt Mum," I begged.

"You have it? All of it?"

"Yes. Yes." He didn't need to know that I was actually quite a bit short of the full amount. Not yet, anyway. "I didn't know where to take it. Your note didn't say."

"What?"

"Your note. It didn't say where I had to take the money."
I was close to babbling, but I desperately tried to slow my
breathing.

I heard him put his hand over the receiver and yell at
someone. Obviously, note-writing had been someone else's job,
but now I knew there were at least two of them.

"Okay. I'll give you another hour." With that he hung up
the call.

Damn! He still hadn't told me where to go!

Approximately one minute later my phone rang again.
Caller unknown.

"Go to Paradise Road," the muffled voice said. "Follow
it out of town for approximately twenty minutes. You'll come to
a yellow gate. Open the gate and follow the drive for
approximately five minutes. Go over the hump, past the cows,
and you'll find a shed. Inside the shed will be the instructions of
where to go from there."

"Okay. Paradise Road, five minutes, cow shed..." Shit,
that didn't sound right!

"No! Paradise Road, twenty minutes, yellow gate, five
minutes. Over the hump, past the cows, and enter the shed!"

"Alright. Paradise Road, twenty minutes, yellow shed,
umm sorry, yellow gate." I heard his sigh over the phone. He
was probably wishing Luke had found the note. "Five minutes," I
continued, "past the cows, and in the shed I'll find the next
instructions."

"Good! Remember you've got an hour." The line went
dead.

My knees gave out, and I sunk to the floor, relieved that
I had more time. Tony kneeled next to me, placing his hand on
my shoulder.

"Are you okay?"

No, I bloody well wasn't okay. I'd moved to Aloha
Lagoon for a new life. One that was fun and relaxed and with my
family. So far it had been far from fun and relaxed. I thought of
my family. They were the most important thing in my life. I
couldn't be here without them.

With Tony's help I stood back up, a renewed energy
filling my spirit. My new life was going to be spent with my

family. No one was taking that away. Not even a stupid kidnapper who didn't know how to write a ransom note!

"Do you have a car?" I asked.

He nodded, and out of habit, rolled his eyes. "It's parked out the back."

"Can I use it please?"

"What are you going to do?"

"Take the money to the kidnappers."

Tony ran his hands over his face, his skin pale in the subtly lit reception area. "You can't do that. It sounds dangerous."

"They have Mum. What other choice do I have?"

"Alright, but I'm coming with you."

I looked at Tony's size and wondered if he would be a help or a hindrance.

"Really?"

"Yes. I know what you're thinking. You think because I'm overweight I'll only get in the way." It appeared that Tony could read minds. "But, you don't know what I'm capable of." The hair on the back of my neck stood up as a look passed through his eyes. "Plus, I have a gun," he added, his genial smile quickly falling back into place.

Now that was a positive.

CHAPTER SIXTEEN

—————

If cars were symbols of wealth, I figured Tony wasn't very wealthy. His green 1994 Honda Civic was pretty beat up with the front bumper missing, a huge gash down the passenger-side door, and a broken headlight. As he started it, it coughed and spluttered. I silently wondered if maybe the bike was a better option after all.

Two minutes into the drive I realized why he had so much damage to his car. He was a shocking driver. Thank goodness it was the early hours of the morning and there weren't too many other cars on the road. I pitied any wildlife that might step into his path though.

We rode in silence, my thoughts only on Mum. I tried Alani's number again, and I tried Casey again. Still both went to messages. Anxiety gnawed at my stomach about what we were doing. I'd never met a kidnapper before, and I knew this was a stupid thing to do. There was no guarantee he would hand Mum over even after I'd given him the money.

Thank goodness I had Tony and his gun. Tony's threat about how they didn't know what he was capable of came to mind. Sneaking a sideways look at him barely fitting behind the steering wheel, I thought he probably considered himself an action hero, but the reality was much different.

The car slowed as he looked for a yellow gate. He turned his headlights to face the driveways that turned off Paradise Road. After the third turn, we found the one we were looking for. I jumped out of the car, made my way through the long roadside grass and debris, and opened the gate, allowing Tony to drive through. I felt the sting of a stray broken branch scratch my leg, but ignored it and closed the gate behind him. I then ran to get back in the car, and we timed our drive for five minutes. I wasn't sure what speed the kidnappers were going when they'd timed it, but Tony was going at snail's pace. At this speed they probably meant ten minutes.

The car bumped over the potholes in the dirt drive leading to the middle of a field. This wasn't a path that got driven on a lot. Tony drove over the hump, and within minutes the road was filled with cows lying around sleeping. A few looked up in the headlights, not liking that we were disturbing their beauty rest. At this distance, and in the glow of the car's lights, the cows looked huge and scary. I prayed they would stay asleep.

Thankfully, a shed came into our view. Tony hadn't even stopped the car when I opened my door and ran to it. There was no moon, so he left the headlights on, and I used the flashlight on my phone to find my way around.

This wasn't a big shed. You definitely couldn't drive a tractor into it. Maybe Tony's car at a push, so that should make it easier to find what we were looking for. To be honest I didn't know what we were looking for, but I was going for a sheet of paper just like the one that had been left at home.

I pulled the door open, the creaking of old wood screaming through the night air. The smell of dust filled my nostrils, and I coughed as Tony moved behind me and across the dirt floor, causing dust to rise around us. His large flashlight was much more effective than my phone.

Ignoring it all, I ran in, my flip-flops slapping the dirt against my bare legs.

"Over here!" shouted Tony, his light illuminating the far wall. He ripped a piece of paper off the wall and turned to me, reading as he moved.

"What does it say?" I asked, checking the time on my watch. It was nearly twelve thirty. I really hoped our next stop wasn't that far away.

"We're to drive behind this shed and stop at the farmhouse. Around the back of the house is an open cellar door. We're to make our way inside."

Alright, that didn't sound like it would take that long to get to. Tony dropped his flashlight to his side, dropping me into the shadow. I couldn't see his face as my eyes needed to adjust, but I heard the hitch in his voice. "These guys don't know what's coming for them."

They didn't? I looked around me wondering if the cavalry had suddenly appeared. I had no idea what he was talking about. As far as I could tell, what was coming for them was a twenty-eight-year-old with her undies full of cash and a fifty-year-old man who was well and truly out of shape. True, he did have a gun. I needed to remember that. They also didn't know I had Tony with me. They thought I was alone.

I hoped there were only the two of them that I'd heard on the phone. I knew if this was Mark, we would maybe be okay. Patrick, on the other hand, I was scared of. But I couldn't dwell on that now. I just needed to get the money to them to keep Mum safe. I didn't have a plan beyond that, and I was kind of hoping Tony did have one.

"Tony, what do we do once we hand over the money?"

"I've been thinking about this. They think it's only you coming. I have my fingers crossed they're not actually watching us from here on, as my plan is that I want you to drive, with me hiding in the backseat just in case they are. Then you're going to go in alone, and I'm going to sneak in behind you with my gun. We'll tie them up and release your mother."

"That sounds dangerous."

"It is. Are you up for it?"

"Yes. But why are you helping me with this?"

"Because."

He turned and made his way back to the car, leaving me standing alone, the only light coming from my phone. I hurried after him. "Because" was not an answer. I knew that for a fact, as many times growing up I'd tried to use it on Mum. Right now though, I didn't have time to argue with him about it. I just needed to accept his help in the spirit he was giving it.

I followed the instructions on the note, taking the fork in the road. I didn't know how far it was to the house, but Tony was squashed safely behind me in the backseat. It was a tight fit, and I really hoped he could get out of there once I'd stopped.

Sitting in the car, fear threatened to consume me. Panic bubbled in my chest, causing my breathing to become ragged.

Adrenalin kicked in, and my whole body started to shake. *Come on, Sam. You can do this! What other choice do you have?*

The farmhouse was old and abandoned. The grass was almost as high as the verandah surrounding it, and it was dark. It did nothing to help my panic attack.

I pulled the car to a stop and checked my phone for a signal. I switched it to silent in case Luke or Casey called whilst I was handing over the money. I might just need the phone once that part was over, and I couldn't risk having it confiscated.

I got out and made my way through the long grass in the dark to the back of the house. The ground was rough, and I struggled to see where I was going, stumbling once or twice, but I used the side of the house to guide myself. The cellar door was easy to spot, as it had light pouring out of it.

Taking three deep breaths, I made my way toward it. My heart was pounding harder than it ever had when I stepped in front of the door and spotted Mum. She was tied to a chair and looked like she wanted to kill someone.

Okay. That might help if we needed it.

"Hello," I called, my voice wobbling far more than I'd hoped it would.

Mum snapped her head up to look at me. Fear shot across her face, and her eyes filled with tears.

"Come in," a voice called.

"No!" yelled Mum. A hand slapped her. A sob escaped my throat, and I hurried down the steps into the old cellar, leaving the doors open behind me.

The glare of the light hurt my eyes as I blinked against it, moving down the steps to Mum. "Are you okay?" I asked before I even looked around the room.

"You shouldn't have come. These guys are idiots!"

"Do you have the money?" said a voice from behind me. It was a voice I recognized. And it didn't belong to Mark or Patrick.

It was Tristan. The manager of the Aloha Ohana facility.

I spun around to face him, taking in my surroundings as I moved. The cellar was reasonably large—larger than Mum's lounge room anyway—the walls were cement, and there was only one way in and out.

"You?" I asked. "You're the one behind all of this?"

"Yes, it's me. And I am not an idiot!" he said, turning to Mum.

"Yes, you are. You couldn't even write a bloody ransom note correctly!"

"That wasn't me. That was Patrick. And you may be right about him being an idiot."

"Excuse me," said Patrick, standing from his place at a small table pushed against the far wall. Mark was nowhere in sight, so I'd obviously been wrong about him, but at least I was right about Patrick being a bad guy.

"Come on," said Tristan. "How hard is it to write a note?"

Patrick grumbled something in response, but it kind of got lost as Tony entered the cellar gun first, tripped, and fell down the steps, his gun firing as he tumbled. So much for him being the knight in shining armor.

"*What the hell?*" yelled Tristan, ducking from the bullet bouncing off the cement walls.

Patrick lunged toward Tony, pulling a gun from a holster on his hip.

"Stop!" Tristan yelled, moving to grab Tony's dropped gun before I had the chance. Tony rolled around on the floor, crying and holding his arm, so I figured he wouldn't have been trying to get it. My mind flicked to Mr. Fathersham and how I really should have signed my will.

Tristan sighed loudly, looking at Tony. "Put your gun down, Patrick," he said over his shoulder. "You're not going to shoot anyone."

Patrick looked uncertainly to Tristan but did as asked.

"So you killed those men?" I asked Tristan, my voice shaky, as he put the safety back on the gun and held it by his side.

"No!" Tristan snapped, sounding offended by my accusation. "I'm not a murderer. I'm just the coordinator. Patrick did the killing," Tristan said, almost offhandedly. "I just wanted the money. I'm six months off retirement, and I don't intend to do that poor. Plus, Kylie is an expensive habit. She likes to be kept in a certain style." I involuntarily shivered as Tristan took a step backward, flicking some dirt off his shirt as he moved. "I've given the last fifteen years of my life to Aloha Ohana, and all I get for retiring is a bloody watch. Who needs a damn watch when they've retired? Isn't the idea that you relax and no longer have to worry about damn time? Now where's the money?" Tristan raised Tony's gun as he spoke.

"I have it," I said quickly. Patrick eyed me suspiciously, and Tony shifted onto his back, his face showing a mixture of anger and pain. He looked like he wanted to say something, but pain was getting the better of him. Judging by the weird angle his wrist was sitting at, I guessed he'd broken it when he fell.

Everyone was getting more agitated than was healthy. Well, healthy for me, Mum, and Tony. The other two could shoot each other, for all I cared.

Tristan moved closer to me and put out his hand. "Come on. Give it to me."

I lifted my nightie and pulled the money out of my undies. It didn't all come in one big bundle. It came in lots of bills, some of which were stuck to me from sweat.

Mum groaned. I knew what she was thinking. Only Samantha would stick money in her underwear.

Tristan grimaced as I gave him a handful of bills and then went back in to retrieve another lot. "Did the bank not have bags?" he asked sarcastically.

"Sorry I didn't have time to bundle it," I snapped, thinking he should be bloody grateful he was getting the money. When I pulled out the last bill, he stared at me openmouthed.

"What do you think this is?"

"Money," I said, wrinkling my brow.

"Where's the rest of it?"

"That's it. That's all there was. I know. I know!" I quickly added. "There should be more. But you did only give me a very short amount of time. It was all I could get my hands on."

Even in the bad light of the cellar, I could see Tristan turn green as he looked at the notes in his hands. His mouth screwed up, and his eyes blazed. "What do you mean—all there was?" he asked quietly, getting up in my face. Patrick fidgeted behind him, his finger obviously itchy to pull a trigger. Despite his obvious pain, Tony let out a bark of laughter.

"Three thousand dollars. That's all there is," said Mum. "I've been telling you—the inheritance hasn't come through yet. But did you listen? No, you didn't. Like I said, you're an idiot. And how did you expect Samantha to get that money out of my bank account tonight?"

Tristan turned away, and we all sat in silence as he paced backward and forward. "But..." he finally said. "But the inheritance should be through by now."

"If you paid more attention Tristan, you would know that inheritances don't come through that quickly," said Mum. "Remember that little thing called *probate*? You're the manager of Aloha Ohana. You should know these things!"

"There's no one to contest it! I know that for a fact," he shouted.

"Yes, but the court still has to allow time for relatives to come out of the woodwork."

Tristan ran a hand through his hair, obviously as frustrated as hell.

"They've had time!"

"Not enough," replied Mum slowly.

"I still want my share," demanded Patrick.

"Oh shut up!" snapped Tristan, throwing the money on the table and rubbing his face. Fatigue showed in the dark bags sitting under his eyes.

"No, I won't shut up. It's still a three-way share."

Tristan glared at him.

"Kylie's done her share, following her around," said Patrick, nodding at me. "If we don't get the money, what's the point?"

"Why was Kylie following Samantha?" asked Mum, her eyes narrowed at Patrick. Tony sat up straight, grabbing his wrist and wincing against the pain.

"She was scoping her out for me," said Tristan. "And to answer your earlier question, *you* were supposed to get the money out of the bank when you found the ransom note. You see, you weren't our target. Samantha was."

I gulped, shocked by this news.

"W...what?" asked Mum, paling.

"The plan was to kidnap Samantha and ransom her to you for the money. But *Stupid* here grabbed the wrong damned person!" yelled Tristan, pointing at Patrick.

Patrick narrowed his eyes and death-stared him. "Don't call me stupid."

"Well, you are! You had one job today! *One!* Kidnap the girl and leave a ransom note."

"That's two jobs. And see how much those two look alike? It was an easy mistake."

Tristan sighed. "See what I have to work with?" He looked at Tony. "If you hadn't double-crossed me, I wouldn't be in the situation where I needed 'Thug for Hire' over there!"

What? Hang on a second—Tony was on our side.

"Go to hell, Tristan," snapped Tony.

"Thug for hire?" asked Patrick.

"Yes. What else are you good for?"

"I got your butt out of trouble once or twice!" yelled Patrick.

"Please," said Tristan, disdain dripping from his every word. "You only did that to save your own butt and get some extra money. At any point I could have told the authorities about you stealing the drugs from Aloha Ohana and selling them. But I only hired you because I needed you."

"So you used me?"

"Of course I did. I wanted to speed up the whole money thing, and I wasn't going to murder those men myself! Anyway, you're getting paid, I might add!" snapped Tristan.

Patrick moved to the table and picked up the money, shoving a handful of it into his jeans pocket and going back for a second load. "Not that well, by the looks of things."

"What do you think you're doing?"

"You promised me a lot more than this. I'll consider it a down payment," sneered Patrick.

"But...but...that's mine!"

"Yeah? Well, it's mine now," replied Patrick, raising his gun to Tristan. "Want to argue about it?"

"Double-crossing bastards!" snapped Tristan, raising his own gun to Patrick and unclicking the safety. Patrick didn't blink. He just adjusted his stance and stared Tristan down. I saw the sweat drip down Tristan's temple, but he held his ground. It appeared we had a standoff.

Now don't get me wrong, —I secretly hoped that Tristan and Patrick would just shoot each other, but I was worried because Tristan was now standing behind Mum and me, which put us both in the line of fire. *And what did he mean by Tony double-crossing him?*

"You're as mad as a cut snake. Both of you," said Tony. He had that right.

Mum whipped her head around and properly looked at Tony, her teeth biting down on her bottom lip. She was thinking something. What that was—I had no idea.

"What is it?" I whispered, watching the confusion cross her face.

"Nothing," she replied. "It's just been a long time since I've heard that saying," she said, still looking at Tony, her eyes narrowed.

He shifted uncomfortably under her gaze. Okay, that was weird. I gave Mum a questioning look, a look that she ignored.

"So what now?" asked Tristan, his gaze firmly on Patrick. "Do we just stand here all night until one of our arms gets tired?" He rolled his shoulder as he spoke. If that was what we were waiting for, I figured we wouldn't be waiting long.

"What happens now is I'm taking this money, and I'm going. You can figure this mess out for yourself." Patrick took a step toward the door.

Silence filled the room, each of us wondering what was going to happen next. Mum sat chewing her lip, I sat nervously wanting to pee, and Tony sat rolling his eyes to the top of his head, occasionally wincing against the pain his wrist must have been putting him through.

Mum's attention hadn't left Tony, her mouth hanging open very unattractively. I really needed to ask her what the heck she was looking at, but right now didn't feel like the appropriate time.

"If you leave now, you won't see any more money," said Tristan. Patrick flinched but stopped. "I promise you that. However, if you stay and help me, I will honor the agreement as soon as I have the money."

"But I really feel like shooting someone," snapped Patrick, his temper flaring. "Maybe I should just shoot the woman." He turned his gun to Mum, and my stomach went into freefall. On instinct I moved in front of her.

"You really are an idiot," said Tony. "If you kill her or Samantha, you'll never get the money." I liked his strategy. If Tristan and Patrick both thought they still needed us, we had a good chance of getting out of here alive.

"Stop calling me an idiot!" Patrick swung the gun from person to person, unsure whom he wanted to shoot the most. "So tell me—how is this going to end?"

Tristan rubbed his eyes with the ball of his fist. "I don't know."

"Well, what was plan B?"

"Plan B?" asked Tristan.

"Yeah. There's always a plan B in case plan A goes wrong. You have a plan B, right?"

"Well...the plan was for us to get the money and then you kill the women. By the time they were found, we'd be long gone. There was no plan B."

Tony laughed. "Idiots," he whispered, almost under his breath. Almost.

"Oh, just shut up, Brian...Tony...whatever the hell your name is?" sneered Tristan. "This is all your fault anyway."

Mum shifted in her seat, anger flashing as she stared at Tony.

"I knew it was you!" she sneered. "The second I saw you. I knew it!"

Tony stared back at her and then slowly nodded *What?*

"Mum, what are you talking about?" I asked, moving to the side of her and wondering if Patrick had knocked her head at some point.

She didn't respond. She just sat staring at Tony, her mouth hanging open. "But...but why? Why are you here? You were always in Australia."

He nodded. "A year ago I found out that you had moved here. So I followed you."

"Why?" she asked.

"What are you talking about?" I still hadn't caught up with the conversation.

"A while back I was involved in a bad accident," continued Tony, ignoring my question. "I nearly died. It made me reassess my life and what I'd done. When I got to the island and saw how you were working so hard to keep a roof over your head, I knew then that I needed to find a way to put things right for you. Tristan gave me the perfect chance to do that."

"*Mum!*" I snapped. "What's going on?"

She pulled her gaze away from Tony and looked at me. She gulped.

Tristan laughed. "So Brian, are you going to tell your daughter who you really are?" he asked.

My head snapped to Tristan. *Daughter?* I looked at Tony. And then back to Mum.

"But…his name's Tony, not Brian," I stammered, completely confused.

Tristan laughed. "His name is Brian Antony Barrett. His ID says so."

"Yeah, tell them how he spilled his guts about the whole family situation the day that he confronted you about Albert's murder," laughed Patrick. Tristan turned and glared at him. The glare suggested that he should shut up.

"Mum, it's not true, is it?"

Her eyes filled with tears, and she slowly nodded.

"But…but…our name is Reynolds. Not Barrett."

"Reynolds is my maiden name. Brian and I never married."

"This is just ridiculous," I scoffed. "If he was my father you would have recognized him. I mean, how many times have you seen him at Aloha Ohana?"

"None," said Tony. "I always made sure we were on different rosters. She never saw me. I made sure of that." He turned to Mum. "I'm sorry, Rita. I treated you badly all those years ago. All the affairs and never being present in the kids' lives. But I always loved you, and for the last year that I've been in Aloha Lagoon, I've been watching over you, making sure you were okay, trying to help you in any way I could."

Tony was my father? How? *How could that be?*

"What do you mean, helping me?" asked Mum, suspicion mingling in the emotions she was showing.

"I made sure that you got all the extra money I could find. Like…like the work raffles that you've been winning. I made that happen. And remember how you won that thousand dollars in the radio competition? Well, you didn't. I did. I just asked them to say that you won it."

Mum nodded. "I knew I didn't enter any radio competition. I don't even listen to the radio. I told them they had it wrong, but they just kept insisting."

"Yes! And the money that kept turning up hidden in your house. That was me. I gave you all the extra money I earned. I only kept enough to live on."

Mum looked flabbergasted. "You broke into my house?"

"Well…yes. But it was all for a good cause. I remembered how you always hid money around the house, and then you'd forget about it. I snuck in and hid it so that when you found it, you would think that you'd put it there."

Mum shook her head. Her mouth was opening and closing again, but no words were coming out. I didn't blame her for being speechless. I was a little bit that way myself.

"I helped, Rita," Tony continued. "I helped any way I could. I'm just sorry it didn't come early enough."

"Oh, look at the touching family reunion," said Patrick mockingly. "Doesn't it just make your heart swell?"

I thought back to the conversation I'd had with Tony when he'd told me that he had a family that he'd lost touch with. Even though I was annoyed that he'd broken into our house and angry about the way I had just found out that he was my father, I believed him when he told me he regretted not knowing us. Maybe we could make up for lost time. Sure, we wouldn't have the relationship we could have had, but it was never too late, right?

"You know what," snapped Tristan. "I've had enough. Tony is *not* the good guy here. Have you asked yourself why your family was named beneficiary of the two murdered men, Rita? It was because *he* was part of a plan."

"Plan?" she asked.

Tony looked at her, tears skimming his lashes. "I was to convince as many residents as possible to change their wills to name *us*," he said, pointing to himself and Tristan, "and then we were to retire rich."

"But it turns out Tony's a double crossing bastard," spat Tristan. "I should have had Patrick kill him days ago, but I figured I should keep him around until I had this sorted. Just in case he had any other tricks up his sleeve that I might need to know about."

Nausea rolled in my stomach. Maybe it was too late.

I heard the cry escape Mum. "Brian, you had those men murdered?"

"No!" shouted Tony—Brian—whichever! "Murder wasn't part of the plan. Those men had no family to leave their money to, so Tristan explained to me that no one was being hurt by it. I knew that the residents trusted me and would listen to my advice. Only I saw a better opportunity. I could help you and Luke with the extra cash." He hung his head in shame. When he looked up again, he had tears in his eyes. "I didn't know that they would be murdered. That was all Tristan."

"But...but...Detective Ray blamed Mum and Luke," I stammered, not really believing what I was hearing.

"Yeah, I know! That wasn't supposed to happen," continued Tony. "Those men were to die of natural causes."

"They did die of natural causes," said Patrick, smiling. "Lack of oxygen and too much insulin is a natural cause." He thought he was hilarious. I thought he was a lunatic.

"You double-crossed me," Tony snarled, looking at Tristan.

"Yeah, but you double-crossed me first!"

Patrick's fingers twitched on the gun.

Horror was etched across Mum's face, her eyes filling with tears.

I sat down on the floor next to her, my stomach cramping.

"I spoke to Albert about how you were my wife once," said Tony, looking at Mum. "I told him how I'd left you with the kids and how I was never faithful to you. He understood my remorse. He had no family, so I suggested he give his money to you. He wanted you to have it, Rita, he really did. But I would never have hurt him to get it!"

"Why didn't you just talk to me?" asked Mum quietly. "Tell me you were here?"

"Because you're better off without me in your lives. I always screwed everything up for you. I thought it would be better to stay away and help from afar. If everything had gone to plan, you would never have known the truth."

"Neither would I!" sneered Tristan. We all turned to look at him. "At least not until it was too late. If everything had gone to your plan, Brian, it could have been years before I found out that I'd been double-crossed."

"Yeah, and I was supposed to be long gone by then," replied Tony quietly.

"But...but what did you do to stop Detective Ray questioning Mum?" I asked.

"I put him onto Patrick. I told him that he was stealing drugs and I thought he'd been the murderer. I knew that Detective Ray could never have found the evidence to pin it on Rita. Turns out I was right about Patrick anyway." Patrick fidgeted, glaring at Tony, hatred causing him to look even uglier.

"What about Jeremy?" I asked. I was trying to understand what Tony-slash-Brian was telling us, but the ringing in my ears was making it very difficult. "If you knew that Albert was murdered because of the money, did you at least try to save him?"

"Of course I did. I knew weasel Tristan wouldn't do the dirty work, and I suspected Patrick, but other than guarding Jeremy myself, I couldn't do anything about it."

"You could have told Detective Ray!" I almost screamed.

"Tristan said that he would have me incriminated in the plan. He said that he'd tell the detective that I was part of it all along, and then Rita and Luke would never see the money. No, I thought it was better if I guarded Jeremy myself, but Patrick overpowered me. Knocked me out cold. When I woke up, Jeremy was gone." Tony really was quite pathetic.

"I don't know what you're all so upset about. Those men were old, sick, and going to die anyway!" scoffed Patrick. "You're making a big song and dance about nothing."

Tristan turned to him. "Yes, you're right. So explain to me again why you chickened out and didn't kill Jeremy on the same night as Albert, like I proposed?"

"I didn't chicken out. I was getting the rat poison from where I'd hid it, when someone was coming. I needed to get out before I got caught. But I went back a few days later and finished the job, didn't I?"

Tristan growled. I didn't think Patrick was about to get the employee-of-the-month award. He then turned to Tony. "If you'd just done your job like planned and got me named as beneficiary, I'd be on my way to the Bahamas by now. But no—you got greedy!" Tristan paced around the room, swinging the gun as he spoke, contempt rolling off him. "What's wrong with this country that you can't even get good help anymore?"

Tears ran down Tony's cheeks. "Rita, I was trying to help you. Those men just weren't supposed to die like that. Please believe me when I say I didn't know about that part of the plan."

"You could have done more to save Jeremy. You could have stopped it if you'd told someone!" Mum snapped.

Tony's head hung low, and loud sobs wracked his body.

I looked at him contemptuously, wondering how this man could be my father.

"I've had enough," spat Patrick. "Now, here's what I suggest we do. I take the money. We agree that Rita gives us the rest as soon as she gets it, we split it, you can all go free, and no one goes to prison. If anyone spills this to the authorities, I go in and shoot them. What do we all think?"

Tony seemed to snap out of his misery, anger burning in his eyes as he turned to Patrick. "I don't think so," he said. "That money belongs to Rita. You're not getting a cent of it!"

The tension in the room grew. Patrick had once again lifted his gun and had it aimed at no one in particular. Tristan saw this and raised his as well.

"You know what? I changed my mind," said Patrick. "I'm taking this money and cutting my losses." With that he turned his weapon to Tristan and pulled the trigger.

The noise in the small cement room was deafening. I heard screams, which in actual fact could have been from me. Tristan apparently didn't like being shot at, so he shot back at Patrick.

I don't know whether he hit him or not, my attention solely on Mum. Blood oozed from her chest, her eyes rolled back, and her head slumped to one side. Patrick's bullet had missed Tristan and got Mum.

No! This couldn't be happening! Mum could not have been shot.

I screamed out to her, undoing the ties that held her hands to the chair, and then pulled her to the floor. I needed to help her. I needed to remember my CPR training. But I couldn't. The noise level in the room had escalated. People were shouting, moving around. Patrick dropped to the floor, his hands out in front of him. Was he shot? I didn't think so, but honestly, I couldn't care. I didn't even turn to see what was happening, my entire universe consisting of only Mum.

"Mum!" I called. "Mum, Mum, please be okay," I cried, lifting her head into my lap. Her skin had gone deathly pale, her breath coming out in short, sharp spurts. She couldn't leave me. She was my rock, one of my best friends, and I wasn't ready to lose her. "Please, Mum, don't die," I whispered, kissing her cheek.

I heard a voice yelling at me to move, to let her go, but I couldn't. I could never let her go. Seconds later, I felt hands under my arms pulling me upward and away from her. I screamed and kicked out, my mind in a blind panic. I wouldn't let anyone hurt her. I wouldn't.

"Sam! Let her go. I need to help her."

The voice broke through my panic, making me stop and look at who was speaking. It was Luke. I had no idea where he'd come from, but I had never been more grateful for him in my life. He moved past me to Mum, laying her flat and checking her pulse. I heard her cough, and then I dissolved into a sobbing heap.

Luke came to me and pulled my arms away from my face as a woman in uniform attended to Mum. "It's okay, Sam. She's been shot in the shoulder. She's okay. It was just shock that made her pass out."

I fell into Luke and watched the room as he held me tight. It appeared that whilst I had been distracted with Mum, the police had moved in, Luke in tow.

"What happened?" I asked in between sobs.

"Alani got your message about the kidnapping, so I found Detective Ray. He tracked the GPS on your phone, and we came here. God, we arrived just as we heard the gunshot."

I felt Luke start to shake. I put my arms around his chest and held on tight. He must have been as scared as I was.

"I didn't know..." he said. "I didn't know if it was you or Mum."

His voice broke on the last word. Luke didn't cry often, and I knew that the memory of this moment would stay with me forever.

* * *

Organized chaos is the only word that could describe the scene around me. Police cars filled the area around the abandoned house, their lights flashing blue and red, causing the night air to feel eerie and strange shadows to dance in their wake.

Three ambulances were slowly making their way down the grass road leading to the house. One was for Tony, one was for Patrick, who apparently got shot, and one was for Mum. Luke stayed with her, waiting for it to arrive. I was asked to step outside to talk to Detective Ray, filling him in on what exactly had happened tonight.

I did my best, but I was tired, emotional, and still hungry. I never did get my leftover pizza from the microwave. Plus, I was cold. The nights in Hawaii might be warm and tropical, but right now, they didn't feel it. Detective Ray barked an order at one of the uniformed officers, and suddenly a blanket appeared and was wrapped around my shoulders.

"You were foolish tonight, Samantha. You should never have followed the kidnappers. This could have been so much worse," he said to me.

I felt the lecture coming on. I didn't need it. Yes, I knew it probably wasn't my best decision, but what choice did I have?

"However," he continued, "I would have done the same thing for my mother."

I looked up at him, surprised.

"In any future incidences, wait for the police though please." He smiled and closed his notebook.

Without a doubt he would have more questions for me, but it seemed tonight, he'd asked enough. I would be eternally grateful.

"Detective, what happens now?" I asked.

"Well, Tristan will be charged with extortion and kidnapping. I'll be looking into exactly how much Kylie knew about all of this. Patrick will be taken to the hospital to have Tristan's bullet removed from his leg. He'll be charged with two counts of murder, plus we already have him under investigation for stealing drugs from Aloha Ohana, so once he's finished at the hospital, I have a few more questions for him. And his associates."

The detective gave me a knowing look. During my recount of tonight's events, I might have mentioned how I thought Mark was involved. Did this mean I was right about him?

The detective's expression softened. "Any investigation into your mum or Luke will be closed. The cash you handed over tonight will have to go into evidence."

I shrugged. "Mum and Luke should have the inheritances soon."

"I'm sorry, Samantha, but I'm sure the money those men left your family in their wills will be tied up in court cases for a long time. I'm not sure if you will ever see any of it."

It didn't matter. Our financial woes were the least of my worries right now.

"What happens to Tony?" I felt my breath hitch as I waited for his response. I was really unsure how I felt about Tony, but time would probably settle that.

"Not much. As far as I can tell, those men changed their wills voluntarily. Tony didn't force them to do anything. He will be questioned in regards to his motives, but at this stage I can't see how he's done anything illegal."

I smiled and wrapped the blanket tighter around my shoulders.

"Now if you'll excuse me please," he finished. "I have a job to complete."

He walked away, leaving me standing alone in the semidarkness. Wow, what a night. Actually, what a few weeks! Yes, I'd only been in Aloha Lagoon for a short while, yet I felt like I'd done more in that time than I had in a lifetime.

I moved closer to the cellar door, wanting to know what was happening with Mum, when a gurney was pushed past me. Tony was strapped to it, sitting up. He spoke to the paramedics, asking for a minute with me. I didn't know what to say to him. Turned out I didn't need to worry about it.

"I just wanted to tell you," he said, stopping to take a deep breath. "I wanted to tell you that I'm proud of you. I'm proud of the person you've become. And before you say anything, I know that you've grown into this person in spite of me not being in your life. But please believe me when I say that I left for your benefit. I wasn't ready to be a husband or a father, even though I tried for four years. I saw the impact I was having on Rita, the impact of my behavior. But I couldn't stop. I don't think I wanted to stop. But I regret it, Samantha. I regret every single minute of my life without you all. I tried to put everything right, to help, but all I managed to do was mess everything up even more and put you all in danger." His eyes filled with tears as Luke stepped up behind me. "I'm truly sorry."

I nodded. I didn't know what to say. Many, many times over the years I'd been growing up, I'd imagined meeting my father again. Never had I imagined it like this.

Luke put his hand on my shoulder, clearly confused as to why Tony was talking to me like this.

Boy, was he in for a shock.

CHAPTER SEVENTEEN

———

It was nearly six a.m. by the time I got home. Luke and I had spent the last few hours at the hospital waiting for Mum to come out of surgery to have the bullet removed. Thankfully, it all went to plan, and we left Mum sleeping peacefully. A good dose of morphine would do that for you.

Whilst waiting, I'd brought Luke up to date with everything that had happened, including the part where I'd found out that Tony, aka Brian, was our father. To say Luke was surprised was an understatement. That surprise turned to anger but then dissipated into sadness. Sadness that Tony had never told him. Had never told any of us. I guessed that we had time now, assuming that what Detective Ray told me about Tony having no charges pressed against him were true. Providing I could get past how he had acted in regards to Jeremy Gibson.

The sun was starting to rise, giving the morning sky an orange glow, as I wrapped myself in a sweater and made my way out to the back deck to watch it.

Footsteps on the timber kitchen floor alerted me to Luke heading my way. Luke had surprised me last night, the way he'd taken control of the situation. I wasn't sure what would have happened if he hadn't turned up.

"Hey," I said, smiling at him.

"Hey."

"Did you get any sleep?"

"No. You?" he asked.

"Same. I kept replaying what happened."

"Yeah, it could have been so much worse. I thought I'd go back and visit Mum after she's had some sleep and they move her to a ward. I know she wanted to come home as quickly as possible, but I'd like her to stay there for as long as she needs."

"She was pretty upset to learn about Mark."

When Mum had been lying on the gurney, waiting to be put into an ambulance, Patrick had spilled the beans about everything, including his involvement with Mark. It turned out he'd been stealing the drugs and Mark had been selling them.

"Yeah, none of this should have ever happened," said Luke, rubbing his hands over his face. "I should have protected her."

"Luke, it's not your job to protect us."

"Yes, it is. Dad told me I had to. He told me it was my job."

"What are you talking about?"

"When we were little, and he left us. I remember the night. He came into my room and told me that I was the man of the house now and to take care of you and Mum."

"Luke, you were four years old. How do you remember that?"

"Some things you remember. But the funny part of it is, I remember him telling me—I just don't remember his face."

We sat in silence for a while. I thought about what he'd just told me and the impact it must have had on him. Luke eventually broke the silence.

"When Mum left Australia for Hawaii, I didn't know who I was supposed to be with. Should I stay in Oz and look out for you, or should I move to Hawaii and look after Mum? At the time you were in a relationship with Jason, so I thought Mum needed me more. I'm sorry I left you, Sam."

Luke's words broke my heart. How could he have been carrying such a huge burden for so long without telling me?

"You have nothing to be sorry for. Mum needed to be here to look after Gran. After Gran passed away, she decided to stay. I needed to be in Australia because that's where my life was. You should have been wherever you wanted to be."

"I wanted to be in both places."

His words sat heavily on me. All the times I had thought he was selfish and inconsiderate, he was actually the most caring person I had ever known.

"Luke, I give you a hard time as a brother, but I love you. You have always taken care of us. You did an amazing job."

He gave me a tight smile. "Thanks."

"You know, at some point though, Mum and I need to take care of ourselves?"

"Yeah, I'm working on that."

I smiled and allowed the comfortable silence to fill the air between us.

"I need to tell to you something," said Luke, his voice gravelly with emotion. "It's about Casey."

My stomach flipped. "What is it?"

"You know how I told Casey to stay away from you?"

"Yes," I replied, a knot rapidly forming in my stomach.

"I also told you he said he was just a friend to you."

"Uh-uh." My breathing was becoming more rapid.

"It wasn't true."

"What?"

"Well, it's true that he said it. It's just not how he really feels. He confessed to me that he thinks he's falling for you."

Okay, my stomach did a full-on somersault, the butterfly circus doing the opening scene.

"Really?" My voice came out on a whisper, all the air vanishing from my lungs.

"Yeah. Really. I'm sorry. He was going to tell you, but I pulled the best-friend card on him and told him to stay away."

I wanted to be angry with Luke for interfering, but I now understood why he had. He was trying to protect me. Whatever his reasons though, I needed to find Casey to tell him how I felt.

"I have to go," I said, standing. "I need to find him."

Luke nodded, then dug into his pocket and pulled out his car keys. "Take the car. Remember though, we drive on the opposite side of the road here. Don't crash it," he said, throwing the keys to me.

I smiled as the keys flew through the air. I put out my hand to catch them, this moment with Luke perfect. Only I forgot that I wasn't very coordinated when I was tired. The keys sailed straight past me and landed in amongst Mum's bromeliads. Geez, I hoped that wasn't an omen.

Other than my short drive the night before, I hadn't driven since I'd arrived here. And being on the opposite side of the car was definitely throwing me. More than once I found myself on the wrong side of the road, the oncoming vehicle blasting me with horns.

I managed to get to Casey's house without any accidents though. I knew he wouldn't be at the resort yet. It was too early. The sun had broken the horizon, the day well and truly underway. I leaped from the car and ran to the front door. My hand shook as I reached out and rang the bell.

Waiting for Casey to appear, I took the time to straighten my clothes. I had bothered to quickly get dressed before running off to find him, but only took enough extra time to brush my hair and clean my teeth. Now I wished I'd applied full makeup and found something better to wear than just shorts and a T-shirt.

My foot tapped impatiently as I looked through his front window, hoping to see him walking toward me. Hmmm, no Casey.

I stepped back and looked up at the balcony off his bedroom, wondering if he was up there.

A boy riding a push bike and doing a paper round threw a newspaper across the front lawn, hitting me in the back with it. Ouch!

I bent to retrieve it, and as I did, the ocean came into my view. It almost beckoned me. I wondered...

I checked that the kid on the bike wasn't heading back down the street before I crossed the road. Standing on the grass looking down over the water, I took a deep breath, relaxing for the first time in days.

Taking one quick look back at Casey's house, just in case he had appeared on the doorstep, I moved to the path leading to the beach. I had a hunch where I might find him.

I ran down the path, almost leaping through the dunes till I got to the water's edge. From there I ran up the beach toward Casey's rock. That was what I'd called it. Sure, I knew that it wasn't the official name, but to me it would always be Casey's rock.

I was surprised by how fit I had become, running all the way there. Okay, I might have stopped to catch my breath once. But that was all. Just once.

The rock jutted out into the water, the tide almost all the way out. Sitting on the very end, looking down into the water, was Casey.

My heart missed a beat as I slowed to a walk.

He didn't turn and see me, his focus on whatever was in the water. I moved slowly and quietly, climbing the rock easily and moving behind him, the sound of the ocean covering any noise I made.

I took a moment to enjoy him, sitting with his back to me, the sunrise reflecting on his skin. *Wow* was the only word I could think of. Casey startled, realizing I was behind him. He turned quickly to look over his shoulder, his thoughts unreadable.

"Hi," I said, my voice quiet and uncertain. I'd raced here in such a hurry wanting to tell him how I felt, but now that he was sitting in front of me, it all seemed so much harder.

"Hi," he replied. "What are you doing here?"

"I came to talk to you. If you don't mind, that is."

He smiled, and the world slipped on its axis. If this conversation turned out the way I hoped it would, I really needed to get used to his smile.

"No, of course I don't mind. I was just thinking about you, actually."

He was? My heart tripped as I attempted to gain some control.

I moved closer to him and sat on the rock, our shoulders nearly touching. The view was magnificent whichever way I looked, but I took a moment to enjoy the water. It calmed me, and from it I could find the courage I needed.

"Have you spoken to Luke today?" I asked.

He shook his head. "Nah, I've had my phone turned off. I don't feel like talking to him just yet though."

"Oh. We had a bad night," I explained.

Casey's eyebrows shot up as he looked at me. I brought him up to date with the night's events. By the time I had finished with the part where Tony gave me his speech, Casey's face was torn with emotion.

"Your mum was shot?" he asked.

I nodded.

"But she's okay?"

I nodded.

He sat quietly for a moment. "And you were going to ride your bike to find the kidnapper?"

Yeah, that did sound pretty ludicrous in the light of day. I nodded again.

Casey swiveled on the rock to face me. His eyes were deep blue, concern dancing in their depths. He opened his mouth to say something and then closed it again. He did this three more times before saying, "So where did you keep the money?"

I'd told him I'd only been wearing my nightshirt and flip-flops, and that was why my legs had scratches and cuts on them. Heat flooded my face, and I wondered how I didn't pass out.

"Well, I…it doesn't matter where I kept the bloody money."

Casey's grin turned to a full-on smile. "Let me guess," he said, teasing me. "You put it in your bra."

"I wasn't wearing a bra." His eyebrows shot up somewhere around his hairline, a small smile playing on his lips.

"Underwear?"

"Of course I was wearing underwear. Geez, what kind of girl do you think I am?"

He let out a bark of laughter, the sound deep and gravelly, which did absolutely nothing to keep my hormones in check.

"You're one of a kind, Samantha," he said, his smile turning sad.

Silence filled the air between us.

"I spoke to Luke this morning," I finally said. "He told me he pulled the best-friend card on you and told you to stay away from me."

Casey looked out over the horizon, his gaze unwavering.

"Last night made him reassess his priorities," I continued.

His gaze whipped to mine, and he looked deep into my eyes.

"Really?"

I nodded. "Really."

Suddenly the air changed and became charged with electricity. All reserves were down, and Casey looked at me like I had never been looked at before. The intensity was beyond anything I had ever felt.

His hand reached out to me, his fingers gently tracing their way around my jaw, skimming my bottom lip on their path. His eyes looked deep into mine, and I felt my world move. My mind went blank, filled only with Casey.

People say that stressful situations can cause emotions to be confused. My emotions weren't confused. They knew exactly what they wanted. And that was Casey. Looking at me like this. Forever.

"Could you see yourself with me, Samantha?" he asked, vulnerability dancing in his eyes as he spoke.

My breath hitched. "Yes," I replied on a whisper. "To infinity and beyond."

ABOUT THE AUTHOR

Beth was born in Manchester, England, but after moving backwards and forwards across the world 13 times in 14 years she decided at the age of 18 that Australia was to be her home. She now lives on the beautiful Sunshine Coast in Queensland, Australia where every day is a good one. She is the lucky mother of two grown-up children, and, along with her ever-patient husband, she is the proud but sometimes flustered owner of four dogs, a cat, and a canary. She has always had a love of reading, and even though her background is in accounting, she has now discovered her love of writing. Her main wish is to write books you can sit back, relax with, and escape from your everyday life…and ones that you walk away from with a smile! When she's not writing you will usually find her at the beach with a coffee in hand, pursuing her favorite pastime—people watching!

To learn more about Beth Prentice, visit her online at:
http://www.bethprentice.com

Visit the official

website!

Trouble in paradise...
Welcome to Aloha Lagoon, one of Hawaii's hidden treasures. A little bit of tropical paradise nestled along the coast of Kauai, this resort town boasts luxurious accommodation, friendly island atmosphere...and only a slightly higher than normal murder rate. While mysterious circumstances may be the norm on our corner of the island, we're certain that our staff and Lagoon natives will make your stay in Aloha Lagoon one you will never forget!

www.alohalagoonmysteries.com

If you enjoyed *Deadly Wipeout*, be sure to pick up these other Aloha Lagoon Mysteries!

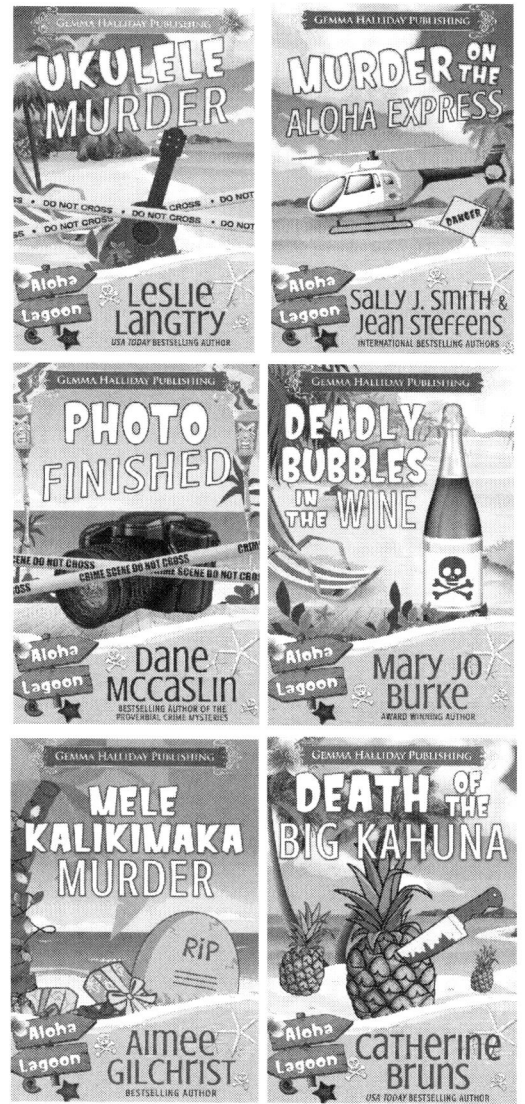

Printed in Great Britain
by Amazon